Was now the time to tell Marcus about the baby?

True, the jail was far from the ideal place. Yet Chloe had hesitated before and lost her chance.

"Hey, Marcus," she said. Her words came between gasping breaths. "You know that call I made to you this morning?"

"Before we showed up here and everything went to hell?" he asked. "Don't tell me, you had a premonition that something bad was about to happen."

"That's not exactly it." Light shone upward from an exhaust that led to a room below. Chloe stared at it.

He did too. "That may be our way out of the jail," he said. "You stay here. I'll check it out."

"Wait." Marcus was brave—it was one of the things she admired most. She had to tell him. Now.

"The call this morning," she repeated. "I needed to tell you something important."

But then all hell broke loose.

Dear Reader,

I can't believe that this is the end of the Wyoming Nights series! I hope you've enjoyed getting to know the residents of Pleasant Pines as much as I've enjoyed writing about them.

There are a few things that I love about this book. First, Chloe Ryder and Marcus Jones finally get the romance that they've deserved from the beginning of the series. They are truly the ultimate power couple—confident, dedicated and, above all, passionate.

And second, we finally get to see what happens with elusive serial killer Darcy Owens. No spoilers from me—but it's explosive.

So thank you, Dear Reader, for joining me on this journey. If it weren't for all of you, none of these characters would ever have had the chance to come to life.

The best to you always,

Jennifer D. Bokal

THE AGENT'S DEADLY LIAISON

Jennifer D. Bokal

HARLEQUIN

ROMANTIC
SUSPENSE

HARLEQUIN®
ROMANTIC SUSPENSE™

Recycling programs
for this product may
not exist in your area.

ISBN-13: 978-1-335-75980-1

The Agent's Deadly Liaison

For questions and comments about the quality of this book, please contact us at CustomerService@Harlequin.com.

Harlequin Enterprises ULC
22 Adelaide St. West, 41st Floor
Toronto, Ontario M5H 4E3, Canada
www.Harlequin.com

Printed in U.S.A.

Jennifer D. Bokal penned her first book at age eight. An early lover of the written word, she decided to follow her passion and become a full-time writer. From then on, she didn't look back. She earned a master of arts in creative writing from Wilkes University and became a member of Romance Writers of America and International Thriller Writers.

She has authored several short stories, novellas and poems. Winner of the Sexy Scribbler in 2015, Jennifer is also the author of the ancient-world historical series the Champions of Rome and the Harlequin Romantic Suspense series Rocky Mountain Justice.

Happily married to her own alpha male for more than twenty years, she enjoys writing stories that explore the wonders of love. Jen and her manly husband live in upstate New York with their three beautiful daughters, two very spoiled dogs and a kitten that aspires to one day become a Chihuahua.

Books by Jennifer D. Bokal

Harlequin Romantic Suspense

Wyoming Nights

Under the Agent's Protection
Agent's Mountain Rescue
Agent's Wyoming Mission
The Agent's Deadly Liaison

The Coltons of Grave Gulch

A Colton Internal Affair

Rocky Mountain Justice

Her Rocky Mountain Hero
Her Rocky Mountain Defender
Rocky Mountain Valor

Visit the Author Profile page at Harlequin.com for more titles.

To John. Always and forever.

Prologue

"The trial's been set."

Darcy Owens looked up at the man who had spoken, her steps faltering. Had it really come to this?

Darcy was engaged in her twice-daily hour of exercise. In reality, she was placed in an enclosed mesh cage atop a concrete slab—not unlike a dog run. Rain, shine or snow, the state of Wyoming allowed her one hundred twenty minutes of fresh air daily, in which she could pace back and forth. Her court-appointed defense attorney, Stuart Riskin, had arrived at the Northern Wyoming Correctional Facility as her hour began. He stood outside of the fencing, where he was allowed to talk to his client.

Stuart reminded Darcy of porridge, gray and lumpy. Leaning on a metal post, he continued, "There's a witness to the murder of Carl Haak, the former sheriff. They're seeking the death penalty."

She'd been charged with six murders by the State of Wyoming. Ever since her arrest and arraignment several months before, she'd known that this moment might come.

Still, it was a shock.

Darcy couldn't breathe. Looping her fingers through the chain links, she held herself upright. "Oh?"

"Is that all you have to say?" Stuart asked. His voice seemed to come from far away. "Don't you want to know about your trial? Your defense?"

"Sure," said Darcy, her mouth numb. "Of course."

"We're still going to try and plead insanity," he said. "We have it well documented that you've suffered from memory lapses. We'll still claim that you have no memories of the crimes."

"I *can't* remember anything." Darcy began to pace again, dragging her feet along the concrete path. Gravel and dust had collected in the seams between the slabs. One of the small stones worked itself into her shoe. Stopping, she bent down and picked the rock free.

"Take it," the Darkness whispered in her ear. "Keep it."

The Darkness had always been with her. It guided her. Protected her. And it was never to be questioned. With the small stone hidden between her ring and middle fingers, she resumed her walk.

"That's good." Stuart glanced over his shoulder. He continued, whispering, "Rule number one for the accused—always maintain your innocence."

A pair of guards stood more than a dozen yards

from the cage. "They can't hear you," Darcy said. She looked at the guards and watched them for a moment before resuming her walk. "They're great rule followers here, and listening to our conversation would violate my attorney-client privilege."

"Anyway," he said, "there's more than Wyoming that concerns me. You've also been charged with murder in Colorado, Nevada and Texas." Stuart shrugged. "Let's just say that the death penalty is a real possibility."

Her throat grew dry. The hidden bit of gravel rubbed her skin raw. Darcy moved her fingers back and forth, trying to work it free from where it was hidden in the webbing of her hand.

"Don't," the Darkness said, speaking to her again. "Follow the plan."

A plan? Now, that was interesting.

Her life had been broken down until she lived hour by hour. For twenty-two of those twenty-four hours each day, she was locked in a ten-by-ten-foot cell by herself. She never spoke to or saw any of the other inmates. Her furniture—a bed, sink, toilet, desk along with a chair—were bolted into the wall or floor. The door to her cell was metal, with a small inset window that was covered in mesh. There was a small slot inside the door that was used to put handcuffs on Darcy if she was taken from her cell and for passing trays of food back and forth.

It was a wholly dehumanizing existence. Then again, she assumed that was the point.

She understood that other inmates had TVs and computers, luxuries that had been provided by family or friends. But Darcy had no one. All her worldly possessions had been provided by the state of Wyoming. She had two shapeless orange jumpsuits. Three pairs of industrial underwear. Two bras with seams inside the cups that rubbed her nipples raw. She also had three pairs of socks and a single pair of foam moccasins.

A band of paper and plastic was wrapped around her wrist. Her name, birthdate, and inmate number were printed on the ID tag, along with her photo and a bar code. Each time Darcy was taken from—or returned to—her cell, the guards scanned the bar code, verifying and recording her identity and whereabouts.

Truly, Darcy had been crushed until she was nothing but dust. As she paced, Stuart continued to talk. Pretrial *this*. Jurisdiction *that*. His words were nothing more than background noise for Darcy as she thought and plotted.

Her original plan to avoid prison had been simple. Claim blackouts. Plead insanity. Get sent to a psychiatric facility instead. There, the Darkness would have guided her, helped her to gain her freedom.

Now, it seemed as if she'd never escape the death sentence.

The Darkness rose within her again, like a seductive song. Her heartbeat thrummed against her ribs, and Darcy understood the absolute perfection of the plan.

"I want to confess," she said abruptly.

"You what?" Stuart's gray pallor looked even more sickly, matching his suit coat perfectly.

"You heard me."

"Are…are you serious? You're willing to confess to fourteen murders?"

Leveling her gaze at Stuart, Darcy said, "I'll give

all the details of *twenty* killings the authorities know about—and a dozen more they don't."

Stuart stepped back from the fence. "You're willing to confess to over thirty murders?"

Good, her news left him rattled. She continued, "All confessions in exchange for life in prison. Can you make that deal?"

After smoothing his tie, the attorney shuffled forward again—uneasily this time. "You know that you have the right to a trial. If you confess and enter a guilty plea, it's done. You won't get a do-over. No judge or jury will ever hear the evidence…"

Is that what Darcy wanted?

The Darkness whispered in her ear. "Make the deal."

She said, "Yes, Stuart, I want to plead guilty. I don't want to go to trial here or in any other state. I just want this to end."

"I need to call the attorney general's office in Laramie and see what kind of deal they're willing to make. They'll send a lawyer to talk with you, I'm sure. But don't worry about that. I'll be with you the whole time…"

"No way," Darcy interrupted, panic rising in her chest. "I'm not talking to someone new. And I don't need you with me, either."

"As your attorney," he said, his voice stern. "I have to advise you against confessing without some kind of legal counsel present."

"When I was arrested, I was told that I had a right to an attorney. Correct?"

"That's right," said Stuart, his tone less certain than before.

"Then I hereby waive that right. I don't want you in the room," she interrupted. "I'll make a confession to Chloe Ryder, the DA from Pleasant Pines, or nobody at all."

He shook his head. "I have to insist that I'm with you every time you speak to the authorities."

The directions given to her by the Darkness were clear. "But you're my attorney. I can fire you. I can defend myself."

"You can go *pro se* if you want…"

"What I *want* is for you to make the deal."

Stuart scowled. He was clearly put out by her growing demands, but also appeared ready to commit to this extreme in order to make his exit. "Fine. Anything else?"

Hell yes, there was. "I want Marcus Jones at the confession, too."

Now the lawyer just looked confused. "The guy who led the team that found and arrested you?"

Before Stuart could ask his obvious question—*why him?*—Darcy continued, "I never thought I'd be caught, much less go to jail. I just want to know how he got to me. Then I can look everyone in the eye and tell them what they want to know. They can understand why everything happened the way it did."

"Marcus Jones." Stuart took a pad and pen from his shirt pocket, then wrote the name in his little book. "I'll make contact with both of them as soon as I get back to my office."

Darcy squeezed the small stone she still held in her hand. "Thanks."

"I'll be honest," he said. "These arrangements might

take a few weeks, or even a month. Like I said before, there are several jurisdictions involved. They'll all have to agree to your terms—"

"Time means nothing to me in here," she said. Now that she'd made up her mind, she wanted nothing more than to get rid of her lawyer—at least for now.

"Alright then, I'll head back to town and get started on these calls." He turned to leave, then glanced back. "Darcy—are you sure about this?"

She met his gaze and held it evenly. "Stuart, I've never been surer of anything in my life."

Chapter 1

Chloe Ryder sat at her desk in the Pleasant Pines County office building and stared at the folder in her hand. Her assistant DA, Jacob Loeb had gone home for the evening. A pile of manila folders sat untouched at Chloe's elbow.

She had a trial scheduled to begin early in the morning. The evidence was set. The witnesses were prepared. Now she only needed her opening remarks. How could she crystalize all the crimes committed a by a group of men who belonged to the Transgressors?

For months, the members of the motorcycle club—really a gang of drug traffickers—had distributed copious amounts of narcotics in Pleasant Pines and the surrounding communities. Yet as far as Chloe was concerned, their real crime was human trafficking.

The setup had been simple. Members of the club had lured unwitting young women to a remote camp in the local forest with the promise of drugs, parties or romance. Then the women were held against their will, and soon after, forced into prostitution.

She massaged her temples in frustration. So many lives had been shattered... Of the dozen defendants, everyone had accepted plea deals and were serving time at NWCF—all except for Luke Winston and Rex Vanguard, that is. They were demanding their right to a trial. As far as Chloe was concerned, both men deserved to be in jail for a long time—and it was her job to make sure that happened. For her, it was more than punishing the guilty, but bringing peace and closure to the victims and their families.

She swiveled her seat from her desk to the credenza that sat next to the wall. The surface was covered with files yet to be reviewed and papers that needed her signature. But there, among the evidence of a busy and productive life, was a single photograph of Chloe and her parents.

Lifting the picture from its spot, she examined all the faces. What would her mom and dad think of her now? Would they be proud? She imagined that her mother would chastise Chloe for working too hard—maybe even harder than her father had worked.

Sadly, they hadn't lived long enough for her mom to make the comparison. Carefully, she set the picture in its spot and turned back to her desk, a wistful smile on her lips.

Her parents had been gone for more than a decade, yet recently they'd come to mind more and more. She knew why. As DA of Pleasant Pines, it had been Chloe's job to meet with the families of those who'd lost a loved one to Darcy Owens. In their anguish of uncertainty, she saw her despair at never knowing who caused the crash that killed her parents.

Sure, there were huge differences between what happened to Chloe's folks and the victims of a notorious serial killer. For one, the families knew who to blame.

Even now, though, a single question nagged Chloe, keeping her awake at night.

Could she make all the murder charges stick?

There was a soft knock at her door. She looked up. Stuart Riskin stood on the threshold. His cheeks were flushed and blotchy. "The guard at the front door said I'd find you here. Can I come in?"

"Sure, Stuart," said Chloe, gesturing to a chair across from her desk. Had he come to make a deal before for the Transgressors? She hoped so. "What can I do for you? Is this about tomorrow's trial?"

"Not that one." The older man dropped into the chair with a sigh. "It's about Darcy Owens."

Oh, really? "You informed your client about the trial date, I assume."

"It's more than that." Stuart hesitated. "She wants to confess—to all of it. She said she'd talk about every murder we know of and some we don't. Here's the kicker. She'll only talk to you."

"To me? Why?" Chloe's heart skipped a beat as she was drawn back into memory. Years before, back in college, Chloe had been a social work intern. Assigned to a local high school, she'd met Darcy, who had alluded to abuse at home in their meetings. Following protocol,

Chloe reported her suspicions to the school. Yet when the administration questioned Darcy, she denied it all.

Was that long-ago association the reason Darcy wanted to speak to Chloe again?

Or was it because Darcy was captured in Chloe's jurisdiction? And after all, she'd spoken to the accused several times already.

Or maybe it was a bit of both.

Did she have a choice but to work with the killer? "Okay."

"There's more," said Stuart.

"Jesus, what else can there be?"

"She also wants to talk to the arresting agent." Stuart paused while he removed a small pad of paper from his shirt pocket. "Marcus Jones. Darcy said that he led the group who finally arrested her. You know this guy?"

"I do," said Chloe.

"Can you give me his number?"

"I'll do you one better," said Chloe. "I'll talk to Marcus first and have him call you."

"That would be great."

"Darcy said she doesn't want me in the room when she speaks to you. I advised her against it, but she doesn't want to listen."

That was a twist Chloe wasn't expecting. "Any idea why?"

"None. It's not common, but it happens often enough."

Stuart was right and they both knew it. "Tell your client that we'll be in touch once we've made arrangements. It might take some time."

"I've warned her." Stuart rose from the chair. "She's

fine waiting. Then again," he asked, "what other choice does she have?"

That was a good question. It left Chloe wondering if there more to Darcy's sudden willingness to cooperate. "My biggest concern is that this is somehow all a legal trick on her part. You know, confess now. Then later, say she was coerced. One complaint to a judge—and boom, she's out of jail." Sure, that outcome wasn't likely. Still, it was Chloe's job—make that her duty—to worry about the worst possible outcome.

"Darcy's shrewd, that's for sure." He paused. "It's my job to represent her, but I'm still an officer of the court. I won't allow her to abuse the system."

Stuart Riskin was an honest man and a good attorney. "I'm glad that we're in agreement." Standing, Chloe continued, "It looks like we've got a lot to keep us busy in the next few weeks. Thanks for the message. We'll see what we can do about this."

She walked him to the entrance, where the guard let him out the front door. Striding back to her suite of offices, Chloe paused. Certainly her mountain of work had just grown. And in all honesty, it wasn't necessarily a bad thing. Chloe had plans and ambitions that took her beyond the district attorney's office in Pleasant Pines.

One day, she intended to be the attorney general for the state of Wyoming. As a law student, she'd clerked with the current AG and was drawn to the office's ability to affect change statewide.

In a world where every case carried weight, not just now but also in the future, the Owens case was a unique opportunity. A well-crafted plea bargain had the ability to launch Chloe's career to the next level. Failed negotiations could end her dreams before she ever got the chance to make them a reality.

Returning to her office, she dropped down into her chair. The opening statement for tomorrow's trial would have to wait a little longer. Darcy's offer to confess changed everything—especially if she handled this just right. And sure, Chloe wanted to celebrate. But first there was more work to do. Picking up the phone, she placed a call to the man who was responsible for Darcy being in jail. The lead operative from Rocky Mountain Justice, Marcus Jones.

Marcus sat in the computer lab on the second floor of RMJ's safe house. The safe house itself was a converted Victorian-era home, located in a residential neighborhood of Pleasant Pines, Wyoming. From the outside, the home looked like any other on the block.

But inside, well, that was a different story. For starters, the safe house was furnished with enough surveillance equipment to see anything for half a mile and listen in on a conversation for over two hundred yards. There was an arsenal of weapons in a fortified room on the first floor. And here, on the second floor, was the computer lab. A server stood against the back wall and hummed with power. Several monitors sat on a semicircular desk, and just as many wireless keyboards sat on the table's top.

Next to Marcus sat Wyatt Thornton. Wyatt was a former employee of the FBI, like Marcus. Whereas Marcus had focused on criminal cases, Wyatt had worked for the behavioral sciences unit out of Quantico, Virginia, as a profiler.

It had been a long day, and Marcus was ready to go home. But before that, he had one final task—a weekly meeting with his boss in Colorado, Ian Wallace. Ian was former MI6. He left the UK after falling in love with Denver-based sports agent Petra Sloane and moved to the United States. From there, Ian started Rocky Mountain Justice, an organization that described their business as *private security*.

But the mission of RMJ was so much more.

Marcus crossed paths with Ian more than a year ago. RMJ was on the hunt for Nikolai Mateev, a Russian drug lord, who sold Afghan opium in the southwestern US. Marcus, the special agent from the FBI's Denver Field Office, also wanted Nikolai Mateev in jail.

Ian wasn't much of a rule follower, which meant that the two men butted heads more than once. Yet even Marcus had to admit that the unconventional methods proved effective. In the end, Ian and the RMJ team brought down Nikolai Mateev. Then the Russian's whole criminal enterprise crumbled.

When Ian began to expand the agency into Wyoming, he asked Marcus to be the operative in charge of that expansion. Marcus was more than a little intrigued by the offer, and he accepted the challenge. Even if he was skeptical about operating in Ian's gray areas, he appreciated the trust the man put in his abilities. And he didn't intend to let him down.

The Darcy Owens case was the first for RMJ in Wyoming. District Attorney Chloe Ryder, was their first client.

Ian rarely came to Wyoming, and this week was no exception. He was confident in Marcus's leadership.

Still, he kept tabs on the Pleasant Pines satellite office with regular teleconferences. Now his face was on a large screen at one end of the room. He spoke, bringing up the next item on the agenda. "What's the news on Darcy Owens?"

Marcus rubbed a hand over his freshly shaved scalp and exchanged glances with Wyatt. "Nothing new to report. Last I heard, a trial date was set, but the judge has given both sides several months to prepare. She was denied bail—no surprise there—and will be in custody until she heads to court."

"Reach out to your local DA," said Ian. "See what more we can do as far as aiding their office with gathering evidence on past crimes."

He felt a small smile tug at his lips. Just hearing Chloe Ryder mentioned had the power to improve his day. And now Ian was directing Marcus to make contact? That'd be an easy order to follow. "Will do."

Ian continued, "Darcy's devious and a high escape risk. I don't want there to be any loopholes for her to slither through."

"That's one of the reasons Wyatt's here tonight. We've been looking into other possible victims whose deaths fit in with Darcy's modus operandi."

"Have you found anything of interest?" Ian asked.

Wyatt brought up an electronic file that filled a computer screen on his desk and was also sent to Ian's computer as well. Names, photos, birthdates and details of their deaths all appeared. "So far, there are four interesting prospects. Two more men in Wyoming. One in Nevada. One from Texas."

"Good work," said Ian. "Keep looking, and if you

find enough for charges to be brought, contact the appropriate jurisdiction. What else have you got for me?"

Marcus paused. That was part of the problem. Sure, there were crimes that happened in Pleasant Pines and the surrounding communities—but enough for an outfit like RMJ? Stifling a sigh, he scanned the list of new clients. "We've gotten two high-level requests for security systems. And a request by that big movie star—he wants to hire the whole crew as bodyguards for a monthlong film shoot in Wyoming. I gave him a quote. From his reaction, I don't think we'll hear back."

"Don't worry if it's slow going," said Ian, obviously understanding Marcus's mood. "That's the nature of our business."

Marcus's phone rang. He checked caller ID. His pulse spiked, and he sat up taller in his seat.

"Who is it?" Wyatt asked.

He glanced up at his companions. "It's Chloe. Um, Chloe Ryder, the DA."

"I'll let you take that, then," said Ian in his crisp accent. "Keep me posted on any updates."

"Will do." The large monitor went black as Marcus swiped the call open. After turning on the speaker function, he said, "Hey, Chloe. I'm with Wyatt, and you're on speakerphone. What's up?"

"I've got news—big news." Chloe paused. "Darcy Owens wants to confess."

Marcus stared at the phone. Then at Wyatt. Then back at the phone. "Are you serious?"

"There's more. According to her lawyer, she only wants to talk to you and me."

It was in Marcus's nature to be skeptical. But

whereas Darcy was concerned, he was downright dubious. "Is this another one of her tricks?"

"Her lawyer came to see me. It's a plea bargain. No death penalty in exchange for a full confession." She added, "Without you and the rest of the team at Rocky Mountain Justice, Darcy would still be at large. You've been a part of this since the beginning, and now we have a chance to bring it to a close. I just wanted you to know first."

Wyatt shook his head, obviously as suspicious as he felt. Marcus nodded and him and spoke. "I want to be happy that she's ready to confess. But Chloe…are you sure about this?"

"Well, obviously I'm going to make sure that every word she says is obtained without creating any questionable legal situations." Marcus could hear the hesitation in Chloe's voice. "It could take a while to make the arrangements. Several weeks. Maybe even a month or two. That worries me, as well. What if I'm too careful, and during the wait, she changes her mind about talking in the first place?"

"That's a risk you'll have to accept, I guess." Now seemed like the perfect time to share what RMJ had found. Marcus continued, "We've been doing some digging into other possible victims. Wyatt's come up with a list of four. We can see if there's anything substantial tying them to Darcy. It might be a way to gauge if she's telling the truth, especially if she really intends to disclose details about these other murders she allegedly committed."

"That's a great plan." He could hear the fatigue in her voice.

"This is good news. You know that, right?"

"Right," she echoed. "Hey, maybe we should grab some dinner in the next few days. Discuss the situation."

"How about now?"

"Oh." She sounded surprised. "Okay. Um...want to meet at Sally's?" she asked, mentioning a diner located next to the town park, and close to her office.

"Count me out," said Wyatt. "Everly and I have plans."

To be honest, Marcus wasn't bothered that Wyatt couldn't make it for dinner—especially since it created a unique opportunity to spend time with Chloe. "I have a better idea," he said. "Let's go to Quinton's."

The centerpiece of life in town was the Pleasant Pines Inn. The two-story hotel was built in the late 1800s of stone and timber. It sat atop a rise at the end of the business district on Main Street. Aside from having dozens of guest rooms and an on-site pub, it also boasted the town's sole upscale restaurant. Marcus had been there once or twice, only on special occasions.

Like a date.

"Quinton's," she said, echoing Marcus. "That seems excessive for a Wednesday night."

"Getting a confession from Darcy Owens is what's excessive."

"We haven't gotten it yet," she said.

He checked his phone for the time. 6:15 p.m. "Meet me there in fifteen minutes," he said. "Since it's a Wednesday, we'll be able to get a table. No problem."

"I have to talk to Julia first," she said, mentioning

the local sheriff. "There's some things we need to go over. Give me two hours."

"See you then." He hung up the phone, more than a little pleased with himself.

Wyatt shook his head and gave a low chuckle.

Marcus gave the other guy a side-eye. "What?"

"That took long enough."

"What d'you mean? What took long enough?"

Wyatt sighed and got to his feet. "For you to ask Chloe out on a date."

"It's not a date." Marcus stood as well. "It's a working dinner."

"You do remember that I'm a behavioral scientist, right?"

"Yeah," he said.

"Well, I know when someone is lying. Even to themselves." He grinned. "Just keep that in mind."

Wyatt had always been a great friend. But sometimes it sucked that his buddy saw everything—and understood even more.

Chloe set the phone down and rose from her desk. A strange sensation tickled the back of her neck, as if she were being watched from the shadows. Aside from the guard and a few other employees, nobody was in the building. But she did know what was wrong.

Despite Stuart's assurances, Chloe didn't trust Darcy. There had to be something that she was hiding. Turning for the main staircase, Chloe climbed to the second floor and stopped in front of the door to the sheriff's office.

Rapping her knuckles on the door, Chloe turned the

handle and entered. The outer office, complete with two desks, was empty and dark. At the back of the room, light shone from the inner office where Sheriff Julia McCloud sat behind her desk.

She glanced up as Chloe approached. "You look about as tired as I feel."

"Then you must be exhausted."

Julia was the newly elected sheriff of Pleasant Pines. Originally appointed to the position after the murder of Carl Haak, Julia ran for the job in a special election and won in a landslide. She used to work with Marcus Jones as an operative for Rocky Mountain Justice, but she resigned from the agency after an attack by Darcy Owens left her with wounds—both physical and emotional—that she believed affected her work as an agent. When an opening in the sheriff's office gave Julia a second chance at a career in law enforcement—and a chance to catch the woman who had tried to kill her— she took it. Reluctantly at first, but now she seemed happily settled into her new job—and her new life.

Resting her elbows on her desk, Julia tucked her injured hand with the missing fingers into the palm of the other, she asked, "What can I do for you?"

"I've got news and a favor to ask." She quickly explained the news about Darcy.

"So, what's the problem? That's great news." Julia took in her friend's expression. "Or…isn't it?"

Chloe rubbed the back of her neck. "I'm not so sure. What if there's more going on here?"

"Darcy doesn't want to face the possibility of the death penalty." Julia tapped her desk. "She knows how the system works—and she's doing just that, using the system."

"What kind of contacts do you have at Northern Wyoming Correctional?" Chloe asked.

"I guess this is where the favor comes in…" Chloe said nothing as Julia deliberated—a tactic she'd picked up from Marcus. "I know the warden. His name is Cal Douglas. He's a former marine and runs a tight ship over there."

A tight ship? Was he the kind of man who'd do a favor if asked? "Can you get a cell searched? I want to know what, if anything, Darcy Owens is hiding."

Chapter 2

The slot window in her door opened. Gretchen, the guard assigned to watch Darcy for the night shift, appeared. "Cell check," she said.

After her offer to confess, Darcy had expected a search. Yet it had been only a couple of hours since her attorney left with terms. The speed with which those on the outside had acted left her hands shaking. Rising from the desk, she approached the door and turned around. Darcy was cuffed, and her wristband was scanned through the slot window. The electronic lock disengaged with a click a second before the door was pulled open. Along with Gretchen, two male guards entered the cell.

Darcy's ankles were shackled. Then a chain was wound through the cuffs and the leg irons before being connected to a leather bellyband at her waist.

"Step into the hallway, please," said one of the male guards.

It was always the same. They were polite, professional and dispassionate.

Shuffling into the hall, she wondered what it would take to make them crack.

Darcy stood by while her cell was ransacked. Her extra clothes were patted down and turned inside out. The blankets and mattress were pulled from her bed. The walls and floor were examined for a seam where she might have pried a tile or brick loose. A K-9 unit was brought in, and the dog sniffed every inch of her cell and all of her meager belongings.

The search took twenty minutes.

"We got nothing," said one of the guards. He was younger than the other. Then he lowered his voice to a whisper. "It's times like this when I wish we could carry a weapon. I don't like being in such tight quarters with a killer like her."

The older guard, a Black man, grunted. "You know why we can't. What if you had a gun and she got a hold of it? Or one of the other inmates? Then what would you do?" He shivered, as if taken with a sudden chill. "Don't even think about it." He called out to Gretchen. "You need to handle the body search."

With a nod, Gretchen gripped Darcy's elbow. "Let's go to the infirmary. The nurse is on hand."

The women's infirmary was located across from the conference room, a place reserved for inmates to meet with their attorneys. The male inmates, who outnumbered the females by twenty to one, had their own hospital wing with over thirty beds and a full-time doctor.

The women only had a wide-hipped nurse in a white smock and pants. She looked up as the door opened.

"We need to search the prisoner," said Gretchen. They crossed the threshold, and the door closed behind them. "Warden Douglas's orders."

The cuffs and leg irons were removed, and Darcy was told to strip.

Standing near the bed, Darcy surreptitiously glanced around the room. She took note of two hospital beds, complete with safety railings. One of the metal slats was loose. An oxygen tank sat in a corner. A locked cabinet, filled with medications and medical equipment, was set into the wall. There was a long counter with a sink. Privacy curtains hung beside each bed.

After slipping on a pair of gloves, the nurse searched Darcy's clothes. Her panties were shaken to prove that they were free of contraband. She held her breath as the nurse examined the bra.

It was given nothing more than a cursory glance, and the nurse placed it atop the pile of clothes. Darcy exhaled.

"She's clean," the nurse said to Gretchen. She handed Darcy her clothes.

"Thanks," said the guard.

Then the scenario played out in reverse. Once dressed, Darcy was cuffed and shackled before being led back to her cell. The bed had been remade and her clothes refolded.

After Gretchen removed both sets of cuffs and scanned the wrist band again, she said, "Sorry about all that."

With a shrug, Darcy said, "I don't mind."

Truly, she didn't. Every action taken by the guards, or the sheriff, or the DA, or even RMJ helped Darcy understand her foes a little bit better. It was how she had survived this long. It was how she would keep surviving.

The search told her that they didn't believe her overture to talk was completely authentic. Yet she would give them no reason to doubt her sincerity about cooperating.

In fact, she would be so compliant that in the end, they *would* trust her. In that trust, their doom would await.

A full half hour had passed since Julia called the correctional facility. For Chloe, each minute passed slowly—as she struggled, not knowing what outcome she wanted. Could Darcy be hiding some clue as to her next move? Or was the killer done playing games?

If Darcy was interested in self-preservation—and therefore truly ready to confess—Chloe could all but guarantee that they might finally be able to end her killing spree and put her away—for good. Assuming she did the work required—and Chloe always went above and beyond where her job was concerned—she was well on her way to a higher office. Closing the Darcy Owens case for good would be the ultimate next step on her career path.

She felt a twinge of guilt, and wondered whether it was crass to tie her ambitions to the fate of a killer as deadly as Darcy Owens. Quickly, though, she shook it off. She'd worked too hard—and had seen too much—to throw all her hard work away with her goals in reach.

Besides, if she held higher office, then she could save people from the same pain she'd suffered at the tragic loss of her parents—and hold those who were guilty to account.

Julia's desk phone rang. She answered it, turning on the speaker function. "Sheriff McCloud here."

"Hey, Sheriff, this is Cal Douglas. I'm calling about that cell check you requested."

"I have DA Ryder with me," said Julia, for the sake of transparency. "And you're on speakerphone. What'd you find?"

"Absolutely nothing," said Warden Douglas.

Chloe leaned toward the phone. "Are you sure?"

"The search was thorough." He continued without pause. "Darcy Owens has nothing in her cell—or on her person—that she shouldn't."

Julia glanced up and shrugged.

Chloe wanted to insist he check again—because she was positive he had to be mistaken—but how could she do so without cause? "Thank you, Warden," she said. "We appreciate your cooperation."

"Anytime," said the warden.

Julia hit a button and ended the call. "I know that it's your decision to make, Chloe. For whatever my opinion is worth, I think you should consider the offer to confess is real."

"You think this offer is legit?" Chloe had a hard time keeping the incredulity out of her voice. After everything that Darcy had done to Julia, she found it hard to believe that the sheriff would have faith in the serial killer.

"Two things. First, Darcy's not dumb—she has some

of the sharpest instincts I've ever seen. And what's more, she'll do anything to survive." Julia held up her injured hand.

"That was one point. What's the other?"

"When you meet with her, don't forget to keep your wits about you—every second."

It was a decent reminder. And besides, Chloe wouldn't be meeting with the killer for weeks at the very least. Why, then, did she still have a tickling at the back her neck? That same eerie feeling of being watched.

She shook it off. "Well, I've got some more calls to make. Plus, I still have to write my opening statement for the Transgressors trial tomorrow." How in the hell would she get it done by nine a.m.? "Thanks again for your help with this." And then, there was the dinner with Marcus. Sure, it was just work, but still, she liked his company—sometimes a little bit too much.

"I'm sure you'll keep me posted as things progress."

Chloe got to her feet and waved as she left the room. While walking back to her office, she mentally listed the different jurisdictions with claims to Darcy. All the other states would have to agree to the offer. Chloe had her work cut out for her to make sure that everyone was on board with the plan.

Then again, when it came to delivering justice, failure was never an option.

Marcus Jones stood in the lobby of the Pleasant Pines Inn and scanned a large bookshelf. The floor-to-ceiling shelves held everything from classic literature, bound in leather, to recent paperback releases, all kept for guests of the hotel. Nothing caught his attention.

Was he too focused on what was next in the Darcy Owens case to be drawn in by a title? Or was there more—like dinner with Chloe? Not for the first time, he reminded himself that this was a meeting—strictly business. Still, he couldn't deny that Chloe was a beautiful woman—and that more than once her challenging demeanor had proven to be as attractive as her looks, if not more so.

Since Chloe first teamed up with Marcus and the other operatives at RMJ to bring Darcy to justice, she'd been the most effective—if unofficial—partner he'd ever worked with in his career. During all those late-night meetings, she'd become...what?

His friend?

Marcus wasn't the kind of guy who hung out playing poker or basketball with the guys—he was too much of a loner. But he liked Chloe. He admired her. He enjoyed being with her—even if the only time they were typically together was spent working.

Friend? Huh. He supposed that the title fit.

Although lately, he'd been a bad friend. Then again, with Darcy in jail, the collaboration waned. But it wasn't just that the case had ended. It was Chloe herself—and the fact that every time she entered a room, Marcus understood what it was to be a man who desperately wanted a woman.

That was even true from the very first time he met Chloe.

His mind wandered from the lobby.

One year earlier

Marcus Jones sat in his office, located in the newly renovated safe house in Pleasant Pines, Wyoming. Having accepted a job with Rocky Mountain Justice, Marcus's first assignment was as team leader for Wyoming, and areas north.

His phone pinged, and he looked at the screen. The reminder read:

Lunch 1:00 p.m. w/District Attorney C. Ryder @ Sally's on Main.

Support staff in the Denver home office had arranged this meeting. It was the first of many that Marcus would, and should, take. He was the new kid in town, and he needed to play nice with everyone. Still, the idea of a musty old attorney regaling him with tales of past trials was not how Marcus wanted to spend the next hour.

He left the safe house, setting the alarm on both the interior door—made of reinforced steel—and the exterior door, which was controlled with a biometric lock. The sky was gray, with storm clouds hanging low. A few stray flakes of snow swirled across the cold and deserted road. Marcus exhaled, his breath freezing into a cloud. He pulled a knit cap low over his freshly shaved scalp. After zipping his jacket, he walked the short distance from his office to the downtown area and the diner.

Opening the front door, he stepped into the restaurant and surveyed his surroundings. A long counter with stools filled one side of the room, with the kitchen behind a chrome-plated wall. A line of booths stood near the windows. Several tables sat in between.

The aroma of coffee and fried food hung in the air, and his stomach gave a painful grumble. Hunger aside, Marcus couldn't help but notice a woman with bright blue eyes, sitting in a booth toward the back of the room. She was pretty—beautiful, really. With a fringe of dark bangs, she had a cosmopolitan look that felt out of place in this rural Wyoming town. In that first moment, he regretted his meeting with the district attorney. It had been a long time since he'd felt a spark, driving him to introduce himself to anyone new. But here of all places? He couldn't explain it. There was something about her...

Looking around the restaurant, he searched for the lawyer he was supposed to meet. The diner was all but empty. A lone rancher sat at the counter and sipped his coffee. Then it occurred to Marcus that he hadn't been told much about the district attorney. He'd only been given a name, C. Ryder. That said nothing about the person's age, or gender.

He looked back to the woman, who smiled and waved him over. When he got to her table, she stood and held out her hand. "Marcus Jones. It's great to see you again. I thought I recognized your name. We met years ago when you spoke to my law school class. I'm Chloe Ryder, the new district attorney."

For the first time in more than a decade, Marcus's heart skipped a beat. Actually, he did recall the pretty law student, who seemed just as confident now as she'd been back then. Holding out his hand, he said, "It's a pleasure to meet you. Again." Their palms touched, and his arm immediately grew warm. He couldn't decide if he was finally thawing after being outside or if it was the woman's touch.

Holy hell, what was he? A kid on his first date?

"Have a seat," she said, returning to her own spot.

Giving a nod of thanks, he slid into a bench across from Chloe.

"So, I spoke to your law school class?" It was a task he did often as the SAC of the Denver Field Office. "How'd I do?"

"I became the DA here, so you didn't scare me away from law enforcement," she said with a smile.

Marcus laughed. Chloe was smart. Charming. Funny. And yeah, she was beautiful.

Maybe this lunch wouldn't be so bad after all.

She continued, "You just moved to Pleasant Pines. How do you like it so far?"

"So far, so good. It's a lot smaller than Denver, but change is good." *Right?*

"Pleasant Pines is a lot smaller than most places. What does your wife think of moving from Denver to an out of the way place like this?"

"No wife. I'm divorced," said Marcus sharing a fact about his past that he usually kept to himself. Clearly, he wanted her to know that he was single. He stole a glance at her left hand. No rings at all. Was she single, too?

This lunch just kept getting better and better.

Chloe reached for her pre-wrapped silverware and picked at the adhesive band. "Yeah, I've heard all the stories about how hard it is to balance family and work in the Bureau. Must be tough on a marriage."

"I'm certainly not going to blame my ex. Turns out I'm not the marrying kind." Marcus gave her a wry smile. "Too focused on work."

"Being DA is basically my life, so I completely understand."

Her words sent a shockwave through Marcus. Did she understand? He felt like he might—and that meeting her was a rare gift.

A rare gift? *Jesus, Jones, pull it together.*

He changed the subject. "I hope you don't mind me saying, but you aren't who I expected to be the district attorney of a place like Pleasant Pines."

"Why?" she asked, a definite challenge in her words. "Because I'm a woman?"

Crap. Now he'd stepped in well, the crap. He wanted to move the topic away from him, not start a fight. He began speaking quickly. "That's not at all what I meant. You're—well—younger than I expected." *Good going, you idiot.* In his defense, though, he'd heard that her predecessor had been a couple of decades older than her. And how old was she, anyway? Thirty-four? Thirty-five? He supposed that wasn't too young—only seven or eight years younger than him, to be fair.

Before Marcus got himself in any more trouble, an elderly woman approached with an order pad in hand. "What can I get for you all?"

Marcus removed a set of menus from the back of the table. He handed one to Chloe before opening his own. "Why don't you go first?" he said to Chloe.

"I'll have the Cobb salad," said Chloe. "And a tea.

Earl Grey." She set the menu at the back of the table. "Thanks."

Marcus then placed his order, adding coffee for his drink. After the waitress left, the two sat in silence. Marcus searched for something to say, some way to learn more about the woman he never expected to meet again.

"I shouldn't have snapped at you earlier about your comment. It was wrong of me to assume what you meant. Although, you'd be surprised how often my gender is an issue."

"No need to apologize. But tell me—how did you end up with the job here?"

"I grew up in the area," she said. "But I've been working in Laramie for the attorney general's office. When the old district attorney retired last year, I ran for his job and won."

"Congratulations," said Marcus. "So, what got you interested in law enforcement—aside from my stellar presentation, I mean?"

It was her turn to laugh. To Marcus, the sound was like music, but a thousand times better. Jesus, what was his problem?

"Actually, my parents were both killed in a hit-and-run accident when I was in college. They never found out who was driving the other car." She blew out a long breath. "It was—is—still devastating. But I decided to turn my loss into something more—something that might be able to help others." She gave another laugh—this one sharp, not languid or musical. "I'm not sure why I just told you that. I never share that story."

"It's staying between me and you."

"Thanks. I appreciate that."

Marcus couldn't help himself—knowing they shared a secret buzzed across his palms. He rubbed his hands together. "Still, it's pretty impressive to be DA at any age."

Chloe waved away his comment. "I'll serve the people of Pleasant Pines for now. But I have bigger plans."

Marcus couldn't help himself; he was intrigued by her candor. "Like what?"

"One day," she said, "I plan to be the attorney general for Wyoming."

The waitress returned and delivered their food. The burger looked juicy. The fries were crispy. Steam rose from the cup of coffee. Picking up a fry, Marcus said, "It sounds like you have a lot of ambitions."

Chloe took a bite of her salad and chewed. After swallowing, she said, "I guess. But don't you? Don't you want more?"

What did he want? Sure, the Mateev case was a win for the good guys. But it had also resulted in an explosion on the outskirts of Denver that destroyed an industrial park. Marcus's career could've survived the debacle—although he'd never accomplish anything beyond being a special agent.

But the thing was, he had a younger brother who followed Marcus into the Bureau. His younger brother had the talent to go far. There were even rumors that one day Jason would one day the deputy director. Yet how far would his baby brother go if he had to live with Marcus's reputation?

The thing was, Marcus had ambitions of his own. He didn't want to be second-in-command. He wanted to run his own operation—which Ian had given him the chance to do at RMJ—and for a moment, he felt as if Chloe Ryder understood. Maybe she was a kindred spirit.

"What about you?" Chloe asked. "What do you want professionally?"

"You were just reading my mind," he said.

"Oh, was I?" She lifted one eyebrow while twirling her fork through her salad. "I knew I was talented, but I didn't know I was a mind reader."

Was Chloe flirting? God, he hoped so. Then again, how could he ask her out without muddying the professional waters, so to speak?

He lifted one shoulder, then let it drop. "I guess I want what everyone wants."

"Oh?" she asked. "What's that?"

"More," said Marcus. "I want more."

For a moment, their gazes held. Marcus's chest grew tight as he stared into her blue eyes.

"I guess we do understand each other." Chloe gave him a half-smile. Marcus fought to keep his expression neutral. It was a losing battle. He smiled in return.

Holding up his cup of coffee, he said, "Here's to our new relationship."

She clinked her mug with his. "To new beginnings."

The next few minutes passed as they finished their food and chatted. By the time they were done eating, Marcus had accomplished what he intended—made contact with the leading law enforcement official in the county. He'd also established the basis for a relationship—even if it would always be of a professional nature.

Still, he was certain they'd work well together. They could be a team.

Chloe wiped her mouth with a napkin and pushed her plate aside.

Sally, the owner of the diner, appeared next to the table. "Do you all need anything else?"

Chloe shook her head. "I'm good. Thanks."

Sally set the bill on the table. "Thanks for stopping by. I hope you come back and visit us soon," she said, before returning to the counter.

Marcus and Chloe both reached for the bill. Their fingers touched. Once again, Marcus felt the heat of contact. "This is on me," he said.

"I can take care of myself."

To Marcus, Chloe seemed to be one of the most capable people he'd met. "I have no doubt that you can," he said. "But at least let me pick up the tab. Besides, I have an expense account."

"Yeah? Me, too." Chloe rose from her seat. "We can split the bill."

Marcus had no choice but to follow, and he stood as well. After they paid, their lunch date was over. As he walked out of the restaurant and back into the cold afternoon, there was only one thing on his mind: Chloe Ryder and when he might see her next.

Chapter 3

The clicking of high heels on tile brought Marcus out of his reverie and back to the lobby of the Pleasant Pines Inn. Turning, he caught sight of Chloe, and his mouth went dry. Damn, she looked good. A silk blouse of light pink draped low at the neckline, giving Marcus a glimpse of the cleavage beneath. The gray skirt she wore hugged her hips and thighs, highlighting her slender curves. Today her straight dark hair was pulled into a low bun, and a fringe of bangs dusted her forehead Small, diamond hoop earrings hung from each lobe.

For a moment, he wondered if the jeans and golf shirt he wore left him underdressed. Just as quickly, Marcus figured that Wyoming was hardly the fashion capital of the world. Besides, hadn't he figured that eating at Quinton's on a Wednesday made their time together a business dinner? And in Pleasant Pines, jeans and golf shirt was about as dressy as it got.

"Chloe," he said while shaking her hand. She smelled of lilacs, and her palm was soft. Yet her grip was firm and confident—just like her. "Glad you could join me on such short notice."

"Thanks for asking."

"Are you ready for tomorrow's trial?" he asked, making polite conversation.

"I still need to write my opening statement. I'll take care of it after dinner, I suppose." Her tone was weary. "But the witnesses are all lined up and ready. You are lined up and ready?" Marcus was the first witness Chloe planned to call.

"I am always ready," he said, leading the way to the hostess stand.

A young woman looked up at their approach. "How many?" she asked, an eyebrow lifted. Had she just sized him up for his attire? *Damn. That'd be harsh.*

"Two," said Marcus.

"Follow me," she said, before leading them through the dining room.

To say that Quinton's was magnificent was an understatement—and that was coming from a guy who'd lived in several major cities while working for the Bureau. One wall was all floor-to-ceiling windows and gave a view of the surrounding woods. A large fireplace filled the back wall, while the others were hung with several Western-themed paintings. More than two dozen tables covered with pristine white cloths filled the room. Only half of them were full.

The hostess stopped in front of a table for two, set

into an alcove. "Will this work?" she asked, setting a pair of menus on the table.

After thanking the hostess, Marcus pulled out Chloe's chair. She gracefully lowered herself into the seat. They both ordered drinks—a glass of merlot for Chloe and two fingers of whiskey for Marcus.

With the hostess gone, Chloe lifted her menu. He picked up his own menu but watched her over the edge. Studied the way she bit her bottom lip as she read.

Marcus shifted in his seat and dropped his gaze.

After a moment, she asked, "What looks good tonight?"

Immediately, his libido answered. *You.*

Thank God his mouth knew enough to filter his thoughts. "I was thinking of ordering the prime rib."

She nodded, yet said nothing.

Setting his menu aside, Marcus said, "Give me all the details. I still can't believe that Darcy wants to confess. What do you think about this, by the way?"

Chloe reached for a pre-poured glass of ice water and took a sip. Setting the glass back on the table, she said, "Frankly, I was so shocked that I went upstairs and ran the news by Julia. She called the warden at Northern Wyoming and requested that Darcy's cell be searched. Before you ask, they found nothing."

Chloe and Julia were top-notch professionals, so he wasn't surprised that they'd taken that initial step. But there was more ground to cover—specifically the demands set in place by Darcy. "What about Darcy wanting to confess, but only to me and you? Does the specificity seem odd?"

"To be honest, it does. Then again, in some ways, it makes sense."

"How so?"

She inclined her head toward Marcus. "You are the reason she's in jail. You—and Rocky Mountain Justice—caught her. Maybe she feels some guilt and wants to explain."

"Her?" Marcus snorted. "Guilt? Unlikely."

"Gloat, then, about all the crimes she committed, where she was never a suspect."

"Possible."

She paused and took another sip of water.

Marcus couldn't help but watch as she drank. A bead of moisture clung to Chloe's lips. She licked it away. It was a natural gesture, but undeniably sexy. Marcus dropped his gaze to the table.

Chloe continued. "She didn't say much when I visited her in custody. I don't know that she would have told me the truth even if she had, to be honest. Kind of the way she lied to me when she was in high school."

He knew the story well, but didn't interrupt. "You think that because she trusted you then, she trusts you now?"

"I'm not sure that she trusted me then, to be honest. Still, the link between us is undeniable." She sighed. "It's thin, but it's all I've got."

The server arrived with their drinks and to take their dinner orders. Marcus waited until they were alone again before asking, "So, what happens next?"

"I have to start working on the parameters of this plea deal. Still, I'm worried about creating a legal loophole with her confession."

"She might not try to create some sort of legal jeopardy, but she could cause other problems."

Chloe took a long swallow of wine and seemed to consider his words. "What else could she do?"

Marcus listed his most immediate concerns. "Once she starts to confess, she'll try to negotiate a reduced sentence. Ask to be sent to a minimum-security prison—and then, pull her usual tricks and escape."

She gave him a sharp look. "It's my job to make sure that none of those options are available to her."

Chloe was a good attorney. He should be happy that Darcy was ready to confess, and he should trust in the DA's abilities to get a conviction in court based on the evidence they were gathering as well. Then why did doubt sit like a rock in his gut?

"According to her lawyer, Darcy alluded to having killed more men than we know about. If she can lead us to their bodies, I'd say that's pretty good."

"How will we be sure that she'll tell us about every one of her victims?"

"You know the answer to that question same as me. We won't." She paused a beat. "But we'll get what we can from her and hope that's enough."

Would it be enough for Marcus?

A tendril of hair had come loose from Chloe's bun. It skimmed her cheek, and his fingers itched with the need to touch her.

Chloe took another sip of wine and gave a short laugh. "I've been so focused on this case—finding and preparing evidence to present in court. When this is all over, I'm not sure what to do next."

"There's tomorrow's trial with the Transgressors.

After that? Another case will come along," he said, repeating the words his boss had spoken only a few hours before.

"Sure," said Chloe. "New case. New jobs."

New jobs? Marcus hadn't mentioned anything about taking another position. Sure, Marcus knew that she had ambitions beyond Pleasant Pines. Was Chloe planning on leaving the area?

Grabbing his drink, he threw back a gulp. The booze burned all the way to his gut. He waited as the slightly anesthetic quality began working on his frayed nerves. And then, it hit him—the reason for his recent dissatisfaction with life.

It was more than the emptiness that was left in the wake of any big case—it was the fact that he wasn't interacting with Chloe every day. A stabbing filled Marcus's chest, until his breastbone ached. He was well acquainted with the feeling—it was regret.

The hunt for Darcy Owens had brought him and Chloe closer together again—and he wasn't ready for to see her walk away just yet.

Chloe took a bite of chicken piccata and chewed. Funny how she had been famished earlier in the evening, and now she was still hungry—but not for food. It wasn't that the meal was bad—in fact, her food was delicious.

It was Marcus.

The dinner discussion stayed on a single topic: how the hunt for Darcy had consumed both of their lives. They'd spent months following leads, working side by side. Sure, during those long weeks—and many late nights—of endless work, Chloe had wondered what it would be like to kiss Marcus. To touch him. She shook her head, clearing away the images before she was overwhelmed with the power of a desire too long denied.

"I want this case closed," said Chloe. "I'm not complaining, but you can't believe how many hours have been dedicated to the investigation."

"I would believe," he said. "I've been right there with you through it all."

She brushed her bangs aside. "I haven't had a weekend off in months. I haven't cleaned my apartment in so long, I think the dust bunnies are going to throw a party soon." This was small talk—and she realized she was terrible at it. Desperate to distract herself from the sensual thoughts crowding her brain, she took another bite of chicken, chewed, swallowed. "What about you?" she asked.

"What about me?"

"What're you going to do if Darcy really does confess?"

He ran his finger up and down the side of his glass. His imagined touch danced across her skin. "Sleep. Maybe go back to New Jersey and visit my folks."

"New Jersey." She made a face. "I thought you were from Denver."

"The Bureau sent me to Denver, but home is good old Morristown."

"Any regrets about leaving the FBI?"

"Pleasant Pines is a nice place." He sighed. "But the pace is a lot slower than what I'm used to—you know?"

She didn't know. She'd lived her whole life in Wyoming. Even places like Cheyenne and Laramie had the feel of a large town—not even big enough to be considered a city. Still, she said, "I can imagine." And then, "What do you miss most about living in a big city? The dating scene?"

Before he could answer, the server returned to remove plates and bring a fresh round of drinks.

"Can I bring you anything else? Coffee? Tea? Do you want to see the dessert menu?"

Chloe took a sip of wine. Her limbs were loose, and her mind was relaxed. "I'm good."

"Nothing for me," said Marcus.

With the server gone, Chloe turned back to Marcus. "Sorry. You were saying—"

"What I miss about the city?" He shook his head. "I don't really know. I'm not exactly the kind of guy who hangs out on dating apps, you know?" Marcus said quickly, then sipped his whiskey. "What about you? Do you date?"

Chloe's wineglass stalled halfway to her lips. "Huh?"

He shrugged. "Sorry. That just slipped out. Just curious, I guess. I know this case has been chaotic—"

She laughed sharply. "That's one way of putting it."

"—but are you seeing anybody?" He leveled his gaze at her.

After taking a sip of wine, she responded, "No. Not that there's anyone available in town. The dating pool is more like a puddle—and a stagnant one, to boot."

"I'm not sure about that anymore," said Marcus. His voice was seductive and smoky. "I'm a nice guy."

Looking up, she met his gaze. His eyes were shaded by a dark brow. His intensity made him look dangerous. Hell, he *was* dangerous—because the fact that they worked together made him the wrong kind of man for her. Yet she couldn't mistake the intent in his tone, or his look.

He wanted her. Did she want him?

In truth, she already knew. She'd felt a pull to Marcus when they'd first met. But Chloe never—ever—got involved with anyone she worked with, and she knew Marcus was just like her in that respect. It had actually made her feel more comfortable working with him. But now their job was done—and things could be different. He'd made her an offer, one she could refuse if she wanted.

But did she?

Marcus was more than just sexy. In every situation, he was always in command and in control. He was a man that people could—and would—follow. It made him a force of nature. It gave him an undeniable allure.

A shiver of anticipation began in her toes. It ran up her legs, through her body, until Chloe felt as if she'd been electrified. Wiping her mouth with a napkin, she asked, "Are you sure that would be a good idea?" They both knew what she meant.

"Only if it's what you want," he said. "If you don't, then no hard feelings. I've been turned down before."

"Let me guess," she said, trying to make light of the situation. "By better women than me."

He held her gaze steadily. "Trust me, Chloe. Nobody is better than you."

"You do know how to sweet-talk a woman," she said, but something about his tone caused a bolt of heat to flare deep inside her. "But… I don't think it's a good idea, Marcus. We still have common interests. Darcy

Owens being one. And there's the Transgressors trial tomorrow." After she presented her still-to-be-written opening statement, Marcus would be her first witness. "After that, there will be other cases. Any—" she hesitated and searched for the right words "—extracurricular communication could make our work together awkward. I don't think we should risk it."

"I get it," he said. "You're a professional."

The server delivered the bill, tucked into a black leather folder. Chloe reached for the tab. "How much do I owe?"

Marcus waved her away. "Tonight's on me. I invited you, remember? I wanted to discuss Darcy and the confession." While taking his wallet from his pocket, he grew serious. "Listen, Chloe—I hope I didn't make a mess out of our working relationship."

"You didn't make a mess out of anything," Chloe said. "You politely offered. I politely declined. I'm sincerely not offended. Are you?"

"Nope," he said with a shake of his head. He grinned and continued, "Disappointed, sure."

His smile danced along her skin.

What she had said was true, yet it wasn't the entire truth. Chloe had been tempted more than she wanted to admit by Marcus's subtle offer for a night together. For far too long, she'd chased away her deepest fears during the Owens investigation with thoughts of Marcus. Of his embrace shielding her, comforting her.

Of his lips on hers. His hands on her breasts. The moment that he entered her fully.

She shook her head. Really, it had been too long

since she'd slept with someone. Maybe, when this case was over and done, she should try dating again.

Especially since taking a cold shower—alone—was starting to get old.

"All set?" he asked, placing several bills in the folder left by the server.

Was she ready? Chloe stood. Lifting her purse from the back of her chair, she draped it over a shoulder. "I need to visit the ladies' room. Can you give me a second?"

She strode from the restaurant and walked through the lobby, the front desk catching her eye. In a split second, she imagined booking a room—just for the night. She could take Marcus with her and create their own sanctuary: a place where the world outside didn't matter.

In the ladies' lounge, Chloe examined her reflection in the mirror. Strands of hair had come loose from her bun, and most of her makeup and worn off during the day. Still, she was pleased with her appearance. Like a woman who made decisions based on deliberation and thought. She was someone who measured all the angles before making a decision.

Not like a woman who acted on impulse or emotion.

Rinsing her hands in the sink, she let the water sluice through her fingers and watched it circle the drain. Running a damp hand over her hair, she smoothed down the loose ends before reapplying her lipstick.

The image of Marcus, his gaze filled with desire and the promise of pleasure, occupied her thoughts. Was it so bad to set all her ambitions aside for one night?

Was it wrong to want to feel his touch on her body?

Besides, one night together—where she created the parameters—might be the prudent way to handle the situation. Working with Marcus and hoping she wouldn't succumb to her desires was what was reckless. One option was a controlled descent. The other was slipping off a cliff.

No. Her mind was made up. She had to get to work on her opening statement. Nothing was more important to Chloe than her job—even a roll in the hay with Marcus Jones.

At the entrance to the restaurant, she paused and pivoted.

The front desk was at the far side of the lobby. A lone clerk stared at a computer screen. What were the odds that a room would be available?

Propelled by the very instincts she so often ignored, Chloe crossed the lobby.

The clerk, a young man with a goatee, looked up as she approached. "Can I help you?"

"I know this is late notice, but do you have a room available?"

"For tonight?" the clerk asked. "Doubtful, but I'll check."

In the moment, Chloe couldn't decide if she'd won the wager—or lost.

A keyboard was set below the desk, and he began to type. "I don't see anything." He paused. "Oh, wait. We had a last-minute cancellation earlier from our website. You're in luck. Do you want it?"

Her mouth went dry. Chloe swallowed, and then without any more thought, she said, "Yes, I do."

Chapter 4

Marcus sat in the restaurant and wanted nothing more than to curse. He'd messed up in a big way. Not only was Chloe a true professional—something that obviously he was not—but the DA's office had been the best client since RMJ opened. Beyond the Darcy Owens case and the Transgressors trial, there could have been other opportunities to collaborate in the future.

But not now.

And it was all because Marcus couldn't keep his libido in check.

After throwing back the last slug of whisky, he cursed under his breath.

Chloe appeared at the door to the restaurant. Their gazes met and held. Damn, she was good-looking. Too bad she'd never be for him.

She moved through the restaurant at a fast clip, the heels of her pumps clicking with each step. Her cheeks were red, her chest flushed.

"You okay?" he asked as she approached the table.

"Yeah," she said, breathless and hoarse. "I'm fine—for the first time in a long while, I'm better than fine."

"Something happen? Did you get an update on Darcy? Or tomorrow's trial?"

"No, it's nothing like that. It's just…" Her words trailed off, and he stood.

"Ready to go?" Marcus was done with the evening. Much as he liked Chloe, he wanted to go home. Still, he was a gentleman. "I'll walk you back to your office."

"That's okay," she began. "You don't need to."

"I insist," he interrupted.

It was then that she set something on the table. For a moment, Marcus didn't recognize what he saw. Chloe slid the key card forward with the tip of her finger. Marcus chest warmed as his gaze traveled from the card to Chloe's face.

Leaning forward, she spoke. Her breath was hot on his ear, and his body hardened. "You don't need to walk me back to my office." She continued, her tone low, "I was thinking about staying overnight and could use a little company."

Chloe stood near the elevator while Marcus pushed the call button. He was so close that she could smell the spice of his aftershave. The doors slid open and without a word, they stepped inside. In her mind, a million different voices spoke at once.

She should set up ground rules for their tryst.

She should say something sexy.

She should touch him. Kiss him.

She shouldn't be here at all.

Before Chloe could speak or act, he wrapped his arm around her waist and pulled her to him. His mouth was on hers, and for Chloe, there was nothing in the world beyond Marcus and the kiss. She tossed her misgivings aside. Tonight was not meant for thinking and analyzing. Chloe wanted to act with abandon and to feel nothing but passion.

Marcus pressed his body against hers. His muscles were strong. It was like iron sculpted into flesh. Cupping her breast, he rubbed his thumb over her nipple. His touch slid over her silken blouse and her lacy bra. She gasped with surprise, and he slipped his tongue into her mouth. He began to savor and taste.

Chloe didn't mind. She was in the mood to be devoured.

The elevator stopped its ascent. There was a ping and the door slid open, ending their embrace. Taking her by the hand, Marcus led Chloe to the room. He swiped the key over the lock and pushed the door open. Her heartbeat raced.

Stepping into the room, Chloe flipped on a light and surveyed her surroundings.

It was a typical hotel room—nothing more. There were two full-size beds with white comforters. A TV on a bureau. A small table and chair. Sconces on the wall. A floor lamp next to the table. Adjacent bathroom.

He pulled the door closed and engaged a trio of locks. For Chloe, the action was symbolic. They truly were shutting the world out and leaving their everyday lives on the other side. More important, they were locked away and able to submit to their deepest desires.

And Chloe did want Marcus.

Yet to pretend that they could have anything beyond tonight was foolish.

"What happens in here tonight, stays in here," she said. "We have a trial together in the morning. Then, there's whatever work we share going forward. This—whatever this is—can't get in the way."

"Understood," said Marcus as he approached her from behind. His breath washed over Chloe's shoulder. "You are so beautiful, Chloe. I've wanted you for the longest damned time."

Turning to face Marcus, she splayed her hands on his chest. "We have all night."

Marcus pressed her into the wall. His fingers scalded her with his touch. He kissed her deeper and harder, leaving Chloe unable to catch her breath.

His hand moved to her breasts, his fingers reaching under her bra. Again, she promised herself it would only be this once.

Just like scratching an itch.

No, there was more to it than that.

She felt as if she were a person who had been too long denied food and then brought to a banquet. She was ravenous and would feast until she was replete. In the morning, her time with Marcus would be a memory.

But not now.

He rolled her nipple between finger and thumb. It was pain enclosed in the velvet sheets of pleasure. She cried out and clung to his shoulders. He gripped her rear with his other hand, lifting her up, and pinning her between his body and the wall. Chloe wrapped her legs around Marcus's waist. Her skirt rode up to her middle. He was hard. She was wet.

Marcus kissed her deeper as he unbuttoned the fly of his jeans. Then he pulled her panties aside, and she gasped as he entered her.

"Chloe," said Marcus. His voice was a growl. "You are damn near perfect." He claimed her once again with a kiss.

He thrust into her harder, faster. She felt herself becoming lighter—illuminated and weightless, both—as if her soul was about to expand from her body. Yet she was still earthbound. She knew the key to her release. Reaching between their bodies, she found the top of her sex, already swollen, and began to rub.

With a curse, Marcus said hoarsely, "Let me."

His touch sent a shock wave of ecstasy through Chloe. Her pulse raced as she watched him enter her, slowly, then slide out with the same agonizingly deliberate rhythm. She began to tremble and couldn't hold on anymore. Rising above herself, Chloe cried out with delight. It was then, as the echoes of her pleasure still radiated out with each beat of her heart, that Marcus's thrusts became harder and more powerful.

Rearing his head back, Marcus let out a low snarl. He ground his hips into her pelvis.

He kissed her again, slowly this time.

Chloe's pulse echoed throughout her body. "That was magnificent," she said.

He smiled against her lips. "That was just the beginning."

* * *

Marcus couldn't recall ever having a more satisfying experience—sexually speaking, that is— than with Chloe. In fact, he could barely wait to take her again. Maybe this time they'd actually make it to the bed.

Chloe wiggled from his grasp and dropped to the floor. One of her shoes had come off, and she kicked off her other pump. He took the time to button himself back into his jeans.

"The beginning?" she echoed his words. Smiling up at him, she asked, "Does that mean you've been conserving energy?"

"Something like that," he said. Chloe was smart, funny, and he liked her company, but tonight he wasn't in the mood to chat. Scooping Chloe up in his arms, he carried her to the bed and laid her on the comforter. "This time," he said, working a button free on her blouse. The tops of her creamy breasts and lacy pink bra were exposed. Marcus was rock-hard again, his erection straining against the fabric of his jeans. He continued, "I'm going to take my time."

He undid each button and opened her blouse. Her skin was soft and smooth. His pulse started to hammer in his ears as he gently kissed her stomach, then dragged his tongue up her torso. Chloe sighed and melted under him.

He was driven to take her again, now, with all their clothes on. With an inhale, Marcus forced his libido to chill. One thing he never doubted about Chloe was her resolve. She had said that tonight was all they had. If that was the case, then he was going to create memories worth keeping.

For too long, Marcus had imagined just such a moment. He'd dreamed of being with her, of the mind-blowing sex they'd surely share. As much as the fantasies had aroused him, they had nothing on reality.

With Chloe on the bed, Marcus placed his mouth atop her bra and scraped her nipple with his teeth. She sucked in a breath and dug her fingers into his back. He wanted to feel her, skin to skin, and he shrugged out of his shirt.

Sitting back on his heels, Marcus drank in the sight. Her blouse was open, and her nipples were hard. Her skirt was still on—a problem to be dealt with in short order—but the fabric hugged her hips and thighs.

She'd look just as sexy buck naked—although she wasn't completely there, not just yet.

Marcus reached for one of her feet and, setting her foot on his shoulder, he pressed his lips on her ankle. It gave him a glimpse of her silky panties. They were the same shade of pink as her bra. He liked that she paid attention to all the details—even the ones that were seldom seen. He worked his fingers up her leg, gently massaging every inch.

Marcus hovered above Chloe. Her skirt had ridden up her legs and was now crumpled around her waist. After tracing his finger over her panties, he slid his finger under the fabric, before slipping his finger inside her.

She moved against him, taking him in deeper. Marcus slipped another finger inside her and used his thumb at the top of her sex. Now that he knew what she liked, he intended to drive her wild.

"Marcus," she groaned. He claimed Chloe's mouth

with his. She was his, damnit, even if it was just for tonight.

Her inner muscles clenched around his fingers as she cried out with her climax. "Marcus. Marcus. Marcus."

Rocking back to the floor, Marcus stripped out of his shoes and jeans, leaving them in a pile on the floor. Chloe watched him through eyes that were half-opened.

"You're gorgeous, you know," he said. "But you have me at a disadvantage. I'm naked. You aren't."

Lifting her hips, Chloe slid out of her skirt. She removed her blouse and threw it aside. "Better now?"

"Much." He moved between her parted thighs and slipped off her panties. Next came the bra. True, he'd promised himself to take his time. But he couldn't wait—not any longer. He found his discarded pants and wallet, where he always kept a condom. After rolling the prophylactic down his length, he kissed Chloe, and entered her in one slow stroke.

Chloe held his shoulders, raking his skin with her fingers. It was an exquisite pain. She was soft, where he was hard.

He reached between their bodies and found the top of her sex. He rubbed her clitoris, and she began to moan. Chloe was claimed with her own climax and her innermost muscles tightened around his cock.

Marcus wanted this night to last forever and focused on keeping his pace slow and even—but it was a losing battle. He drove into her harder, faster, deeper. A burning began at the back of his neck.

He was on the verge of coming.

It was like stumbling off the edge of a cliff—and

there was no way to keep from falling. A great wave of pleasure undulated through him, turning his vision cloudy and filling his hearing with only the sounds of Chloe's breath and his own racing heartbeat.

Marcus placed his lips on Chloe's. He wanted to say something, but what?

"That was mind-blowing." Her words becoming part of the kiss.

"Mind-blowing?" He rolled off Chloe and pulled the comforter up and around them. "I like the sound of that. Give me a bit to recharge. Then, I can blow your mind again—at least."

She snuggled into the covers and closed her eyes. "I like the sound of that," she said, her voice husky with sleep. "You'll wake me?"

He draped an arm around her and placed a kiss on her bare shoulder. "I will because it's not as much fun on my own."

She gave a quiet laugh. Then, Chloe's breath came deep and slow.

Had she fallen asleep already? Maybe it was okay. Sure, Marcus had wanted Chloe from the moment they became reacquainted and that was more than a year ago. But it was more than giving in to their physical desires. They'd lived through the terror that was the hunt for Darcy Owens. Now that the case was over, it was time for a final release—in all ways.

Still, Marcus wasn't sure he was ready to examine how he felt about Chloe and what their single night together meant. Or worse yet, what he might accidentally reveal about those feelings.

* * *

Chloe woke, suddenly aware of her unusual surroundings—and her bedmate. Marcus lay on his back, the covers pulled up to his waist. A black sprinkling of hair covered his pecs before narrowing into a line down the middle of his tight abs and then disappearing under the comforter. The muscles in his arms and shoulders were well defined.

His cheeks and chin were covered in stubble. Dark lashes lay beneath his dark brow. His lips were parted slightly as he slept. She longed to kiss him—just once more.

As memories of the previous evening came to Chloe, she was filled with two unique notions. First, she wasn't sorry that she'd taken Marcus up on his offer. After all, he was gorgeous. And as it turned out, incredible in bed. Second, she knew that their lovemaking could never happen again. It left her disheartened to know that their relationship—or at least, this aspect of it— was pretty much over before it started.

A bedside table held a clock showing the time in an otherworldly green glow. 5:45 a.m. Damn it. She'd slept later than usual. On top of that, she still had to prepare her opening remarks for the trial that began later in the morning.

Slipping out of bed, she searched the darkened floor for her discarded clothing before tiptoeing to the bathroom. Without the benefit of a light, she redressed and washed off yesterday's makeup.

Her shoes lay near the door. Holding on to the wall, she slipped on a pump.

"Were you planning to sneak out?"

It was exactly what she planned to do. Her bag had been dropped near her shoes, and she picked that up as well. "It's early," she whispered. "I didn't want to wake you."

"What time is it?" Marcus looked at his phone and answered his own question. "Almost six." He held up the covers. "Come back here. Room service opens in an hour. We can order breakfast in bed. Until then, we can find a way to keep occupied."

"I can't. I still have opening arguments to prepare. I have to get home and take a shower."

"There's a shower in the bathroom. I can even wash your hair."

It was an enticing offer. Biting her lip, she said, "I was serious. No matter how fabulous last night was, Marcus, it can't go any further."

"It can—if you want it to." He folded a pillow behind his head and stared at the ceiling.

"We can't complicate our lives. To do my job, I need to be able to work with Rocky Mountain Justice. The two of us sleeping together could undermine both of us professionally."

"I get it," said Marcus, glancing at her. And she knew he did. But still, she felt awkward.

Because you know you're lying through your teeth, and so does he.

Chloe rested her hand on the door handle. "I hate to abandon you, but I really do have to get going. I'll see you in court, okay?"

"Yeah, sure," he said, before adding, "Anything you need."

Chloe pulled the door open and stopped. Turning

back to the room, she said, "Thanks for everything, sincerely. Our night together was perfect."

He gave her a flat smile. "Glad to hear it."

Then she stepped into the hallway and closed the door.

For a moment, Chloe stared at nothing. With an inhale, she made her way down the hall, down the elevator, and out of the inn's front door. The sky was soft gray. It was the moment when night had already ended, but the day had not yet begun. Mist clung to the surrounding woods, and Main Street was deserted between the inn and her office.

At least she wouldn't have to face anyone she knew. Or worse yet—answer any questions about why she was doing the walk of shame through the town square.

A pang of regret stabbed her chest. Was she disappointed that she'd given in to her desire to sleep with Marcus? Or was it because she wasn't willing to risk a relationship—even one that promised to be more passionate than any she'd ever been in?

She knew the answer but refused to think about last night. Refused to let her thoughts drift to Marcus in bed, his arms open to her, kisses trailing down her back...

Shaking her head, Chloe cleared the image from her mind. Her car was parked in the small lot behind her office. After opening the door, she slid behind the steering wheel and started the engine. If all went well, and it should, she could get home, shower, change and be back at the office in less than an hour. It would give her two hours to prepare before the trial started.

As she pulled onto the street, Chloe realized that

her thighs were sticky—which could only mean one thing. Marcus hadn't worn a condom the first time they had sex.

And to make the already complex situation worse, Chloe couldn't recall the last time she'd faithfully taken her birth control pills.

The courtroom could hold more than fifty spectators. Yet for this trial, it was nearly empty. There were those associated the trial: the codefendants, their counsel—Stuart Riskin, the judge, with his assorted courtroom staff, a paralegal from the DA's office and Chloe. The witnesses had been sequestered in the DA's office and would be brought in as needed.

Peter Knowles, editor of the *Pleasant Pines Gazette*, sat alone in the gallery. A former boyfriend of Darcy Owens, Robert Carpenter, had become dangerously obsessed with Darcy's murders—and had begun to commit copycat crimes of his own in a twisted attempt to clear her name. His scheme failed, though, and resulted in his own death.

"We are here for the people versus Luke Winston and Rex Vanguard," said Judge Harrington. The defendants had chosen a bench trial—meaning that they wouldn't face a jury. Only a judge would hear the case. As far as Chloe was concerned, it was brilliant move on Riskin's part. The community was not sympathetic to the Transgressors. "Are the defendants present and with counsel?"

The two men had been charged in the same indictment and had not moved to sever their trial—a fact for which Chloe grateful. It saved her the extra work of a second court date and saved Pleasant Pines the additional cost.

Stuart rose from his seat. "They are, your honor."

Luke Winston and Rex Vanguard wore the orange jumpsuit of all inmates of the NWCF. Their wrists were shackled together in front of them.

Once the opening statements had been made, the lawyers were ready to try the case.

The door at the back of the courtroom opened and closed with a whisper. Chloe looked over her shoulder. Marcus had slipped into a seat in the back row. He wore a dark suit, a crisp white shirt and a tie. Of course, he was her first witness and had obviously dressed for a court appearance.

Their gazes met. Despite her best efforts to remain neutral, Chloe couldn't keep the heat from pooling in her belly at the thought of Marcus's touch on her skin—

"Is there something I can help you with, Ms. Ryder?" the judge asked.

Damn, she'd been busted staring at Marcus. "No, your honor."

"Is the defense ready with their opening statement?"

Stuart sat between Luke and Rex. He rose to his feet and cleared his throat. "As you know, your honor, it is my job to provide legal counsel to those who have been charged with a crime but cannot afford an attorney. That being said, I do give my clients the best advice I have to offer…"

Chloe tried to focus on what Stuart had to say, but she couldn't—not with Marcus sitting just a few rows behind the prosecution table. Her thoughts wandered back to last night—to his mouth as he claimed her with kisses. To his hands as he explored her. To the sweat as it glistened on his body.

"District Attorney Ryder?" The judge's question rang out like a shot.

Chloe sat up straight. "Your honor?"

"Call your first witness."

She glanced at the list, despite the fact that she had memorized the order of those called to testify. "I call Marcus D. Jones to the stand."

Marcus rose and walked to the witness box. After he'd taken the oath and was seated, Chloe moved to stand before him. "Mr. Jones, can you tell the court where you work and the nature of your employment?"

"I am the lead operative for a private security firm based in Denver with a satellite office in Pleasant Pines," Marcus said. "My agency is called Rocky Mountain Justice."

Chloe moved back to the table. "Can you describe what you do at this…private security agency?"

Chloe never asked a question in court to which she didn't already know the answer—especially when she had worked to prep the witness. So it came as no surprise when Marcus said, "RMJ can be hired by individuals or government agencies for a variety of tasks. Personal security. Sometimes government agencies will contract with RMJ for assistance with investigations."

"Give the court an example, please."

"Your office, the district attorney's office, hired RMJ to assist in the search for Darcy Owens, a serial killer who had remained at large for several months. The sheriff's office in Pleasant Pines is small and didn't have the manpower to handle the hunt on their own."

Sure, there were other law enforcement agencies that she could have asked for help. Then again, Wyoming was a big state. The closest FBI field office was in Denver. Even with every deputy working overtime, Chloe still needed help solving crimes.

She asked, "And what do you know of the motorcycle club known as the Transgressors?"

Marcus cleared his throat. "My agency was contacted by Pleasant Pines Deputy Travis Cooper last spring, seeking assistance. He had been to their compound and had reason to believe that the members were producing drugs. He also had visual confirmation that there were women on site who were being held against their will."

Chloe asked Marcus about the night RMJ and Deputy Cooper raided the Transgressor's compound. She had established that the motorcycle club had locked a group of women in a RV and that the only way to get those women freed was through force.

After thirty minutes, in which they thoroughly reviewed the incident, she turned to the judge and said, "I have no further questions for this witness."

"Does the defense have any questions?" Judge Harrington asked.

Stuart waved away the judge's offer. "No questions, your honor."

Marcus was excused from the witness stand.

She turned in her seat and watched as Marcus walked down the long aisle of the gallery and pushed open the door at the rear of the courtroom. Then he was gone.

There was no time to think about last night. Or how

things were left between them—really, how she'd left things. She had a job to do.

Over the next two hours, Chloe went steadily through her list of witnesses. As each one testified—a gas station attendant who had seen some of the gang with the women; the owner of a small convenience store out on the highway who had sold them liquor and overheard them talking about "parties" involving the women and the money they'd earn—she felt her case grow stronger. Before lunch, she felt her doubts melt away.

She was on the verge of another win. She knew it. The thought of a victory for the victims in her case thrummed in her veins—

"Before we proceed," said Stuart, interrupting her reverie, "I would like to confer with the judge and the district attorney."

"This is highly unusual," the judge snapped. Then he sighed. "We'll meet in my chambers. Bailiff, take the defendants away."

A court security officer led the two defendants to a holding cell adjacent to the court room.

Chloe was still watching the door, her skin tingling—but this time not with Marcus's remembered touches, as the words registered. *Confer with the judge and the district attorney...*

What was Stuart up to?

Was he about to offer a plea deal on behalf of his clients? Or was Stuart about to outmaneuver Chloe with some legal wrangling?

Chapter 5

Judge Harrington's chamber was a small space, accessed through a door at the back of the courtroom. There was room for a large bookshelf on one wall, full of dusty legal tomes, along with a large desk and two wingback chairs.

Between the Transgressors hearings leading to today's trial, plus various motions for the Owens case, she'd had more than one conference in the chamber over the past several months.

"I'll get right to the point," said Riskin as he settled into a seat. "This trial isn't going well for my clients, your honor. You've seen all the pretrial evidence and read all the transcripts the state will be presenting." He rubbed a hand over his face. "I really don't have a defense to mount."

Judge Harrington asked, "I assume that's why you brought us here—to discuss a deal?"

Stuart straightened his tie before looking at Chloe. "What is it that you want?"

There were ten counts of kidnapping. Human trafficking. Production and distribution of narcotics. Really, a century behind bars was too good for the defendants. But as little as she thought of Luke and Rex, she knew they wouldn't accept something tantamount to a life sentence.

She quickly did the math on Wyoming's sentencing guidelines. Human trafficking came with 120 months in prison. Another eight years for distribution of narcotics. If the sentences were served consecutively, it'd put the defendant behind bars for a couple of decades. She felt a deep sense of victory for her office—and all the victims and their families. "Twenty years without parole in Wyoming's state penitentiary," Chloe said.

The public defender sat back in his chair. "I'll go for ten years, with time already served being counted. Parole in eight years with good behavior."

Chloe stood. "You've got to be kidding. Ten years is a joke, considering the charges on the table." She shook her head. "Let's get back to the courtroom and finish this trial. The state's case is strong. Why would I ever accept those terms?"

Although if she were being honest with herself, the last thing Chloe wanted to do was force the victims to testify. It would be a brutal and harrowing experience for the women who'd already been through so much. If she could save them from that last bit of trauma, she would.

Judge Harrington said, "Well, Stuart? You might want to think about taking the DA's offer to your clients."

"Alright," said the defense attorney. "I know when I'm beat. Twenty years with the possibility of parole after twelve."

"No parole and you have yourself a deal," said Chloe.

"Deal."

Judge Harrington said, "Ms. Ryder, if the defendants agree and your office sends me the paperwork, I'll sign the plea deal. Right now, the maximum-security prison at Rawlins is at capacity. I'll have the defendants remanded to NWCF if space is available."

Northern Wyoming Correctional Facility was secure enough for the likes of Luke and Rex. What's more, they had a cell block where violent offenders were housed. The two gang members would be kept separated, and wouldn't even be a threat to the rest of the population. "Agreed," she said.

The lawyers and the judge returned to the courtroom and waited while the defendants were brought back by the bailiff. Chloe sat at her table and pretended to write on a legal pad. All the while, Stuart explained the details of the deal to his client.

"The DA is willing to offer you twenty years in prison without parole."

"Willing to offer?" Luke spat. "The hell with that. I want a trial. Then we can see what the judge says."

"The judge has agreed to the plea deal," said Stuart. "Rex, you've been quiet. What do you think?"

Chloe looked over her shoulder. Marcus sat in the

back row. Since he was done testifying, he was free to watch the trial.

He lifted a brow, and Chloe's cheeks grew warm. She quickly looked away.

"Chloe?"

She started and looked up. Stuart stood in front of her table. "The defendants want to be eligible for parole in fifteen years."

She understood that the judge wanted some kind of agreement. All the same, could she really go back to the victims of the Transgressors and tell them their abusers might be free in a few short years? Chloe already knew the answer. "Not a chance."

She glanced at the defense table. Rex looked down at his hands. Luke glared directly at Chloe. She refused to be cowed and held his gaze before adding, "It's twenty years from me or it's going to be a life sentence from the judge."

"I'll talk to them," said Stuart.

"We can hear you just fine," called Luke. "And that sounds like a lousy deal. Tell her *no*."

"I don't know about that," said Rex. "Twenty years is a long time, but it's better than we're going to get."

Her throat suddenly felt dry. She picked up the glass of water that sat on her table and drained the contents. "It's up to you." After rising to her feet, she glanced at Marcus. Truth was, she couldn't look away. Then to Stuart, she said, "I'll give you a minute to discuss your options in private. When I get back, you can tell me what you've decided."

She turned for the railing that separated the well of the courtroom from the gallery for spectators. For a moment, Chloe was weightless. Her feet left the ground, and as she slammed into the floor, she realized that she'd been struck from behind.

A body pinned her down. It all happened so fast that she didn't have time to panic. There was yelling. Someone called for the bailiff—who was with the judge in his chambers. She heard feet running across the tile floor. The slap of shoe leather was sharper than gunfire.

Somehow, although she would never truly understand how, Chloe knew that Luke Winston was her attacker. Beyond that, every other thought left her mind. There was a flash of movement, and Luke was knocked to the ground. Chloe scrambled to her feet.

Marcus and Luke wrestled on the floor. With his hands still cuffed together, Luke punched Marcus in the jaw. His head snapped back, and the blow left his lip bloody. Luke rolled to the side and got to his feet. Lifting his heel, he aimed at Marcus's head, and kicked.

Marcus caught the other man's foot inches before it made contact and twisted. Luke screamed in pain as he toppled to the ground.

Sidearm drawn, the bailiff and aimed at Luke. "Lay, facedown, on the ground."

Luke lifted his palms in surrender and flipped to his stomach.

Chloe dropped into the chair at the prosecution's table. Her heart beat wildly against her chest. Bile rose in the back of her throat. Yet she'd be damned before she got sick in the courtroom.

"Are you okay?" Marcus knelt next to Chloe and gently rubbed her shoulder.

She was far from okay. What Chloe wanted—no, needed—was to lean into Marcus's embrace.

Yet that wouldn't do. Not here. Not now. Not ever. She'd known letting herself be vulnerable to emotion, to passion, even for one short night, was potentially dangerous, but she hadn't realized how literally dangerous it could be. Who would have thought that a momentary glance could have opened her up to attack?

No, she only had one choice. There was one way to get through this moment, and that was to face it alone.

Just as she'd warned Marcus last night, he was a distraction she couldn't risk. And whatever she might feel for him now—and in the future—were emotions best ignored.

It was late, and Chloe still sat in her office. Her neck was sore. Her head hurt. Her eyes burned. She knew that she should go home—her staff had left hours earlier. But she couldn't bring herself to leave the office. Why? It wasn't like she was afraid to be in her apartment alone. Still, it hurt to breathe every time she imagined Luke knocking her to the ground.

The faint sounds of footsteps in the outer office caught her attention. Her pulse spiked, and she reached for the phone, ready to call the front desk guard.

"Who's there?" Even Chloe heard the tremor in her voice.

"Hey, Chloe. It's me. Marcus."

With a sigh, she slouched back in her chair and set the phone on the cradle. "Come on in."

Marcus crossed the threshold. He wore the same suit from earlier in the day, but he'd removed the tie.

Leaning against the wall, he folded his arms across his chest. "Hey."

Her chest grew warm at the sight of Marcus. She gave him a wan smile. "Hey, yourself."

"How're you doing? That trial this morning was wild."

"Wild is one way to put it. I guess it's a win, though. The plea deal has already been signed. Both men will spend the next two decades in jail."

Marcus rubbed the back of his neck. "I'm glad that the scumbags are being sent away, but how are you? Really?"

"You know." Her eyes burned with fatigue. "Tired."

He was quiet for a minute. "So, I was just across the street at Sally's and saw the light on in your office. You want to grab some dinner?"

"It's been a long day." She powered down her computer. "I was just packing up and heading out."

"Perfect time for dinner, then."

"Marcus, I can't."

"Can't what? Eat?"

"After last night." She shook her head, not knowing exactly what she wanted to say. "I've never made it a secret what I want out of life."

"To be attorney general for Wyoming, I know." He grinned. "Not to mention where you could go from there."

"I can't be distracted. Not by you or anyone else. Or anything else. It's just not worth it."

She regretted the words as soon as they were out of her mouth. Sure, she meant them—but not the way they were likely to land. And Marcus—she *did* care about him. It was just the wrong time. She just couldn't make room in her life right now for the kind of emotional upheaval a relationship might bring.

His expression shifted, but just as quickly, the mask returned. "Ouch. That'll take some time to heal."

Damn it. Now I'm the bad guy. "Listen, that came out too harsh. But I am focused—and you know why. And unfortunately, you're a distraction."

"You want to do right by the memory of your parents." Marcus nodded slowly. "I get it."

"Do you?" Chloe wasn't sure that she understood herself.

"Actually, Chloe… I don't." He paused a beat. "Lots of people have fulfilling careers, and they find time to date. Hell, some of them even get married." He held up his hands. "And please don't think that I'm proposing." He paused again. "Look, today was pretty harrowing. I just came over to check on you. I know what happened last night can change everything, but it doesn't have to. We can still be friends, you know?"

"Friends." The word tasted sour. "Right. We can be friends." But could they simply be friends after all the passion they shared? Maybe. Maybe not.

"Alright, then. You'll be in touch regarding the plea deal from Darcy Owens?"

"As soon as I get something from her lawyer, I'll reach out."

Marcus nodded. "G'night, then."

"Good night," she called after him, but it didn't matter. Marcus was already gone. She remained at her seat, staring at her reflection in the darkened computer monitor, and her mind traveled to this same place, but a very different time.

Eight months earlier

"A serial killer? In Pleasant Pines?" Chloe sat behind her desk in the DA's office and repeated what just had been said. Marcus had taken a chair directly across from her. He wore a sweater in forest green and a T-shirt in lighter shade of the same color underneath. His eyes matched the sweater, and butterflies were fluttering madly in her stomach. Still, a meeting about several killings was hardly the time to be distracted by a man—even one as handsome as Marcus Jones. "Are you sure?" she asked, focusing on the topic at hand—murder.

Marcus nodded. "Unfortunately, I am."

He spent the next few minutes covering the basics of the case. For years, law enforcement agents had been tracking a person who'd been murdering men by means of alcohol poisoning. The killings originally surfaced in Las Vegas, but after falling off the grid, they'd recently appeared in Pleasant Pines—following an investigator from the behavioral sciences unit who'd left the FBI and relocated outside town. The sister of the latest victim suspected foul play.

That had set off a series of events that ended with the death of two more people—a cook from the Pleasant Pines Inn, and the local sheriff, Carl Haak. The suspected killer had been shot by the former FBI agent

Wyatt Thornton. Despite the fact that she was wounded, the murderer escaped and was still at large.

A narrow window overlooked the back of the building and a parking lot filled with cars. As Marcus spoke, Chloe watched the falling snow as it blanketed everything in white. It was like they were cocooned in her office. Yet her chest was tight as she listened in disbelief.

Marcus continued, "We've identified the killer. Now we're trying to piece together her life and figure out where she might go, or who might help her." He set down a tablet computer. The screen was filled with the picture of a woman. "Her name is Darcy Owens…"

Chloe gasped. Her chest constricted further, making it hard for her to breathe. She reached for the computer as her hands began to shake. "Say that name again?" she handed him back the tablet.

"Darcy Owens. We have some information about her background." He read from an electronic file. "She attended Slippery Rock High School."

Chloe went numb. "I know her," she said. "I knew her when she was in high school." She stared at the picture. It was her, Darcy. "My undergraduate degree is in social work. When I was in my last year of college, I was an intern at the high school she attended."

Marcus stared. "My God. Do you remember her at all?"

"Do I ever." She sighed heavily. "She came to me one time and it seemed that she really needed to talk, like something was seriously wrong. In our conversation, she insinuated that her father had been sexually abusing her for years. I did what I was trained to do and told the principal and the school's counselor. They called her into the office and asked about what she'd told me. Here's the thing. The administration talked to Darcy's parents. The police. She continued to deny everything. I was then told by the administration that I'd been mistaken in what she had said."

"Were you?"

"I didn't think so then. I don't think so now, either."

"What did you do?"

Chloe's throat was tight and raw. She coughed. "Sadly, nothing."

"Nothing?"

It felt as though the cold from outside was seeping into Chloe's bones. She rose from her seat. "Care for a hot tea to drink? I can brew it by the cup. It only takes a minute."

"Sure," said Marcus.

Chloe moved to the brewing station. The reservoir for the water was nearly filled, and several mugs sat on a tray. "I have lots of different teas. What kind do you like?"

"*Like* is a pretty big word."

She gave a small laugh.

Marcus asked, "You wouldn't happen to have coffee, would you?"

"Sorry," Chloe said. "No."

"I'll drink anything that doesn't taste like grass clippings."

Chloe brewed Marcus a cup of black tea and then a cup of Earl Grey for herself. The pause in the briefing gave her time to reflect. "Back then, I offered to talk to Darcy again, you know." She handed Marcus his mug. "I wanted to see what she'd say to me, not just the principal."

"I'm guessing that you didn't."

Blowing on the tea, she shook her head. "I was told that asking Darcy about the reported abuse could be considered harassment. Not only my internship, but my whole college career, would be in jeopardy."

"It sounds like you really didn't have a choice."

Chloe moved back to her desk and took her seat. "I'm not sure that I agree. We always have a choice."

"Darcy never spoke to you again?"

With a shake of her head, she said, "Never. In fact, she avoided me at school. Not long after, her father died. Then a few months later, her mother committed suicide. She dropped out of school a few weeks after that. My internship ended, and I went back to college. Graduated. Then went to law school."

"How'd her father die? Do you remember?"

Chloe sipped her tea. The liquid burned her mouth and scalded her gullet. The pain seemed like payment for her sins. "I do, actually. Her dad drank too much one night—not unusual. When I worked in the school, we'd learned that he tended to drink. It was part of the insinuations she'd made. Anyway, it seems he got lost in the woods and died of exposure."

"Just like the other victims." Marcus shook his head. "That's a hell of a thing. Do you think she's copying her father's death with all of the other men?"

"Or he's her original kill."

Marcus sipped his tea, grimaced, and placed the cup on the edge of Chloe's desk.

"What's more, her mother hanged herself."

Marcus cursed. "The cook at the Pleasant Pines Inn hanged himself. That guy had been a friend and, unfortunately for him, a possible accomplice of Darcy's."

Chloe swore that she wouldn't cry. Yet tears stung her eyes and left her vision blurry. She wiped her face with the side of her hand. "Sorry," she said. "I just can't help wondering what would have happened if I'd insisted that I wasn't wrong. What if I called the police myself? Or social services? Would things be different for Darcy? Maybe all her victims would be alive today. Or at least some of them."

"You can't blame yourself. You know that, right?"

Chloe heard his words and understood their meaning. But she shook her head. "I became a lawyer to help people and serve justice."

"Sure, like a superhero."

"Yeah, just no tights or a cape."

"I bet you'd rock both."

Chloe couldn't help but chuckle. She paused. "All jokes aside, I've never quite gotten over the feeling that there's more that I could have—or should have—done to help her."

Marcus walked around Chloe's desk and laid his hand on her wrist. His grip was warm and reassuring. "You are not responsible for the actions of a deranged killer. Do you hear me?"

"I hear you."

Chloe glanced at the picture of her parents. If they were here, what advice would they give? For some reason, she imagined it would be much like what Marcus was telling her now.

"Do you believe me?"

She wanted to look at Marcus but was afraid that if she let her gaze meet his, she might never look away. "I'm trying but not doing a great job."

He touched her face and tilted her head up so that they looked each other in the eye. It was an extremely bold and personal move. Then again, she'd just made a bold and personal confession. A fluttering filled her stomach as she imagined more than his fingertips on more than just her chin. In her mind, his mouth was on hers. His hand was splayed across her naked thigh. His breath came hot and ragged in her ear.

Good Lord, Chloe needed to get out more often. Rising from her seat, she said, "You're being too kind, and I'm being ridiculous."

Marcus remained at her side. "I don't think you're being ridiculous. I think you feel guilty about what Darcy's done, but your guilt is misplaced. You couldn't have imagined that a teen in that situation would become a serial killer." He paused. "I know what it's like to misjudge a situation."

Chloe heard his words, yet she snorted. "Doubt it."

"We've known each other for a while, but I never did tell you how I came to be a part of RMJ."

She shook her head, intrigued about what he might say next. Then again, everything about Marcus Jones was intriguing. "You never did. What happened?"

"Long story short, I hired RMJ to help the FBI find and arrest a Russian drug lord. We got the guy, but things went sideways in the end. A whole industrial park went up in flames—literally."

She drew her brows together, confused. "And the FBI got rid of you? That seems harsh."

"That's not exactly what happened but I was damaged goods. The thing is, I have a younger brother who's also an agent. He has the talent to go the distance in the Bureau. I couldn't have him fighting my reputation on his way to the top."

"That's very noble of you."

He shrugged. "The thing is—you did what was right as well with Darcy. It's not always easy and it doesn't always work out the way want. But you've got no choice other than to move forward."

Marcus's words had made her feel better. "Thanks for sharing your story."

"I don't tell many people, but I figured you'd understand." Marcus moved back to his seat. Picking up the mug of tea, he took a drink. Swallowed. Again, he grimaced.

"You don't have to finish the cup just to be polite."

He exhaled. "Thanks. I really can't stand the stuff."

"I'll make sure I have coffee on hand for you next time."

"Maybe we can do this another time when we're both off the clock?"

It was hard to miss the interest in his voice.

"Maybe," she said. She could suggest they go out for another lunch—or better yet, a dinner. They had the serial killer case in common. Certainly there was more that she could learn about Darcy from Marcus. "I hope so."

Then again, she knew the real reason she wanted to get together with the handsome operative, and it had nothing to do with work.

Chloe immediately chastised herself. She couldn't

get involved with anyone associated with work. She wanted to be attorney general of Wyoming one day in the not too distant future. How much would she damage her chances if she were surrounded by rumors of an office affair?

So, it really didn't matter that his lips were undeniably kissable. He was her friend. Her confidant. A valuable member of her team. And that was all.

"You hope so," he echoed. "When? Where?"

Chloe cleared her throat and took a drink of tea. "The other day, you said that your agency…"

"Rocky Mountain Justice."

Oh yeah. How could she have forgotten? "You said that your agency does private security. But it's not really the kind of operation that monitors some of the big houses in the mountains, or provides protection for movie stars, right?"

"I mean, we do protection when we have to. Let's just say it isn't our specialty." He paused. "What are you thinking?"

"I'm thinking," said Chloe as adrenaline coursed through her veins. This was a case that she couldn't let get away. "That what I want is for your agency to find Darcy Owens. Without Carl Haak, the sheriff's department is going to be overwhelmed with the day-to-day law enforcement needs in the community."

Marcus said, "The FBI has been called in. The Wyoming Highway Patrol, too."

"If hired, you could coordinate with both agencies, correct?"

"Sure," he said with a shrug. "That's what RMJ does. Among other things."

"I want you and your operatives to be involved on behalf of my office. Hell, I want you to find Darcy and bring her in."

"Yesterday, when she had a showdown with Sheriff Haak she was wounded. It's been chilly all day and was downright freezing last night." Marcus continued, "We might be looking for a corpse."

Chloe shook her head. "If nothing else, Darcy knows how to survive. She's out there."

"If that's true," said Marcus, "RMJ will find her." He stood. "I'll keep you updated."

"Please do."

Then he was gone. The scent of his cologne lingered in the air, and she inhaled the scent deeply. A pad of paper sat on her desk. After picking up a pen, she began to take notes from the meeting. After listing every fact that she could recall, Chloe made one more notation before underlining the words and circling them twice.

Get single-brew coffee pods for Marcus.

Chapter 6

In the two weeks since Chloe had heard from Darcy's lawyer with her offer to confess, one of the conference rooms in DA's office suite had been converted to what the staff was calling the war room. The walls were papered with photos of Darcy Owens and her victims. White boards stood on easels, each containing information about a victim. Their names, hometowns—and cause of death.

Of course, there was more to each man than a name, a job, a place of residence. There were the families and friends who had been left behind, who needed closure and answers. Chloe didn't want to lose sight of her real task—to deliver justice.

This afternoon, Julia McCloud, Wyatt Thornton and Marcus Jones were had joined Chloe to strategize.

It had been six days, eight hours and nineteen minutes since she'd left him in the hotel room. After all that time, she could still feel his lips on hers. She could also feel Luke Wilson's strong hands holding her down—along with the knowledge that allowing Marcus to be a momentary distraction almost cost Chloe her life.

"I've received an official offer from Stuart Riskin, Darcy's lawyer." A pile of papers sat in front of Chloe. She shuffled through the stack, scanning each one. The letter from Riskin wasn't there. She reached for a stack of folders, reading the tabs of each as she spoke. "The offer is simple and to the point. A complete confession for life in prison. I'll be honest, it's a prosecutor's dream. Which is what bothers me."

"How so?" It was Wyatt who'd asked the question. In many ways, he was the key to the entire case. Years earlier, when Wyatt worked for the FBI, he'd been assigned to a string of killings in Las Vegas. At the time, a male perpetrator was suspected—and wrongly accused. Though the suspect never went to jail, Wyatt lost his job over the misstep.

Darcy had come to enjoy what she saw as a game between herself and Wyatt. So when he moved to Pleasant Pines—close to where she'd been brought up—Darcy relocated as well and began killing, hoping to lure Wyatt back to the chase.

Chloe looked at Wyatt. He wore a button-down shirt and trousers, kept his hair neat. Still the clean-cut Fed, even after all these years. "Darcy is anything but simple. There has to be an angle." She exhaled. "You're the expert on Darcy. Am I right to be worried?"

"You're right to be cautious, that's for sure." Wyatt

tapped a pen on the table for a few beats. "We can all agree that Darcy's calculating. She won't make a move without knowing the ramifications, correct?"

"I'd agree," said Julia.

As always, Julia wore her blond hair up in a ponytail. A brown jacket from the sheriff's department hung over the back of her chair. She wore a brown T-shirt with the gold star of her office embroidered over the left breast.

Julia always appeared both professional and ready for action. Chloe tried to dress the part of the district attorney—silk blouses, tailored skirts and slacks. But recently, nothing fit right. She shifted in her chair.

"What does she gain by confessing?" Wyatt asked.

"She avoids ever facing the death penalty, for one," said Marcus. It was one of the first times he'd spoken since arriving—unusual for him by all standards. Hell, he'd barely grumbled a greeting when he arrived. Chloe glanced his way. He regarded her with a steely intensity that left her sweating.

She still couldn't bring herself to regret making love to Marcus. But she cursed the fact that their intimacy had driven a wedge between them—just as she'd feared it might—and she'd lost the camaraderie they once shared.

"True," said Chloe. "Is that enough?"

"You need to keep one thing in mind about Darcy," said Wyatt. "She's not stupid."

"About that plea offer…" Marcus said. "Can we see it?"

Chloe glanced at the papers in her hand. The letter from Stuart Riskin sat atop the folder. When had she become so scattered? "Here it is." She slid it across the table.

Marcus picked it up and read it, his dark brows drawn together. "I think this is best we can hope for under the circumstances."

He handed the letter to Julia. She read silently for a moment. "I agree with Marcus."

Wyatt was the last to read the missive. "I'm not a lawyer, but I can't imagine that you want anything else."

"Here's my concern." Chloe leaned forward. "Darcy wants something."

"You might be right," said Wyatt. "But it could be that she simply knows she's been beat."

"I don't trust Darcy, either." Marcus sat back in his chair and stretched out his legs. "But there are other questions you need to be asking."

"Yeah? Like what?"

He pinned her with his gaze. "Like, are you willing to pass on this agreement?"

"Of course not." Chloe knew where Marcus was going and finished his argument for him. "So I have no choice but at accept this deal."

He shrugged.

"Let's move to the other item on the agenda. Wyatt, do you have a report about other possible victims?"

"I do." He had a stack of folders and handed four to both Chloe and Julia. "These are the men we believe Darcy killed but have never been linked to her. If she says that she's willing to tell you about everything, then these men should be on the list."

Chloe opened each file and scanned the names of

the victims. Nothing stuck. "Sure, but what if you're wrong?"

"Excuse me?" Marcus's tone carried an edge.

It was Chloe's turn to shrug. "You don't know that these men were killed by Darcy—you just suspect that they were. You could be wrong."

"We could be," Marcus agreed. "But Darcy has an attraction to a certain kind of victim. Male. Caucasian. Late-twenties to mid-thirties in age. Everyone was on vacation, and therefore not readily missed by family or friends. There's also the fact each and every man died of exposure after ingesting too much alcohol. You have to admit, it fits her M.O."

She wasn't in the mood to be chastised in her own office and glanced at Julia for support.

The sheriff had none to give. "RMJ is top-shelf. They aren't wrong."

"Alright. I'll take this all under advisement. But after she confesses—that's where I'll need RMJ to step in. Everything she says will have to be corroborated. Can you do that?"

"Absolutely," said Marcus, piercing Chloe with his gaze. "We'll look into anything that Darcy tells us and make sure we have evidence to back it up."

That's what she needed to hear. Chloe stood, ending the meeting. "Thank you all for your help."

Wyatt and Marcus rose as well. "You'll keep us updated, right?" asked Wyatt.

"Right."

Marcus paused at the door. He turned, glanced at Chloe, nodded once. Then he was gone. Chloe exhaled, her hands unfurling from fists. Maybe Chloe did regret sleeping with Marcus—especially if there was going to be animosity between them.

Thank goodness she had the plea deal to keep her mind occupied.

With just Julia in the room, Chloe leaned back in her seat. "This case is getting to me. I've started stress-eating, and now none of my clothes fit."

Stretching out in the chair, Julia tossed the folders onto the table. "If we're lucky, it'll all be over soon."

Darcy had almost killed Julia once before. Did the sheriff actually think that they could get lucky? "Do you really believe that we'll ever be done with Darcy?"

She held up her injured hand, as if the loss of her fingers proved a point. In way, Chloe supposed that the wounds did—Julia had faced Darcy and survived.

The sheriff spoke. "There were days—hell, weeks— when I wanted to give up. That would've been the easy route. But I fought for my physical and mental health. Part of that fight is to expect that things will get better. That good will win. You know what I mean?"

Chloe did know. Too bad she had none of Julia's optimism. "I hope that you're right."

"Hope. That's a good place to start."

Yet there was something else that bothered Chloe. "You used to work pretty closely with Marcus. Does he seem off to you?"

"Marcus? Off?" Julia shrugged. "Not really. Why?"

"He's usually friendlier, I guess." Sure, Chloe knew that having sex with Marcus had the ability to completely ruin their relationship. But she didn't want to believe that it had.

"Marcus has definitely chilled since he moved to

Wyoming, but he's always been an intense guy. I knew him back when he was in the Bureau. He was wound super tight then. Rigid."

"Marcus. Rigid?" Chloe couldn't help herself. Her mind went back to the hotel room. Her legs were wrapped around Marcus's middle as he pumped into her hard. Her face grew hot. She used the file as a fan.

"You okay?" Julia asked. "You look a little annoyed."

Chloe shook her head. "It's all of this stress. You said Marcus was rigid." The word caught in her throat. "How so?"

"Well, the first time I worked with him, he was still with the FBI, and a serious by-the-book agent. I guess he was what you'd expect of a Fed."

"Except?" Chloe coaxed.

"Except, we were working on the Mateev case. And a dangerous mobster almost got away because Marcus had his protocol to follow. He refused to step outside the lines—regardless of the situation."

"I see." But did she? "So, Marcus left the FBI to... what? Have more freedom? Make his own rules?"

"Make a bigger impact." She paused. "I don't think he liked living under his little brother's shadow—professionally speaking. The kid was—is, I suppose—on a fast-track to the head office, if you know what I mean. With RMJ, Marcus gets to be his own boss."

Chloe nodded while taking in what Julia had said. In truth, she felt as if she'd been given a glimpse into Marcus's head. But to what end?

After today's meeting she was exhausted—like she'd worked for days and not just a few hours. What's more, she knew why. In sleeping with Marcus, Chloe had lost more than a working partnership, but a friend as well.

Adrenaline coursed through Marcus's veins until his hands shook. Tossing the set of keys to Wyatt, he said, "You drive."

"Sure thing." And then Wyatt asked, "You okay, man?" while opening the doors with the key fob. "You seemed distracted in there."

"Distracted?" To be honest, Marcus was more than distracted. It was all he could do to keep his thoughts off his desire for Chloe. Sure, they'd slept together two weeks ago. Since then, he'd tried convincing himself that taking her to bed was like an itch that needed scratching, but he wanted her now more than ever. To be in the room with her and not acknowledge what passed between them was a living hell.

But it was more even than the sexual past they shared. Before taking her to bed, he'd been able to talk to Chloe. In a world where Marcus didn't have a lot of close relationships, the loss of his partnership with Chloe was a personal blow.

"Marcus?" Wyatt called from the driver's seat of Marcus's black SUV.

"What?" He pulled his own door open and slipped into the passenger seat.

"Is it about Darcy?" Wyatt asked. "You think that her confession is all a plot to get out of jail?"

"It's not the Owens case that's bothering me."

"What is it, then?"

For a split second, Marcus considered confiding in Wyatt. In fact, Wyatt was more than a coworker. He was a friend—or Marcus's closest approximation of a friend. Surely he'd understand. He'd recently found love with Everly Baker, a woman who had lost her brother to Darcy's killing spree. Together, they'd traced her steps, and with assistance from RMJ, they'd managed to keep Darcy from killing Everly. Unfortunately, the killer had escaped into the forest—and continued to wreak havoc for weeks.

Wyatt would understand that Marcus had developed feelings for Chloe. Feelings that he had no business acknowledging—especially while they were still working together.

Then again, was he ready to admit that Chloe didn't want him in return? And maybe that was really the crux of the problem.

In coming to Wyoming, Marcus craved the freedom to pursue his ambitions. Professionally, things were slow going. And his love life? That was non-existent.

He wasn't like Liam, Julia and Luis, who liked to hang out together, watching baseball or having barbecues in Liam and his fiancée Holly's backyard. Hell, he wasn't even like Wyatt, who was a loner to the extreme, but at least had a girlfriend and a dog.

Is that what Marcus needed? A puppy? He thought not. Clearing his throat, he said, "It's all of it, I guess."

Wyatt maneuvered the SUV away from the curb where it'd been parked. As he drove down the street, he glanced at Marcus. "All of what?"

Marcus drew in a breath. He supposed that there was more bothering him than just what happened with Chloe. "If we're right, the Owens case will soon be closed. The Transgressors are all just about done with trial and sentencing. I just have to ask myself, what now?"

Wyatt continued to drive and said nothing.

After a moment, Marcus answered his own question. "Are we supposed to spend our days setting up security systems for the superrich and their second homes? Babysitting a movie star who owns a ranch nearby?" He cursed and looked out the window. "I didn't leave the Bureau for this kind of work." Maybe coming to Wyoming had all been a big mistake.

"Something'll come up," Wyatt said with a smile. "It always does."

"You're quite the optimist," Marcus grumbled.

"Look on the bright side. Christopher Booth is still at large. I'm pretty sure we'll be called in to assist with the search for him." Booth was the leader of the local Transgressors club. He'd escaped in the raid where most of the other members had been captured. Booth was last seen outside of Pleasant Pines when he attacked and nearly killed a local deputy, Travis Cooper.

It was Marcus's turn to smile. "You're right, we can." And then, "Man, what kind of messed up life do I have when the thought of another manhunt improves my day?"

It had taken a full month of work, with constant late nights and negotiations with the attorney general of all four states, but finally, Chloe had done it. She'd brokered a deal that would put Darcy in prison for the rest of her days.

It was 6:15 a.m. Chloe was already dressed in a pantsuit—the only thing in her closet that still fit—and behind the wheel of her small SUV. She drove to her office. The sun had yet to rise, and most of the businesses in downtown Pleasant Pines were closed.

Her stomach roiled. If she were to get through the day, she needed caffeine and something to settle her belly. Chloe parked near the door of a twenty-four-hour drugstore.

She pushed the door open and stepped inside. Several coffee dispensers stood along the wall. Chloe poured herself a cup of cold brew on ice and added a generous helping of cream. Swirling her coffee as she walked, she wandered down the aisle marked Health and Beauty.

She scanned the shelves for antacids and stopped midstride.

Taking a step backward, she stared at the bottom shelf. There were two varieties of pregnancy tests. Her stomach flipped and threatened to revolt. Thinking back over the past several weeks, she had a sudden realization. Her period was late…but only by a couple of days…right?

Wrong.

Her last cycle had been more than six weeks ago. Standing in the middle of the store, staring at the pregnancy tests, she let her mind wander back several months…

Chloe closed her eyes and rubbed the back of her neck. It was well past quitting time for her staff, yet she had a stack of cases still to review. Most of the crimes committed were minor. Public intoxication. Shoplifting. Disorderly conduct. Then, there was the big one. The Darcy Owens case.

She was suspected of committing five murders in Pleasant Pines alone. There was an open investigation in Las Vegas and a strong link to half of a dozen more killings in Colorado.

The killer was in custody, yet she claimed to know nothing about any of the crimes, instead telling the attorneys that she had lapses in memory. Chloe brought in a psychologist. Even after several interviews, the psychologist could neither prove nor disprove Darcy's claims.

What was worse, Darcy confessed to killing William "Billy" Dawson, a serial rapist who had kept Darcy hidden in an underground bunker for almost a month. In the end, Darcy killed Billy. It was a crime for which she had total recall.

In short, it would be a nightmare of a trial.

The only bright spot in Chloe's otherwise bleak and difficult professional life was Marcus Jones. Over the past several weeks, they'd conferred daily, often speaking on the phone, once Chloe was home and finally decompressing from her day. Talking to him at such late hours left Marcus occupying many of her dreams. His voice. His laugh. His uncanny ability to see everything in a room without ever seeming to look. The way he never asked a question, just stated a fact. And then waited for someone to provide more information.

Yet not all of Chloe's dreams focused on Marcus's intellectual prowess.

She had noticed his green eyes. His dark brows. His

full lips. His broad shoulders, well-defined pecs and strong arms. His tight rear.

A soft knocking roused her, and she looked up.

As if he had materialized from her thoughts, Marcus stood at the door. He wore a black button-up shirt and a pair of jeans. "I noticed your car in the back lot," he said. "The guard told me you were still working and said that I could come back."

"Still working," she echoed with a sigh. "I feel like I'm always working and it never stops."

Hooking a thumb over his shoulder, Marcus said, "I was heading over to Sally's to grab some dinner. Want to join me?"

"Is it the whole team going?" Chloe was always eager to talk shop with the operatives from RMJ. "Is there a new development? Please tell me that we have a witness—or someone who Darcy told about her crimes."

"No development. No witness. Not even anyone from the team. Just me needing to get some grub and not wanting to eat alone."

Chloe still had hours of work in front of her, and she knew the right thing to do was decline. Then again, she'd be more productive if she ate. "Sure," she said. "I haven't eaten since breakfast and could definitely use a bite."

Hours earlier, she'd slipped out of her high-heeled pumps and blazer. Now she put on her shoes before standing. After donning her blazer, Chloe grabbed her purse from the floor beside her desk. "Ready," she said.

Marcus moved from the door. "It's a shame that we're only going to Sally's," he said.

"Why is that?"

"Because you look too beautiful for a place as simple as the local diner."

She began to protest. Undoubtedly, her makeup was smudged and her clothes were rumpled from her long day. But…how often did anyone really look at her, compliment her? She felt flattered in spite of her desire to keep her focus at all times. "Thanks," she said. "You don't look too shabby yourself," she continued, accidentally brushing against him as he held the door for her.

She knew he'd only meant the friendly gesture to be just that, but the moment her shoulder grazed the fabric of his shirt, she knew how wrong she had been. Her skin warmed and tingled. Her breath caught in her chest. Marcus looked at her face. His brows were drawn over his eyes. His pulse raced at the base of his throat and he sucked in a breath.

Swallowing, she said, "You know, I really do have a lot of work. Maybe I should just stay and finish up."

"You'll feel better after getting away from your desk," he said. "Besides, skipping one meal is unhealthy. I don't know what that makes missing two meals."

Chloe said nothing, despite the fact that he was right. There was just a small problem. Now they both knew that there was a spark between them. She felt deeply drawn to him. And she had no idea what to do next.

He was strong and powerful. Physically. Intellectually. Emotionally. He was handsome, sure. But what drew her in was the very maleness of Marcus. The fact that he hummed with energy and vitality.

Moreover, that made her keenly aware of the fact

that she hadn't slept with anyone in a long time. And that she wanted Marcus Jones.

Badly.

Her thoughts were unprofessional. Acting on her desires could damage her career ambitions. In fact, a tryst between them had the power to ruin the Darcy Owens prosecution. What would happen if a liaison became public? Would Stuart Riskin claim prosecutorial misconduct? In giving in to what she wanted, would Chloe be handing Darcy Owens the key to her freedom?

What was worse? In the moment, Chloe didn't care.

Then again, Chloe wasn't unable to control her cravings.

Forcing her desires aside, she folded her arms across her chest. "You're right. I'll feel better after I eat. Thanks for getting me out of the office."

They walked down a darkened corridor in the county office building to the front entrance. A night guard sat behind a desk and unlocked the door as they approached. "Evening Ms. Ryder. You think you'll be back tonight?"

Chloe thought about the stack of files waiting on her desk. She'd never been one to procrastinate, but perhaps she could ignore her pending TBD pile for one evening. "I'm not sure, but don't worry. I'll use my key to let myself into the building if I come back," she said, stepping out into the cool evening air.

Without speaking, they walked across the street. Marcus held the door open to Sally's on Main, the go-to diner in downtown Pleasant Pines. No matter the time of day, Sally's always smelled the same. Coffee. Bacon. Cinnamon. Apples.

"Evening." Sally, the owner of the restaurant looked up as Chloe and Marcus entered. "Just you two, or will there be more?"

"Just us," said Marcus.

As had become that owner's practice with RMJ agents, she sat Chloe and Marcus in a table at the back of the restaurant and well away from other patrons. She set down two menus with the nightly specials. "I'll be back in a minute for your order."

Then they were alone.

For Chloe, it didn't matter who else was in the restaurant. Marcus Jones had become the only person in the room. Hell, he could be the only other person in the world, and she'd be content.

"A lot going on at work?" Marcus asked.

"Always," said Chloe.

Sally returned. "What can I get for you?"

"Let me guess," said Marcus, grinning. "You're having the Cobb salad and an Earl Grey tea."

Sure, she often ordered the same thing, yet he'd bothered to take note of her favorites. How long had it been since someone cared enough to know what she liked best? In all honesty, Chloe couldn't recall. Her chest warmed and her face flamed hot. What she did know is that she needed to wall off her emotions, and libido, from Marcus.

She cleared her throat. "I guess that means you're going to have a burger with fries and coffee, then."

"You two know each other too well," said Sally, writing down the order.

Marcus picked up a pre-poured glass of water. "What should we toast to tonight?"

"It's funny, I was just thinking about that time you came to my law school class," she said, speaking before she'd really thought out where she wanted the conversation to go.

"And what were you thinking about?"

"I remembered you. But did you remember me? I know you said that you did, but did you—really?" After all, there were more than fifty students in that lecture hall.

"Honestly? I did."

"Yeah? What if I say that I don't believe you? What if I say that you're just trying to be nice?"

Marcus cleared his throat. "You asked me about intent—one of the harder things to prove in any case. How can you know what someone really intends to do—I think was your question."

It had been. "I'm impressed that you remember."

"I'm impressed that you keyed in on such an important topic as a law school student."

Chloe lifted her glass. "Here's to being impressed."

Marcus touched the lip of his glass to hers. "Always."

"Here you go." Sally returned with their food.

As they ate, Chloe couldn't be sure what they talked about, only that the conversation flowed, and she hadn't been this relaxed in months. Marcus, ever the gentleman, insisted on walking Chloe back to her office—even though it was simply across the street and up by a few buildings. At that time of the evening, the only business open was Sally's. The restaurant's light spilled onto the empty sidewalk. A slight breeze blew, pulling Chloe's hair across her face.

Standing in front of her office building, she was

so keenly aware of Marcus that her skin tingled. He reached up and brushed a strand of her hair aside, taking a moment to tuck it behind her ear. His hand lingered on her cheek, and Chloe's flesh warmed to his touch. He stepped toward her, erasing the distance between them. She didn't back away.

Leaning forward, she knew he was about to kiss her. What would his lips feel like against hers? And if he kissed her now, would she ever be able to stop?

For Chloe, there was no place she wanted to be other than in Marcus's arms. Yet she took a step back even before realizing that she'd decided. "Thanks for dinner." Hooking a thumb over her shoulder, she continued, "I need to get back to work."

Marcus shoved his hands into the pockets of his jeans. "Sure. You're welcome."

She held out her hand for him to shake. They touched and the tingling increased, collecting in Chloe's middle.

Now, months later, Chloe was back in the drugstore. As she reached for the pregnancy test, she couldn't help but wonder if that delicious feeling in her middle had been foreshadowing this exact moment, when she would wonder if Marcus had gotten her pregnant.

Chapter 7

The county office building had yet to open. Chloe stood beside her desk as her stomach roiled and threatened to empty. She'd let herself into the office with her passkey. She scanned the agreement, signed by both Darcy and her lawyer, one more time. If the serial killer actually confessed, this would be a huge win—and not just for Chloe's career, but everyone involved.

With everything that had happened over the past several weeks, it was no wonder that Chloe's stomach had been slightly off. It was also no wonder that she had been exhausted, unable to avoid falling into bed early nearly every night, sometimes as early as nine. What she couldn't explain was why all of her bras were suddenly too tight. Or why her period was now late.

The pregnancy test she bought sat in her tote bag,

along with her antacids. Staring out the window, she told herself that a positive result was unlikely. She was just…ruling things out. Being safe. Covering the bases.

She took a sip of coffee. It tasted like soil, and she gagged.

Certainly it was nerves. Unless it wasn't. After all, she and Marcus had been reckless and didn't bother with protection the first time they had sex. The possibility that she was going to have a child was small, but it was there nonetheless.

Grabbing her purse from her desk, she strode down the empty hallway to the women's lavatory. Shutting herself into a stall, she leaned on the door and opened the box. Chloe read the directions once and then a second time for good measure. There was a results window, where she'd find out her fate in minutes. A plus sign meant she was pregnant. Negative sign, not pregnant.

She took the test, and time passed like an eternity. Finally, the timer she'd set on her watch dinged, and she picked up the stick to check her fate.

The window filled with a bright blue cross.

Positive.

She was pregnant.

Her hands began to tremble. What was she going to do now? Hell, she didn't even know what to do with the used pregnancy test. Could she throw it away in the public bathroom? How soon before someone noticed it sitting in the waste bin and began to wonder who it belonged to?

Grabbing a wad of toilet paper, Chloe wrapped up the test and shoved it into her bag. Stumbling from the stall, Chloe realized that she didn't know the first thing about children. Or parenting.

Or whether she wanted to *be* a parent. What about her job? What about her goals? How would a child fit into the life she'd built for herself, the future she'd envisioned?

She stared blankly into the mirror over the sink as the realization hit her.

Good God, she was going to have to tell Marcus.

What should she say? How would he react?

She pulled her phone from her bag. After finding Marcus's contact, she placed the call. It rang five times before his voice mail answered.

"Marcus," she said. Even she could hear the anxiety in her voice, the panic that she could barely hold back. "It's Chloe. Something's…come up. It's…big." But was it? Sure, a baby would change everything in her life, but she could handle it—couldn't she? Then again—what if Marcus didn't want it? Or didn't want to be a father?

Chloe wasn't sure what to think—her emotions were churning, and the timing couldn't be worse, since she was due at the prison to meet with Darcy in a little while. She swallowed and drew in a deep breath. What else was there to say when she wasn't willing to leave such important news in a message? "It's not about Darcy," she added quickly. "But we need to talk privately. Call me."

Darcy Owens sat on her bed, staring at the dull gray walls that surrounded her. She wore the same shapeless orange jumpsuit. For months, this had been her life—her entire universe.

Today, all of that ended.

The small inset window opened. Darcy looked up. It was Gretchen, the guard who monitored her overnight. "Morning."

Gretchen made a point to speak to her every day. Darcy supposed that was what others would call a kindness. The guard was younger than Darcy, but only by a few years—yet her caring made her seem almost childlike. Or maybe it was naivete. Still, she preferred Gretchen to the male guards who never looked in her direction, much less bothered to speak to her.

Rising from the bed, Darcy approached the mesh-covered window. "What time is it?" she asked. The light seeping in from the single window wasn't bright enough yet for breakfast.

"Seven o'clock. Today you get breakfast early. Are you ready to talk to the district attorney and that other guy? They'll be here in an hour."

"I guess I'll find out."

"You'll do just fine." Gretchen gave a quick smile. In an instant, she decided that the guard was ill-suited for her job. "You're doing the right thing. You don't want to be dragged all over the country for all those trials. I shouldn't be telling you this, but you're smart to confess."

"If I was so smart, then I wouldn't be in jail."

Gretchen shook her head with a quiet laugh. "Got you the oatmeal you asked for."

A metal tray, filled with a bowl of oatmeal and cartons of both juice and milk, appeared through the trapdoor. Taking the tray, Darcy pivoted and took a step toward her desk and chair.

She stopped and faced Gretchen a second time. "Why are you so nice to me?" she asked. "You actually treat me like a person."

The guard shrugged. "I was brought up to believe that everyone has value."

"Everyone?"

"It was what my Grandma Ruth always said while she was raising me."

So. Gretchen The Guard had been brought up by a grandparent. It was an interesting fact and one that Darcy committed to memory.

Then again, what Gretchen said had brought up an interesting question. Did everyone have value? Was that the same thing as being useful? Turning away from the door, she moved to the desk and sat.

Darcy stirred her oatmeal for a moment. Then she waited a moment more, making certain that there wouldn't be any interruptions and that Gretchen was no longer looking into the cell. Standing, she pulled down the top of her jumpsuit and removed her bra. The white fabric of her undergarment had turned gray from use and sweat. It stank of body odor and, inexplicably, motor oil. It had been four weeks since she'd had this particular garment laundered. To avoid suspicion, she always sent her spare bra with the dirty clothes.

Inside each cup was a loose thread. She pulled one free and then the other, revealing a wad of tissue stuffed inside the cup. Inside each tissue was a scoop of dirt.

For the past month, Darcy had collected soil and bits of gravel whenever she'd gone outside. It was never a lot. Yet over time, it had added up.

She only hoped it was enough to make this impor-

tant step of her plan work. After dumping the contents
of each tissue onto her oatmeal, Darcy stirred it in to
blend everything, then took a big bite. She immediately
gagged from the muddy taste. Screwing her eyes shut,
she stomped the floor as she swallowed.

The effort left her breathless. Sweat coated her brow
as the oatmeal threatened to return. It didn't. But clearly
this next step in her plan was going to be harder to take
than even she had imagined.

Finishing her horrifying meal, she re-dressed—this
time donning her clean bra. After tucking the old bra
into her laundry bag, she sat back at the desk. Unable
to get the awful taste of the tainted oatmeal out of her
mouth, she started to gag again. Vomit rose in the back
of her throat.

"Don't!" The Darkness screamed, the single word
echoing in Darcy's mind. *"Not now. If you do, you'll
ruin it all."*

Of course, the Darkness was right. She drew in deep
gulps of air, waiting for the sensation to pass. Now
Darcy could only hope that her will remained strong.
Without perfect timing, all of her plans would be for
nothing.

And she simply couldn't allow that to happen.

Marcus Jones stepped from the shower and toweled
his scalp dry. Wrapping the towel around his waist, he
wandered to his adjacent bedroom. Despite his simple
routine, he knew enough to know that today was important. It meant he had to wear a suit. At least this was
Wyoming and he didn't need to wear a tie.

In his years as an agent with the FBI, Marcus had

interviewed hundreds of suspects. Most of them were, like Darcy, willing to admit to certain crimes for leniency in sentencing. Plea bargains happened so often that he considered them a matter of course in almost every criminal case.

Too bad this one wasn't routine.

Then again, they were well-prepared to interview the notorious serial killer. Marcus's team had gathered enough information about the four other victims who Darcy might have murdered.

Chloe's prep for their visit had been thorough. She'd covered every possible angle, and had been tough but fair in the arrangements for Darcy's imprisonment—but didn't leave an inch of room for Darcy to wiggle free.

The killer would give a complete confession today, or Chloe would take the case to trial. And he'd seen the district attorney in court—he knew she would win.

Damn. Just thinking about Chloe left his throat raw. It was too bad that things had been strained between them over the last month. Maybe now was the time for him to try and make peace again.

He hated to admit that she might have been right— that giving in to their desire for each other put a crimp in their working relationship. Because even though he knew damn well there was no one better in front of a jury, now he also knew how she tasted. How she'd dug her nails into his back as he drove into her so hard that he'd forgotten his own name. How she gave a little cry as she came.

Hell, just thinking about being between her thighs left Marcus stiff.

For Chloe's part, she never let on that anything had happened between them. In fact, she acted almost the same as before. Polite. Professional. Friendly—but now a little distant. As though they'd never spoken on the phone for hours. Never shared a late dinner at Sally's. It was almost as if she didn't remember their passionate night together—or maybe she didn't care.

Now that was a boner-killer of a thought.

After dressing in suit pants, shirt and coat, Marcus lifted his phone from the charging station on his nightstand.

One missed call from ten minutes ago when he'd been in the shower, along with a single voice mail.

Both were from Chloe.

He opened the app and listened.

"Marcus." She was breathless and her voice was tight with anxiety. "It's Chloe. Something's happened. It's big." She paused. Drew a shaky breath, then continued, "It's not about Darcy, but we need to talk privately. Call me."

Without thought, he returned the call. After two rings, her voice mail picked up. "You've reached Chloe Ryder…"

The sound of her voice landed in Marcus's chest. Gripping his phone tighter, he hung up. After all, he didn't really need to leave a message—she'd see the missed call and know that he'd reached out.

Dropping the phone into his coat's interior pocket, he grabbed his car keys. He'd wait and talk to Chloe in person.

He was concerned, though. If her panicked call wasn't about Darcy, then what in the hell was going on?

* * *

Chloe drove from her office to the jail, located twenty miles outside of town. The trip took less than thirty minutes, and it gave her time to think.

After the death of her parents, Chloe vowed to spend her life protecting the vulnerable and putting away those who broke the law. It was the only way she knew to honor their legacy. But Chloe had greater ambitions, too.

Certainly, raising a child would complicate her life's plans. Yet somewhere deep inside her chest, a sense of wonderment was already beginning to take root. Was she really going to have a baby? Her career had always been at the forefront of her mind, had always been more important to her than anything else—including romances and a family.

Like today.

Then again, there was the undeniable truth that having a child would also honor the memory of her parents—that in Chloe giving birth, the shared DNA from her folks would live on. For a moment she wondered about naming the baby after her parents. Heather if it was a girl. Franklin for a boy.

She wondered, too, what Marcus would think about all of this. If he would want to be a father to his—*their*—child. Or if he would choose to step back and leave her to be a single mom.

Not knowing was daunting. She'd never backed down from a challenge—but this was…different.

As she drove, she forced her thoughts to the upcoming interview with Darcy Owens. That brought up a whole different set of worries. Sure, in some ways it was a huge plus for their case that Darcy wanted to confess. But her nagging fears were still there. Was there evidence that they'd somehow missed? Were there more victims? Because Chloe was eager for the win—and she desperately wanted to bring closure to the families—were there of other victims out there? Or other people who still didn't know what happened to their loved ones?

Should she have dug deeper?

True, Wyatt had come up with four possible victims. Sure, forensic testing needed to take place. But in a way, those men were a litmus test for Darcy. If she confessed to those killings, she was telling the truth. If the men were omitted, well—what then?

Chloe could charge Darcy with making a false statement. But did a charge like that really matter in the face of being accused of murder?

Soon the correctional facility came into view. It was the only building that occupied an open plain. A paved, single-lane drive led from the road to a building of gray brick that was more than a quarter of a mile away.

The layout was perfect for security purposes. If an inmate did manage to escape, they'd be spotted before reaching the road. That was if they made it out of the compound at all. Tall fences, topped with razor wire, surrounded the property. The gate was shut, and Chloe pulled to a stop. An intercom sat atop a metal pole, and a disembodied voice crackled through the speaker as she approached. A camera was affixed to the fencing.

"State your name and business."

"Chloe Ryder, District Attorney." She held up a picture ID with the official seal of her office. Then she paused, not sure how to categorize such an important task. "I have an appointment."

The gate rumbled and slid open. Chloe eased her foot off the brake and drove up to the front of the building. She pulled into a parking space near the front door marked Visitors Only. After slipping out of the driver's seat, she collected her tote from the back. Glancing around the parking lot, Chloe looked for Marcus's black SUV with the dark-tinted windows. He had yet to arrive.

As far as she was concerned, Chloe was fine with a few minutes to organize her thoughts. A thick metal door, also controlled by an electronic lock that unlatched as she approached, led to a small lobby. She pulled open the door and stepped inside. The walls were off-white, as was the ceiling. The floor was covered with gray tile. A metal detector stood sentinel before another set of doors that led to the inside of the jail. Someone had thought enough about the decor to place a large fern in the corner. There wasn't even an exterior window.

A male guard sat behind a thick pane of glass in a control room. He stood as Chloe approached. "Place all of your personal belongings inside the metal drawer, please."

Chloe knew the drill. Because everything that came into the jail had to be searched, she'd learned to bring only the basics with her. Tote bag. Phone. Legal pad. Pens. Keys. She lifted her bag to the drawer and stopped. Damn. Her pregnancy test was shoved into an inside pocket of her bag. Would the guard see it? For a moment, Chloe thought about returning to her car and stashing the test into the glove box.

Wiping a bead of sweat from her brow, she dropped her bag into the open drawer. Saying a silent prayer that the guard didn't look too closely at the tissues, Chloe stopped at the metal detector.

"You can step on through," said the guard. "I'll give you your belongings on the other side."

"Thanks."

"Big day," said the guard. His name tag read Jeff Stone.

Had everyone heard that Darcy Owens was about to confess to avoid a trial? Chloe supposed so. After all, the guards were certain to gossip. "Yeah," Chloe agreed. "Big day."

Then again, that was a total understatement. Between Darcy's confession—and the positive pregnancy test—today was one of the biggest days in Chloe's life.

Chapter 8

A buzzer sounded as the guard unlocked a door that led to the bowels of the jail. Pulling open the door, she stepped into the corridor. There was another large window to the guard's room that overlooked the hallway.

Chloe had made enough visits to the jail that she was familiar with the layout. Beyond the guard station was another set of doors controlled by electronic locks and monitored by more corrections officers. That led to half a dozen cell blocks that housed around twenty inmates each. Every cell block had its own security, based on the threat level on the inmate. Inside the guard's small cubicle, a bank of monitors, three screens high and four across, sat atop a desk. The images changed every thirty seconds. There were images of the cafeteria. Exercise yard. A hallway that ran through one of the cell blocks.

Chloe watched as Marcus's SUV ~~turned off the~~ county ~~road and~~ approached the jail.

"He with you?" Jeff asked. The image of Marcus's SUV slowing at the gate was visible on one of the monitors.

"He is," said Chloe.

"Well, once he gets in here, I'll call back to the cell block and have the prisoner brought to the conference room." Jeff hit a button on a control panel and the gate opened. "But the warden wanted to chat with you first. You mind?"

"Not a problem." Chloe stepped away from the guard's office as Jeff placed a call and then let Marcus through security.

Marcus opened the door that separated the lobby from the corridor. Their gazes met and held—his step faltered. "Hey," he said, crossing the threshold and letting the door close behind him.

Damn. Marcus looked good. He wore a black suit and a starched white shirt—open at the collar. A bit of flesh and chest hair were exposed at his neck. She recalled licking the salt from the base of his throat. Her face grew warm. She swallowed. "Hey, yourself."

"You ready for this?"

Of course, he was asking about talking to Darcy Owens. Yet Chloe's immediately thought of the positive pregnancy test. "As ready as I'm going to be," she said before adding, "The warden wants to talk to us first, though."

He stepped closer and lowered his voice. "I got your message. Is that what the message is all about? Talking to the warden?"

"No. It's not that…" This was hardly the time or place to tell him about the baby!

Before Chloe decided what to say, Marcus continued. "Have you met the warden before? What d'you know about him?"

"I haven't met him, but Julia knows him." She shrugged. "She tells me he's a good man. I do know that Cal Douglas runs a well-maintained jail."

Before she could say more, Jeff tapped on the glass.

"The warden will see you now. You have to cut through this room to get to the administrative suites." He opened the door to let Chloe and Marcus enter. On the far side of the cramped office was another door. Jeff pointed. "Just go that way."

True, Chloe was an elected official. And sure, she came to the jail with some regularity to interview inmates. Yet in all the times that she'd visited NWCF, she'd never been allowed into the administrative wing, nor had she met the warden.

She pushed the door open and stepped into what appeared to be a typical reception area. A white-haired assistant sat behind a wooden desk. There was a sofa and chair in matching blue vinyl. Half a dozen filing cabinets lined the wall.

Standing in the middle of the room was the warden. Cal Douglas wore a brown suit, in a color reminiscent of a marine's service uniform. Despite his age—somewhere north of sixty years—he had broad shoulders and a powerful build. A fringe of gray hair clung to his otherwise bald head.

He held out his hand for a shake. "Chloe. It's a pleasure." Then he shook hands with Marcus. "I've heard some stories about your outfit—what's it called? Rocky Mountain Justice."

"Stories, eh?" Marcus smirked. "I bet some are even true."

The warden let out a loud laugh and slapped Marcus on the shoulder before handing him a business card. "Come with me into my office." Another door led to a short hallway that was lined with more filing cabinets. "I keep hard copies of the intake paperwork on each inmate. I have files that go back for a more than a decade—and I only shred the files if the inmate isn't still serving a long-term sentence."

"You know, they have computers for things like this," said Marcus. His tone was light, so the warden didn't take offense to the comment.

"I know. I know. I hate the damned things, though. Give me an old-fashioned piece of paper any day. It's kind of like this jail—the state redid the whole building a few years back. Now, I'm not saying there weren't issues before, but I'm not sure that the improvements really improved things, if you know what I mean." They passed a door, partially open. Inside, two conference tables had been pushed together and were surrounded by chairs. Chloe also noted a fridge, microwave and lockers. "That's the guards' break room." There was another door—this one closed. "And this," he stopped at the end of the hallway, "is my office."

He opened the door and allowed Chloe and Marcus to enter. A large wooden desk sat in front of an American and a Wyoming state flag. A framed picture of the governor sat between the two. The walls were covered with an impressive number of commendations—from the marine corps and the state of Wyoming. On the far side of the room was a seating arrangement in matching blue vinyl that served as the reception area. Cal gestured to the sofa. "Make yourselves comfortable."

Chloe and Marcus sat as the warden took a seat in a chair.

Douglas began to speak. "I make it a point to let everyone do their job. The way I figure it, I have enough on my plate with running this jail, and I don't need to second-guess anyone's decision."

"Fair enough," said Chloe.

"But I gotta ask, when do you plan on moving Darcy Owens? I want her in Rawlins as soon as possible."

There were several regional facilities that housed inmates all over the state. But the main penitentiary was in Rawlins and was the place where Darcy would spend the rest of her life. "As soon as Darcy confesses, her guilty plea is entered, and the judge accepts—she'll be moved. I can't tell you how long these interviews may take. Days. Weeks. Hopefully, not months. Then again, you already know that."

"Why can't you interview her in Rawlins?" Warden Doulas asked.

Marcus spoke up. "You said that you have concerns about your facility's security. Why didn't you say something when the initial arrangements were being made? Should we be concerned, too?"

"Concerned is a bit harsh," Warden Douglas corrected him. "A few years back—hell, maybe it was more than a decade now—the state sent a bunch of engineers, and they turned all the locks in this place electrical. We've got high tech security now, that's for sure. We're completely off the grid and got our own power supply in the basement. A backup generator in case things really go sideways. But me, I want a lock and key—something I can trust and understand."

"Sure," said Chloe, not entirely certain what the warden wanted her to say or do. "But don't locks eventually break? Can't keys get lost?"

"True on both counts, which is why the state did the upgrade." He paused a beat. "And to be fair, they did add this suite of offices and such, which are nice. I just don't trust technology. Call me a luddite. I don't mind."

"So, your issue with Darcy Owens remaining at Northern Wyoming has nothing to do with the facility itself, correct?" she asked, just to clarify.

"Correct."

Now she was truly puzzled. "What is it, then?"

"Darcy's a bit of a celebrity. We get contacted about her all the time. Reporters who want to interview her. Psychologists who want to study her." Cal held up his hand. "I don't know if we have the staff to handle that mess, is all. And before you go biting my head off," he continued, seeming to read her mind, "I'm just asking you to consider my position—and see what you can do."

"Fair enough," said Chloe. Then again, what could she do? Nothing in this moment, but maybe in a few months—or years, Darcy could be transferred. "After we're done today, I'll talk to both the public defender and the judge."

"That's all I'm asking for." The warden stood. Chloe and Marcus stood as well. "Now, are you two ready to meet with her?"

"Of course," Chloe said, giving no thought to her answer. Despite everything, she was truly prepared.

A guard was summoned, and he led Chloe and Marcus from the warden's office, down the hallway, through the room with all of the monitors and finally, to the conference room, where inmates typically met with their attorneys. He unlocked the door and held the door opened as they passed. "Knock if you need anything."

"Will do," said Marcus.

The guard left, letting the door clang shut. Then, Chloe and Marcus were alone.

A square with cinder block walls, the conference room had one small window, covered in frosted glass that was reinforced with wire between dual panes. There was a metal table and four metal chairs. One side of the table had a large iron loop fastened to the top.

Chloe hooked her finger through the loop and pulled.

"You know, Darcy's going to be handcuffed, shackled, and then both sets of cuffs will be attached to the table and the floor," said Marcus. "She's not going anywhere—and I'd never let her get close to you anyway."

With a nod of understanding, she said, "Thanks. But this isn't my first rodeo, you know."

He blinked. "I'm aware of that. I wasn't implying—"

She put up a hand. "I know, Marcus. I'm just a little keyed up, that's all." She sat in one of the chairs and removed several notepads and pens. She intended to get Darcy to write as much as possible in her own words. What she wasn't willing to put to paper, Chloe would transcribe. "I wish she would've agreed to the interview being videotaped. That way there would never be any question about what was said or not."

"You pressed. She refused," said Marcus. "There wasn't much more you could do."

Chloe lined up the pens and the notebooks. "Maybe. Maybe not. I also wish her attorney was here."

"Same thing. She waived her right to counsel. You can't force her to use a lawyer if she doesn't want one."

Marcus removed his jacket, draping it over the back of his chair, and sat next to Chloe. As he rolled up his shirtsleeves, she stared at the cords of muscle in his arms. She tried not think of how it felt to have him hold her, yet the memories of their one night together had been tattooed on Chloe's brain.

"And speaking of problems." Clearing his throat, Marcus continued, "That call this morning…what was it about? You said it had nothing to do with Darcy."

Chloe shrugged. Now that they were face-to-face, what should she say? "It didn't," she said, hedging. She hated to be evasive. But how could she tell him about the baby here? Now? She couldn't even think of the right way to break the news. *Hey, guess what? I'm preggers* seemed too glib. *I have news* was too formal—especially since Chloe wasn't sure that the news was bad. But she also knew that Marcus wasn't likely to let the call go.

"I haven't been feeling well," she began.

"Yeah," said Marcus. "You said you were keyed up. It's completely understandable. That's some heavy pressure and stress. Frankly, a lot of people are watching you."

"It's more than that," started Chloe, but just then, the door opened and Darcy Owens shuffled in. Months ago, the killer had colored her blond hair to dark brown to change her appearance. The dye job was starting to grow out, leaving chestnut-colored ends on golden roots. Her eyes were downcast, and she had the air of someone who'd been defeated.

No, Chloe decided. It wasn't that. There was something else there...but she couldn't quite put her finger on what it was.

A female guard led Darcy to the chair, pushing her into it while loosening the chain that ran from her handcuffs to the shackles at her ankles. This was pulled through the loops on the table and the floor before being reattached to the cuffs at Darcy's wrists.

The guard gave a hard tug on the chain to make sure it was secure.

"She's all yours," she said before leaving the room.

"Mr. Jones," said Darcy, looking at Marcus. Then she met Chloe's eyes. "District Attorney Ryder."

Sure, Chloe was sitting across from a serial killer—a woman who had taken multiple lives without any thought, and definitely no feelings of guilt. Still, she had to build a rapport with the suspect if she wanted a full confession. "We've known each other for a long time, Darcy. You can call me Chloe."

The killer ran her tongue along her teeth, as if tasting the name. "Okay, Chloe."

Shoving a pen and pad of paper across the table, Chloe said, "We're here because you've agreed to confess to your crimes in detail. In return for your truthful confession, all jurisdictions will allow you to enter a guilty plea, not face trial and you will spend the rest of your life in state penitentiary in Rawlins, Wyoming." She paused a beat. Chloe had to make sure that Darcy's choice to confess without her attorney present was deliberate. "Stuart said you waived your right to legal counsel."

"Yep. I did."

"We can still call him and have him sit in on this confession," she urged.

"Absolutely not." Darcy picked up a pen and placed it on the paper. A drop of sweat fell from her forehead to the notepad. The lines blurred as the perspiration was absorbed.

Chloe couldn't help but look at the serial killer and see the teenaged girl who'd come to her for help. A pang of regret resonated in her chest. "Are you okay?"

She lifted one shoulder and let it drop. "I guess."

Chloe waited a moment for the killer to say something more. She didn't. "It doesn't feel like it right now," she began. "But I am here to help you."

With a mirthless laugh, Darcy jangled the chains on her wrists. "Yeah, this is real helpful."

"You came to us, remember," said Marcus, his tone curt. "All of this is to keep you from going to trial and from facing a death penalty. If you don't want to talk and you'll take your chances with a jury, fine. Tell me now and we'll go. I'm sure the DA has some trial prep she needs to start."

"I'll talk," Darcy mumbled. "I'm just not sure where to begin is all."

Fair enough. Chloe drew in a deep breath. "Tell us about the first murder you committed."

"This is just hard for me. What should I write?"

Chloe tamped down a bubble of annoyance that rose from her gut. She was determined to say no more. First, she worried that Darcy was simply trying to waste time by bringing both her and Marcus to the jail. Second, if Chloe said too much about the crimes, Darcy could later claim she was led to confessing to certain murders, and they could later be thrown out by a judge.

Seconds ticked off the clock. Marcus spoke. "I'm not sitting here all day." He pushed the paper toward Darcy. "And if I leave now, I won't come back."

Darcy pressed the pen into the paper. "My dad." Her voice was little more than a whisper.

"What about your dad?" Chloe asked.

"He was the first person I killed. But I swear, he had it coming. The world is a better place without him in it."

Chloe exhaled. Tension she'd been carrying for months slipped from her shoulders. "Finally, we're getting somewhere." Using a pen to point to the pad, Chloe encouraged Darcy, "Now write it down."

Head bent, Darcy began to write. Chloe watched the time slip away. Ten minutes. Twenty. Half an hour. In the baggy jumpsuit, two-toned hair and handcuffs, Darcy hardly looked like a threat. Then Chloe realized what she'd been missing. Darcy Owens looked ill. Her pallor was gray and blotchy. A sheen of sweat covered her brow.

"I…" said Darcy, looking up from her pad. "I…"

"You what?" asked Marcus.

Rivulets of sweat ran down Darcy's face. She opened her mouth but didn't utter a word. From somewhere in her chest, there came a deep groan. Chloe rose from the table and stepped back.

It wasn't a moment too soon.

Chapter 9

The Darkness whispered in Darcy's ear. *"Hold it. Hold it. You can't be too hasty."*

Yet the moment had come, and she could no longer obey. With one great belch, Darcy emptied her stomach. The cramps and sweats and pain ended. Marcus Jones, the bastard from RMJ, was on his feet and beating at the door. "Guard! We need a guard in here!"

Chloe moved to Darcy's side. "Are you okay? It'll be okay." All the while trying to avoid the large pool of vomit spreading to the table's edge. If she hadn't felt so damned lousy, Darcy might've enjoyed all the chaos.

The door flew open. A male guard paused on the threshold. His tanned face paled at the sight. "I need to get the inmate to the infirmary," he said, though that much was obvious. Using a mic on his shoulder, he said, "Gretchen, we need a female guard to stay with the prisoner in the infirmary." Then he called a janitor. "There's a mess in the conference room. We need you quick."

The Darkness need not speak anymore. Darcy knew their plan had worked. A smile crept across her face. She gave a fake heave to hide her expression.

Hustling from somewhere down the hallway, Gretchen entered the room. She took one look at the table, another at Darcy, and recoiled.

"Holy crap," she said. She donned gloves and unlocked the chain connecting Darcy to the table. With the guard's hand on Darcy's elbow, she was ushered across the hall.

The round-hipped nurse looked up as they entered. Aside from the middle-aged woman, the room was empty. "What happened?" she asked.

"I don't feel so well," said Darcy, giving another phony heave.

"Let's get you on the bed," said the nurse. "Gretchen, help me get her settled."

Darcy let her knees go limp as the women hefted her onto a narrow stretcher. Next, Gretchen unfastened the handcuffs before removing the scanner from a holder on her belt. The guard swiped it over the bracelet on her arm. In one movement, she hooked one metal ring around the bed's railing and then attached the other cuff to Darcy's wrist.

Handcuffed to the bed?

Damn. Lying quietly, she waited for the Darkness to tell her what to do. But the voice remained silent. Darcy knew that her plan would never work—not if she were chained to the bed.

In a flash of memory that she could not escape, Darcy was thrust back into the dank, underground cell where she'd been held captive by Billy Dawson. She gave an involuntary shiver and scanned the room. She'd escaped that underground bunker, and she was going to get out of this jail, too.

"What happened?" asked the nurse.

Gretchen said, "All I know is that she threw up."

"What'd she have for breakfast?"

"Just oatmeal. That shouldn't make her sick."

The nurse cursed under her breath. "I hope we don't have another stomach virus going through the jail. Two years ago, everyone got the flu. It was disgusting. Before it was all over, we had to remove all the inmates and disinfect the entire place, cell block by cell block."

"This inmate's been in solitary for months, so I don't know where she'd get exposed to any infection."

"You'd be surprised how those things spread."

"Maybe it's her nerves," said Gretchen. "Today's the day she's supposed to talk to the district attorney."

The nurse grunted. "Maybe. Hopefully."

To Darcy, it seemed like the guard constantly saw the silver lining to every cloud, no matter how ominous. It was a trait Darcy fully intended to exploit.

"Now," the Darkness whispered. *"This is your chance."*

Darcy began to thrash, rolling her eyes into the back of her head. Her arms and legs shook. Her stomach was sore from retching, but she bucked on the bed.

"Oh my God," Gretchen gasped. "A seizure. Do I call the doctor from the hospital wing?"

"We don't have time. Unlock her cuff," ordered the nurse. "Do it quickly! We have to get her on her side."

"I can't do that."

"If she aspirates, we could both get fired. Or worse—sued."

The nurse held Darcy's shoulders as Gretchen fumbled with the lock on the handcuff. Darcy continued to writhe. Once her hand was free, she gripped the back of the nurse's hair and slammed her head into the metal railing. The woman screamed and stumbled back. A cut split her forehead in two. Blood streamed from her hairline and down the side of her face.

Gretchen lunged for a touchtone phone on the wall and lifted the receiver.

Vaulting over the bedside, Darcy jerked the loose slat on the railing free. Gripping the nurse by the wrist, she pinned the older woman's arm behind her back. Then she pressed a jagged slat from the rail to the nurse's throat.

"Hang up the damned phone," said Darcy.

Gretchen stared at Darcy, her finger hovering over the keypad.

Pressing the shank's edge to the soft flesh at the nurse's throat, Darcy drew a pinprick of blood.

The nurse screamed.

Darcy said, "I will gut her like a pig if you don't hang up that damned phone."

Wordlessly, Gretchen placed the earpiece back onto the receiver.

"Throw me the keys to the handcuffs," said Darcy.

"I... I... I can't."

"You think I'm joking around?" Darcy drove the sharp metal into the nurse's throat, leaving a gash that wept blood. Looking back at Gretchen, she softened her tone. "You know who I am. You know what I've done. But if you give me the keys, then all of this will be over in a few minutes. I promise."

"You promise?" Gretchen asked.

"I swear."

The guard tossed the keys to Darcy. They landed by her feet. "We are going to bend down and get the keys," she said to the nurse. "You fight me, you die. Understand?"

The older woman sobbed quietly. "I understand."

Bending at the knees, Darcy kept the makeshift knife at her hostage's throat as she picked up the keys to the handcuffs. Holding the shank with her cuffed hand, she worked the key into the lock. Once open, the cuffs fell to the floor. Darcy kicked them toward the guard. "Gretchen, put them on."

The other woman shook her head. She glanced at the camera on the wall. "No. I can't."

The camera had been placed in a corner above Darcy's head. She needed to take only a few steps back before being able to push the lens so it faced the wall. Hopefully, the guards were still dealing with the conference room and wouldn't notice that anything was amiss—until it was too late, that is. Without hope of help arriving anytime soon, she turned back to Gretchen.

"Put on the freaking cuffs."

"I can't."

"You can and you will."

Gretchen looked at the door again. Darcy could well imagine that the guard was thinking of how she could get help. Yet she wouldn't. Darcy somehow knew that, too. She'd never leave the nurse alone with a killer. "The handcuffs, Gretchen."

Kneeling, the guard retrieved the cuffs from the floor. She slipped them around her wrists and clamped the rings shut.

"Now sit in the corner. On the floor."

Gretchen did as she'd been told.

With a deep inhale, Darcy plunged the sharp edge of the metal railing into the nurse's neck. A spray of blood shot across the room, painting a wall with gore.

Darcy's hands were awash in the woman's life-blood—warmer than bathwater. Still, she pushed the shank harder. The nurse let out a single scream, an exclamation point at the end of her life.

The older woman became heavy as she lost the strength to hold her own weight. Darcy lowered the body to the ground. Blood pooled around them as the life literally drained away. Her eyes were open, staring at nothing. Her mouth gaped in a silenced scream.

Next, she took a bulky set of keys from the nurse's pocket and opened one of the cabinets of medical equipment. She found a scalpel—a much more dignified weapon than a bit of metal.

Gretchen huddled in the corner and stared at the dead nurse. Grabbing the guard by her arm, Darcy lifted the other woman to her feet. She pressed the scalpel to her throat. "Do exactly as I say, and we can both walk out of here. You understand?"

"You killed her," Gretchen said. Her voice cracked on each word. "You promised me you wouldn't kill her. Why did you do that? Why did you lie to me?"

"I can't control you both at the same time," she said, keeping her voice as soothing as she could manage. True, Darcy had recognized Gretchen as being kind. Thank goodness the guard was also naive. "For me to escape, someone had to die. I want *you* to live. You've been good to me. And you'll keep living, so long as you follow my directions."

Gretchen drew a breath that shook her entire body. "Okay. Okay. What do I need to do?"

"You are going to make a phone call and repeat what I say, word for word." Darcy then told Gretchen what needed to be said.

"I won't," said the guard, with a little hiccup. Tears slipped down her cheeks. "I can't."

Darcy's patience was wearing thin. How long would she have to calm this crybaby to get her to make a simple call? "Your pity party is annoying. Do you want to survive? Or not?"

The other woman said nothing, just cried harder.

Darcy sighed, then with lighting speed, shoved the scalpel into the guard's throat. "You know what I want you to say. To do." She lessened the pressure of the blade.

"Yes."

"If you want to live, you have to make that call. Got it?" Darcy asked.

Tears streaming down her cheeks, Gretchen nodded. "Got it."

Darcy steered them toward the phone. "Lift the handset and say everything just like I said."

Placing the receiver to her ear, Gretchen said, "Hi, it's me." Her voice was whisper-soft. Darcy pressed the scalpel harder into her throat. Closing her eyes, the guard bit her lip. A tear snaked down her cheek, but when she spoke next, her voice was stronger and without a hint of distress. "I need you to do something for me…"

As she listened to Gretchen speak the words she'd scripted, the Darkness smiled.

The time of judgment was about to begin. Fire would rain from the sky, the earth would open and hell would consume all who thought they could control Darcy and the Darkness.

A crew of maintenance workers arrived with mops and buckets to clean the mess in the conference room. They ushered Chloe and Marcus to the hallway, and then the duo was directed to the small foyer at the front of the building. Standing in the lobby, Marcus watched Chloe from the periphery of his vision. She leaned on the wall, with her arms folded across her chest. Her oversize leather tote teetered drunkenly by her feet.

He wondered what she was thinking. Him? He had several concerns. Like how soon they might be able to interview Darcy Owens again. Or perhaps, more important, whether they'd be able to talk to her at all. They'd both worked too long, and too hard, to end up without a conviction in this case.

Yet there was another pressing issue. "So, should

we revisit our discussion about the message you left this morning?"

Chloe looked up. She stared at him with her bright blue eyes. "What about it?"

Her slightly evasive answer set his teeth on edge. After all, she was the one who'd called him. He wasn't in the wrong to be concerned. "What did you want to tell me?" he asked. "It sounded important."

She glanced over her shoulder. The glass-enclosed guard room was empty. No doubt the staff was still dealing with Darcy and the mess. Chloe turned back to Marcus but didn't look up. "I guess I was just upset by this interview. That's all."

He wasn't buying it. Last month she'd been attacked by a defendant during a trial. At the time, she hadn't done much more than flinch. No, she was lying to him now. But why? Marcus had to wonder—what was so important that Chloe couldn't tell him the truth?

One thing Marcus learned long ago was that suspects would talk, so long as you gave them enough time. More than that, they'd eventually get around to telling the truth so long as they weren't provided with an alternative story.

His years in law enforcement taught him to be a patient man. Yet as he watched Chloe, Marcus shifted his weight from one foot to the other and back again. His tolerance wore thin, and he had to wonder—what was it about this woman that kept him agitated? What's more, how could she stand there and pretend she had no feelings for him? Especially since he'd experienced her passionate nature. And unless his radar needed repair, he knew in his gut that they'd had a connection. An undeniable one that was more than merely physical.

"Something's happened," she said after a pause that had gone on for far too long.

"I gathered that," he said. "What is it?"

"Remember that night?" Chloe asked. "When we went out to dinner at Quinton's?"

Dinner? Was that how she characterized their time together at the Pleasant Pines Inn? *Ouch*. She did know how to wound a guy. "Of course, I remember. I remember a lot about that night, Chloe." He watched her pale skin flush and knew he'd gotten to her. "What about it?"

Chloe worked her bottom lip between her teeth. "It's just that…"

The door that led from the lobby to the jail opened, and Chloe's words trailed off as she turned to look. A middle-aged male guard held the handle and leaned past the threshold. "I just got a call from the guard, Gretchen," he said. "Darcy feels up to talking, but the nurse wants her to stay in the infirmary."

Chloe and Marcus looked at each other and shrugged. "Alright," he said. "Let's go."

"Not you, buddy. Sorry," said the guard. "Just the district attorney. Must be a girl thing."

"Girl thing?" Chloe echoed. "It doesn't seem like protocol to speak to an inmate in the infirmary."

"It's not forbidden, if that's what you're thinking." The guard shrugged.

Glancing at Marcus, Chloe shrugged as well.

He offered, "I can go with you. Darcy can deal."

"Or she can refuse to speak now—and later," said Chloe. She shook her head. "There've been enough problems already this morning. I want to hear what she has to say—no matter where the interview takes place. We owe it to the victims and their families to finally get this closure."

Marcus hated to admit that Chloe was right. "You sure?"

Chloe smoothed down the front of her blouse. "I'll text once I get a better idea of what's going on," she said while picking up her bag.

Marcus was left in the lobby, with nothing more than a bedraggled fern for company. He didn't like Chloe talking to Darcy without him. Sure, she was a thoroughly capable woman, and at least one guard would be present for protection—two, he hoped fervently. Still, it was their case—something they had worked on together. So, yeah, it got on his nerves that he'd been left out of the interview.

On top of all that was the fact that Chloe was keeping something from him. And he was determined to find out what it was.

Chloe retraced her steps back through the metal detector and the door controlled by the electronic lock. The guard entered a code into a keypad on a door that was marked as infirmary. The lock clicked, and the door opened slightly.

Chloe gave him a small smile and a nod. "Thanks," she said.

Pushing open the door, Chloe stepped into the room. The first thing she noticed was the scent of heated copper. And—the room was empty, the beds bare. No sign of Darcy.

Vomit rose in the back of her throat. Chloe pressed a hand to her mouth, fearful that she, too, was going to retch.

Had there been a mistake? Was Chloe supposed to have been escorted to Darcy's cell? Or back to the conference room? Looking around the room, her gaze was drawn to the floor. A hand—that was connected to a wrist and presumably an arm—lay at the foot of the bed. Chloe went cold. Her heartbeat raced.

"Hello?" Her voice quavered. Had someone passed out? "Are you okay?"

Stepping forward, she rounded the end of the small bed.

The nurse was sprawled across the dingy tile. Her white uniform was covered with red, and a pool of blood surrounded her body.

"Oh my God!" Chloe dropped to the floor and reached for the other woman's wrist. Her flesh was warm, yet she could find no pulse. Chloe wasn't surprised. The woman's eyes were open, yet she saw nothing. A piece of broken metal protruded from her neck. Chloe tried to focus on the facts.

The nurse was dead—but hadn't been for long. A few minutes, no more.

Where was Darcy? Where was the guard who had summoned Chloe?

Think, damn it. Concentrate.

Rocking back on her heels, Chloe reached for her bag and her phone. She needed to call Marcus—or better, the warden. They were the experts, and would know what to do.

The door closed with a crack. Chloe turned and

slowly rose to her feet. Nothing that she saw made sense.

The guard, Gretchen, stood there, wearing a set of handcuffs. A glint of silver at her throat, reflected the overhead light. It took Chloe only a moment to recognize it as a razor-sharp blade. Gretchen took one slow step forward and then another.

Darcy stood at the guard's back, holding the scalpel to the other woman's neck. Her orange jumpsuit was covered in vomit and blood.

Chloe swallowed down her revulsion. "You did this, Darcy? Why?"

"Guilty as charged," she said, her voice carrying a singsongy lilt. "Will you ask me to write that on your notepad, too?"

A deep chill ran down her spine. "What do you want?"

"What do you think I want?" Darcy asked. "To get out of here."

What was Chloe supposed to say to that? "You're a smart woman. You know that nobody will let you get away. Not now. Not ever." After swallowing down her rising panic, she continued, "If you plan to take hostages and get them to release you, it won't work." Chloe scanned the room. She had to get help. But how?

"You don't know what I have planned," said Darcy with a sneer.

"You took advantage of your illness and tried to overpower the nurse. Things got out of hand," said Chloe, trying to read the scene and recreate the scenario. "If you stop now, I can help you."

Darcy interrupted with a snort. "I wasn't sick by accident."

The statement made no sense. "What?"

"You don't get it, do you? I made myself sick. I fooled you guys. God, you are so gullible."

Gretchen's bottom lip continued to tremble. "What? How?"

"You two are so stupid," said Darcy. "It's almost boring. Now, here's what we're going to do. Gretchen, you need to unlock the leg irons around my ankles and give them to Chloe."

The guard began to cry silent tears. "No," she said. "You promised to let me go if I made the call."

"You're right," said Darcy. "Now you're free."

Chloe screamed. "Stop!"

It wasn't enough. The killer drew the blade across the guard's throat. An arc of blood shot across the room, covering the wall and spraying the ceiling. Gretchen's eyes went wide. She opened her mouth, as if to scream, but no sound came out. The gush of blood weakened to a stream before exploding again, being pushed out with each beat of the woman's fading heart.

Despite wearing handcuffs, she lifted her hands to her open throat, trying to stanch the flow. It did no good. Blood seeped through her fingers, dripping down her arms and staining the front of her uniform.

Chloe lunged forward, reaching for Gretchen as another fountain of blood escaped from the woman's throat. Red sprayed across Chloe's clothes, her face, her hair. The floor was slick. In her pumps and pants, Chloe had little traction, and she skidded while reaching forward.

Darcy let go of Gretchen's shoulder. The guard dropped to her knees before falling face down on the floor. Chloe knelt at her side. "Gretchen, can you hear me?"

One wheezing breath escaped the other woman's mouth. Then another. And then, there were no more.

Chloe's heart began to race. She finally recognized the mysterious scents she had noticed upon entering the room: they were terror and death.

Chapter 10

Chloe's arms felt heavy, and her feet refused to move. Her thoughts came to her in disjointed snapshots. Yet she knew that the danger was real, and if she didn't act, she too would die.

Darcy removed the handcuffs from her own ankles and held them out. "Put these on."

For the span of a heartbeat, Chloe wanted to comply. Like maybe if she cooperated, then everything would turn out alright. But she knew better.

Darcy held out the cuffs further. "Put these on. Now."

"The hell I will."

Gritting her teeth, the killer snarled. "You don't want to force me to act."

Dropping her bag, Chloe kicked off her pumps.

Standing barefoot in a puddle of blood, she lifted her chin. "You want those on me, come over here and put them on yourself."

Sure, challenging a killer was never a good idea—it was an even worse idea since she was pregnant. But Chloe would be damned before she let herself—and her baby—be taken as a hostage.

Darcy launched herself forward and grabbed Chloe around the middle. The impact drove the air from Chloe's lungs as both women tumbled to the ground. Darcy landed on top of Chloe. She lifted her scalpel, ready to strike.

Chloe grabbed Darcy's wrist. She needed more than her wits to defend herself. If she wanted to make it out alive—and protect the life of her baby, then she had to fight. She looked wildly for something—anything—to use as a weapon. Her pump lay nearby. Chloe grabbed the shoe with one hand and brought it up and around. She slammed the sharp heel into Darcy's face, just missing her eye.

With a screech, Darcy wrenched the shoe from Chloe's hand. She screamed in rage and frustration as the shoe slipped from her grasp and fell to the floor.

Bringing up her feet, Chloe kicked Darcy in the side of the head. The killer lost her balance as Chloe clawed her way forward, reaching for Gretchen's belt. Guards were typically unarmed, so there was little to be used as a weapon. Darcy leaped for her. Spinning to her back, Chloe swung around the plastic-and-metal scanner. She slammed the device into Darcy's cheek. Then Chloe hit Darcy on the back of the head. The killer pulled back, but Chloe refused to let her go. She had to survive not just for herself, but for the child that she carried. Gripping Darcy's wrists with both hands, she jerked her to the side.

The blade slipped from the killer's hand and clattered to the floor.

"No," Darcy snarled.

Chloe's fingers grazed the scalpel, and she flipped around, ready to strike. Darcy pounced again, pinning her arm to the ground. Chloe struggled to get up, to find something else to use as a weapon.

There was nothing other than her bag.

Chloe reached for the straps and brought the tote up and around. The leather connected with Darcy's head as the contents tumbled onto the bloody floor. Keys. Phone. Notebook. Pens. Lipstick. Sunglasses case.

That wasn't all. They both saw it, and for a moment they both froze.

The pregnancy test rolled across the floor, loosened from its toilet paper wrapping. It stopped with the results window facing the ceiling, the plus sign staring up into the room.

For an instant, Chloe couldn't breathe. The moment of distraction was to be her doom. Bringing her head down, Darcy caught Chloe on the bridge of her nose. The pain was intense, and her eyes flooded with tears.

Darcy grabbed the scalpel. She pressed it not to Chloe's throat, but to her stomach. "Get up slowly or else."

Chloe went cold. Lifting her hands, she rose to her knees before standing. Her clothes were stained and red. Her hair was sticky. Blood was smeared across her face. Darcy was a mess as well. But for now, the fight was done. Chloe had more than lost. She'd given up in order to save her baby.

A set of lockers stood at the back of the room.

"See what's in those," said Darcy, gesturing with her knife.

"What? Why?"

"You want to stay covered in blood?"

"No, of course not."

"Neither do I. Now, see what's in those lockers."

Chloe lifted the handle and opened the door to one. Inside was another set of nurse's scrubs, folded and on a shelf, along with set of street clothes dangling from a hanger.

"Put on the clothes." Using the scalpel, the killer pointed to the counter and the sink. "Get cleaned up first. I'm giving you a single kindness," Darcy continued. "Don't make me regret being nice to you by doing something stupid. You won't get past me alive."

Chloe nodded. It took her only a few minutes to wash in the sink and change her clothes. She'd donned a pair of leggings and sweatshirt. There was even a pair of flip-flops that seemed to be a decent fit.

While Chloe cleaned and changed, Darcy attached one side of the leg irons to the bed's railing. "Get on the mattress."

Without a word, Chloe complied.

"Attach the free end to your wrist," Darcy said.

She struggled to comply, but fear was beginning to set in, and her hands were shaking. "You won't escape. You know that. You've killed two innocent women today. This only adds to your body count. Soon this jail is going to be on lockdown, and whatever you have planned won't work. You'll never walk out of this room—much less the building," Chloe said, her words filled with more bravado than she felt.

Yet she had to keep living. She had a baby to protect. She thought about Marcus. He was in the lobby, not so far away from where she sat.

Did he know what happened?

Did anyone?

Chloe's thoughts skipped, like a record's needle jumping the groove. Darcy was smart enough to know that law enforcement would soon be involved. Even with a hostage, she could hardly hope to fend off dozens of armed police who would likely be arriving at the prison soon.

Which meant what?

Darcy had an agenda that ran deeper than just escaping. Chloe knew it in her bones. She and Marcus had both sensed it, feared it, earlier that morning. So how could she discover the truth? Especially since she was in no position to barter or make demands?

There were several blanks in Darcy's story that Chloe wanted filled. Maybe she could start there.

"Why'd you stay in Wyoming?" she asked.

"What do you mean? I live here." She stripped out of her own blood covered jumpsuit and washed in the sink.

"You had the opportunity to get away after escaping from Billy Dawson. You could have left the state. It wouldn't have taken much to cross the border make your way into Canada."

Darcy put on the scrubs and unplugged a floor lamp. Using the scalpel, she cut the cord off the base. "You mean go into another country without a passport? Are you suggesting that I break the law, District Attorney?"

"You can stop trying to be cute. You could've disappeared if you wanted, but you didn't. I'm just wondering why, that's all."

Setting the cord aside, Darcy moved to the body of the nurse. Grabbing the other woman under the arms, she hauled the corpse to the far side of the room. Her feet dragged through the puddle of blood, leaving a smear of red across the floor. She did the same with the guard. Then she pulled the curtains closed, hiding the dead bodies. Chloe's question as to why Darcy would stay in Wyoming was all but forgotten.

"So, you're the DA in Pleasant Pines." Darcy lifted a tank of air and moved it to the door. From there, she placed it atop a stool on wheels.

"I am," said Chloe, not certain where the conversation was going.

"I didn't know until the night that the cook at the inn died," she said.

"You mean the night you killed him?"

"Marcus Jones was there, and he mentioned your name. I immediately remembered you from when I was in high school." Darcy used the frayed electrical cord to tie the door shut before wrapping the end through the tank's release valve.

She couldn't figure out what Darcy was doing—but Chloe did know that she had to keep the other woman talking. "Is that why you remained in Wyoming? To confront me?"

"What do you think?" She stood to the side of the air tank. "Pretty cool, right?"

"That's a lousy barricade." What was going on? "One kick to the door and that thing will topple over."

"Oh." She laughed. "I don't think that anyone is going to kick in this door anytime soon."

"You don't? How long before you're missed? Or me? Or how long before someone wonders what happened to Gretchen? You also haven't thought about what happens when another inmate needs medical care. Really, Darcy, someone is going to come looking for you—and soon."

Chloe watched as Darcy pulled on the cord. The tension was enough to open the release valve. A stream of oxygen hissed. Chloe went cold. Darcy hadn't been putting together a barricade. She'd engineered something much more effective—and deadly.

After tightening and closing the handle again, Darcy inserted the plug into a socket. An electric current began to spark at the frayed end the cord.

"What have you done?" Chloe asked, her voice holding a tremor of terror. "Have you made a bomb?"

"You like it? But it's actually pretty simple. If the door opens, the oxygen will be released. When the electric current from the frayed cord is hit with the gas, it will create a spark that will ignite and cause the whole canister to explode."

She tried to swallow, but couldn't. "You're going to kill us all. Is that what you want? To die?"

The killer seemed to ignore the question. Was that what this was all about? Suicide by bomb?

Chloe's phone still lay upon the ground in a pool of blood. Darcy picked it up from the floor and tossed it onto the bed. "Open your phone and reset the password," Darcy said, giving a new six-digit code. "Then we're going to send a message to your boyfriend."

Chloe wiped the phone's case clean. "Boyfriend? I don't have a boyfriend."

"You know who I mean. Marcus Jones, the bastard from RMJ."

Chloe's body betrayed her as her cheeks flamed red and hot.

Darcy moved in so close that Chloe could smell her vomit-laced breath. "Are you blushing? Is he really your boyfriend? Is he your baby daddy?"

"Don't be ridiculous." Even she knew that tone was less than resolute.

"Oh, this is even better than I hoped. Chloe Ryder got knocked up by Marcus Jones. Since you're still carrying around a pregnancy test, you must've just found out. Does he know? Did you have a chance to tell him yet?"

Chloe dropped her gaze and assessed her situation. It was beyond horrible. Nobody was going to be able to get through the door to rescue her without Darcy's makeshift bomb exploding.

Which meant only one thing. If Chloe wanted to survive, she was going to have to save herself.

Marcus paced the floor of the lobby. He usually thought of himself as a patient man. But he was more than a little curious about what was happening with Darcy. The need to get the confession and officially close the case was gnawing at Marcus's gut.

How long had Chloe been gone? It seemed like hours. In reality, it'd been less than ten minutes—yet it was still long enough that he felt he should send a text and see what was going on. Just as he was about to do so, his phone pinged with an incoming message. He pulled the phone from his pocket and glanced at the screen, relieved to see the text was from Chloe.

"Mystery solved," he muttered, sliding the message open.

It was a series of three pictures and two lines of text. The first photo was of Chloe, sitting on an infirmary bed. She wore a shirt and leggings—not the pantsuit from before, which to him seemed odd. Then he looked closer and stifled a curse. She wasn't merely sitting on the bed—she was handcuffed to the railing.

Taking in a deep breath, he examined the next photo in the series. If the first picture had gotten him shaken, the second one left him shocked. It was a picture of two dead women. One was the guard, Gretchen. The other woman wore a blood-covered set of scrubs, and he guessed that she was the nurse.

The final picture stole Marcus's breath. It was of a door, booby-trapped with a homemade bomb. The last message was a line of text: 7Million, US currency, and a jet that will land outside jail and take me to Argentina. You have 2 hours, or I will blow up the whole freaking jail.

How in the hell was Marcus supposed to get a plane willing to take a serial killer out of the country? Never mind being able to find millions of dollars. And all of it in a couple of hours?

It was impossible.

Then again, Darcy had to know that her demands were unreasonable.

Which meant she really wanted something else. But what?

Marcus's pulse spiked. There was a lot to consider and do. First, the jail had to be evacuated, which meant he had to alert the warden. The glass-enclosed office was empty. He beat on the door. There was no response. He removed a business card from his pocket. Cal Douglas. NWCF, Warden. He entered the number into his phone. The call was answered on the third ring. "Hello? Who is this?"

"This is Marcus Jones with Rocky Mountain Justice."

"Of course," said the warden. "What can I do for you?"

"I'm standing in your lobby." Marcus didn't have time to waste with small talk and continued, "You need to evacuate this facility immediately. I don't know how it happened yet, but Darcy Owens has killed one guard and another woman—the nurse, I think. She's taken the district attorney hostage. They're holed up in the infirmary, and Darcy has booby-trapped the door with a homemade explosive device."

"What the f— A bomb? Are you kidding me? Tell me this is the sorriest excuse for a joke in the world."

"I wish there was a punchline, but everything is deadly serious. She used Chloe's phone and sent me several photos and a message. I'm forwarding them to you now." Marcus used the speaker feature, talking as he sent the texts.

"Got them," Douglas said, a moment before he began to curse.

"Stay where you are. I'll be to you in a minute," the warden said before ending the call.

Using the speaker function, Marcus placed a call to RMJ. Wyatt answered the phone. "You have to put the team together and get out to NWCF." He sent the texts as he spoke. Marcus only had a few seconds to get his teammate up to speed before the warden would come out of his office.

"What the… Is that a freaking bomb?" Wyatt asked as the message was received.

"Just gather the team and get out here. You might need to help evacuate the prison. But first, we have to get the hostage away from Darcy and get the killer back into custody." Marcus ended the call.

The warden hustled into the lobby. "What in the world happened?"

Marcus outlined the facts as he knew them. As he recounted the morning's events—Darcy's illness, Chloe being summoned to the infirmary—he began to burn in anger. His best guess—Darcy's confession was a trap all along.

"Did she have inside help?"

"Your guess is as good as mine."

Douglas cussed like the retired marine that he was. "Tell me that you've figured out a way to neutralize Darcy before she blows my jail to kingdom come."

With a shake of his head, Marcus said, "I'm at a loss right now."

"What about putting concrete barriers in the hallway and using a drone to push the door open? The bomb goes off. All the explosion is contained in the room. No more Darcy. No more problem."

Marcus had been filled with a white-hot fury before. But as the warden spoke, the blood in his veins turned icy.

"You're forgetting about Chloe Ryder. She'll get blown to hell and back, too."

Douglas swallowed. "I'm not exactly forgetting, but we have to expect some collateral damage."

Marcus spoke through gritted teeth. "No way."

"You have to consider all the options…"

"*Not* that one."

There was no way he'd ever put Chloe in jeopardy. She was…well, now was not the time to think about his feelings. He continued, "We'll get Darcy—and save Chloe."

"How? She has a freaking bomb. How do we combat that?"

"We can't fight at first, only prepare. My initial concern is for everyone in the building. I hate to say it, but you have to evacuate the jail. If that thing explodes, a lot of people are going to die." He lifted the phone and stared at the photo of Chloe, shackled to the bedrail. His chest was tight.

Douglas drew in a breath. "You're right. I'll start putting people on the prison bus. It only holds forty-four. We're at capacity right now. Which means that I have exactly a hundred and twenty-three inmates."

"You might need to call other counties and borrow their buses."

"Good idea," said the warden. "I'll get started right away. What are you going to do?"

"Me? My team from Rocky Mountain Justice is on the way. Darcy might've started this fight," he said. "But RMJ is going to finish it."

Chapter 11

Chloe had worked with law enforcement for long enough that she knew the steps they would take to secure the facility and ensure the safety of the other inmates.

She also knew that Darcy's demands would be passed on—probably to the FBI—and negotiations would begin. And there was no doubt that a team would be assembled to breach the room. She assumed that the team would consist of RMJ operatives and be led by Marcus Jones.

Chloe watched as Darcy climbed onto the counter and batted down the sensor for the overhead sprinkler system to the floor. The sensor let out a series of beeps, each one growing in volume. Jumping from the counter, Darcy crushed the plastic casing with her heel. The pile of rubble let out a single, ear-splitting shriek—and then fell silent.

Okay, Chloe understood Darcy building a bomb as a way to keep anyone—especially Marcus and the rest of the operatives from RMJ—from trying to breach the infirmary. But what was up with disabling the sprinkler system? "What happens if your bomb goes off by accident and starts a fire? You really will kill us both. Is that what you want?"

Darcy dusted her hands on the back of her pants. "It'd seem kinda fitting if I did, don't you think?"

"No. I don't think it'd be fitting at all." The metallic taste of panic filled her mouth. Her voice was tight, a thread about to break. "What is it that you want?"

"I want," said Darcy, her voice calm and low, "for you to suffer."

"Me? Why me?"

"After all these years, you know." She kicked the broken sensor into a corner.

"Is all of this because of what you said to me while you were in high school?"

"I've only ever trusted one person. And that was you."

It had been years since Chloe was a social work student. Still, that long-ago training kicked in. *Build rapport with your clients, but be honest.* Chloe softened her tone. "You didn't trust me, though."

With a snort, Darcy turned back to the counter. "You knew and did nothing."

"Me? Nothing? I talked to the school's principal and the counselor, too. When they questioned you, you denied everything. What else was I supposed to do?"

"Something. Anything." Darcy's eyes were moist. Were those tears? "I was just a kid. You were supposed to protect me."

"I tried to get you help." How could Chloe make Darcy understand? Did she even want to understand? "In fact, I begged the principal to let me speak to you again. But they wouldn't let me. If I talked to you again, it'd be considered harassment, and I'd be kicked out of the social work program. Expelled from school."

"Are you giving me an excuse?" Then she scoffed. "Of course, your precious education was so much more important than my safety."

The statement hit Chloe like a slap. Was her failure with Darcy one of the reasons she'd jumped from social work to the law? Was it her inability to help back then—of not being the person making the decisions—that had driven her forward each and every day? Had that episode from years ago shaped Chloe into the person she was now?

The possibility made her head ache. Yet it wouldn't do to wallow now.

"Believe me." Chloe pressed her free hand to her chest. "I wanted to help you, I did."

"Back then, I didn't know what was real—or not." Darcy mumbled something that Chloe couldn't understand.

"What'd you say?"

"This is all your fault, you know. All of it. The abuse I suffered. The deaths of all those people. It's all because of you—and your *help*." She spat the last words before wiping her mouth with the back of her hand.

Before Darcy could say—or do—anything more, Chloe's phone began to ring.

The other woman glanced at the screen. With a snort, she said, "It's Marcus Jones. Obviously." After swiping the call open, Darcy turned on the speaker function. "Is my plane on the way? Do you have my money?"

"I need to speak to Chloe." His voice landed in her chest and sent Chloe's pulse racing with hope. "How do I know she's even alive?"

"I sent you a picture, didn't I? You saw for yourself that she was alive and well."

"That was a few minutes ago. I need to know that she's okay *now*. It's called proof of life, and if you want a goddamn plane, you'd better put her on." His tone was commanding. Whatever he was feeling, he definitely wasn't letting it show.

Darcy held out the phone. "Say hello to your boyfriend."

God, why hadn't she told him about the baby when she had the chance? There was no way that she'd share the news in front of Darcy. But if the unthinkable happened, she'd want him to know. Chloe leaned toward the phone. "Marcus? It's me."

Marcus's voice was easily heard through the small speaker. "Chloe, are you hurt? What's happening in the room? Tell me—"

Darcy asked, "Satisfied?"

Chloe could still hear Marcus's part of the conversation. "Not really. Put her back on the phone."

"I don't think so," she continued. "Besides, there are more important things for us to discuss."

"Like what?"

"Shouldn't you be asking me other questions? Like, what's my plan after I get out of jail? How am I going to get from the infirmary to the plane?"

"I assume you chose Argentina because they don't have an extradition treaty with the United States. You want money to support yourself," said Marcus. "As far as getting from the infirmary to the plane, that's why Chloe's a hostage."

"Since you're such a smart boy, I don't have to remind you that the clock is ticking. One hour and forty-five minutes. Get me seven million dollars and a plane, or I set off the bomb."

"That would kill you, too."

"You think I want to live if I'm going to be in jail for the rest of my life?"

"You have to be reasonable about both a plane and the money. I used to work for the FBI. They don't give in to demands—it's policy."

"It looks like they're going to have to change how they do things, won't they?" She ended the call with a smile.

Sure, Chloe had little she could actively do. All the same, she was the only person on the inside. There was more to Darcy's scheme than freedom and cash, Chloe was sure.

Darcy examined her homemade bomb, testing the casters on the rolling stool.

"Be careful," Chloe called out.

Darcy glanced over her shoulder. "You can't be concerned with my well-being."

"Not really," Chloe said. At least she knew enough to be honest. "But if you detonate your bomb, people will get hurt. And then the FBI will definitely refuse to give you anything you've asked for."

"The only person in this hellhole who treated me halfway decent was Gretchen—and I slit her throat. I really don't give a damn about the rest of you."

Chloe recalled the wide-eyed look of horror on Gretchen's face as the blade was drawn across her neck. The gurgling sound, as she drowned in her own blood. Or the absolute stillness that followed after Gretchen breathed her last.

"Why'd you do it?" Chloe asked. "Why'd you kill her, if you say she was so good to you?"

"Why do you care?"

Chloe's eyes burned, but she knew enough not to beg or cry. Neither would change Darcy's ultimate plan. Still, it was hard to face her own demise—especially since there was a new life growing inside of her. "Because I'm worried that you're going to kill me, too."

Without speaking, Darcy cut a long strip of fabric from the bedsheet. She then tore the cover into smaller pieces. Rolling each piece between finger and thumb, she created a frayed strip. Each strip was tied to the valve on the oxygen tank.

Chloe watched in horror and fascination. What was Darcy really trying to accomplish? Was the bomb truly a way to keep everyone out of the room? Or was she hoping that it really would explode?

If Chloe was right and the jail was being evacuated as she sat on the bed, doing nothing, it also meant that very few people would be inside—only those who were actively working on apprehending Darcy.

The thought left Chloe chilled to the core.

Everything that had transpired this morning wasn't about Darcy escaping. In fact, it was just the opposite. The killer wanted revenge. Holding Chloe as a hostage and making unreasonable demands was only a ploy to bide her time—waiting until everyone who'd been a party to her capture and arrest was in the jail. Then she'd turn the correctional facility into their tomb.

All the same, having information without a way to pass it on really was next to useless. What Chloe needed was a way to warn Marcus.

With the team from RMJ on the way and the evacuation beginning, Marcus and the warden had to decide on the next steps.

"Call the FBI," said Warden Douglas. "The ATF. The CIA. The National Guard. Call the damned President of the United States if it means capturing Darcy Owens with a minimal loss of life."

To Marcus it sounded like the warden wanted to use a chainsaw to cut away rot when the precision of a razor was needed. "I'll call the FBI if you insist."

"I insist," the older man said.

Marcus stared at his phone for moment before placing the call.

It was answered after the second ring. "Big brother, that you? It's good to hear from you, man. What's going on?"

Just hearing his brother's voice filled Marcus's chest with affection and pride. "Jason, we have a problem. It's Darcy Owens."

His brother was back in D.C. and reported to the director. "What now?"

Marcus filled his brother in on all the details. Jason cursed. "I'll have to brief the director. It could take some time to get an ops plan and get agents to you. You are out in the middle of nowhere, after all."

Some time? Was his brother kidding? Marcus gritted his teeth. "In little less than two hours, that bomb is going to go off, and probably kill the DA. Not to mention we don't know how powerful it is or how many inmates might still be in the place when it goes off."

"I'd like to tell you to stand down, but I know you won't listen."

"You got that right."

"Keep your phone on you," said Jason. "I'll be in touch."

Marcus managed to grumble, "Thanks," before ending the call. He looked at the warden. "You hear that?"

"Most of it, sure." Warden Douglas folded his arms across his barrel of a chest. "This is my facility, and every soul in the building is my responsibility. We can't let Darcy blow up the jail while the troops get organized. What can your agency do for me here and now?"

"Lots," said Marcus.

"Then let's make this happen."

After pulling up the contact, Marcus placed a call to Ian, his boss at RMJ. As the call went through, Marcus had a few seconds to mentally chastise himself. Since hindsight provided perfect vision and all, Marcus knew he should have accompanied Chloe to the infirmary. He should have known—or at least suspected—that something was wrong.

Finally, Ian answered the call.

"Marcus," he said. His British accent was unmistakable. "Tell me you have some information from the Darcy Owens confession. I'm eagerly waiting for news."

"I have quite the update," said Marcus. "But nothing is good." He quickly brought Ian up to speed. For his part, the Brit asked only a few questions. By the time he was done speaking, Marcus could see Wyatt Thornton's pickup truck racing up the drive that connected the jail to the main road. Behind him Liam Alexander drove the white van that served as the mobile HQ for RMJ. Luis Martinez was in his SUV, and finally Julia McCloud's official truck with the insignia of the Pleasant Pines sheriff's department.

The troops had arrived.

"What are you going to do?" Ian asked.

"We need schematics of the building. There has to be another egress from the infirmary…"

"Which may be booby-trapped as well," Ian interrupted. "I don't want anyone to risk their lives."

"Tell you the truth," said Marcus. "I respect the hell out of you, Ian. But if I hadn't been bald before, I sure would have been after working the Mateev case with you. You were reckless in Denver. The things you did—you crossed the line plenty of times, man. And why? Because you were seeking justice and the rules—or even your own personal safety—didn't matter in comparison."

"Sure, I did all of those things. But for me, catching Nikolai Mateev was personal."

Marcus watched on one of the monitors as his team was gathering in the parking lot. These were all good people—his coworkers, his comrades in arms, his friends—and Darcy Owens had somehow wreaked havoc in the lives of each of them. "It's personal for every one of us, too."

Ian was silent for a moment. "What if I tell you to call the FBI and wait for them to come and take over?"

"I've already called. Besides, they can't be here for three hours, and that's at the earliest. The warden asked for our help. Even if our help wasn't requested, I wouldn't stand down." It was Marcus's turn to pause. Should he share his relationship to Chloe? And if he did, would it help his argument to run the case—or ruin it? "Darcy's hostage…" Marcus began.

"The district attorney?"

Marcus had to say something. Even if he didn't know exactly how he felt about Chloe, he knew that she was more than a colleague. She was even more than a friend. "We've become close over the last few months. Working long hours, you know the drill."

"Do I know the drill?"

"What d'you want me to say?"

The line went silent. Had the call dropped?

After a moment, Ian said, "It's settled then."

"What's settled?"

"The company has access to a jet plane, and we have money on hand. I can be there in under two hours."

Marcus blanched. "Are you out of your damn mind? We can't give in to Darcy's demands. She won't stop killing unless she's behind bars—you know that. And what about the families of her victims? They deserve justice, too."

"The way I see it," said Ian, "we have to get her peacefully out of the jail—otherwise Chloe's life will be over."

Ian was right. What was Marcus supposed to tell his team? The good guys always won, except when they didn't? He refused to believe that was true. And what's more, he'd never give up if it was. "There has to be more to your plan than to acquiesce."

"There is. I can copilot the flight. Once airborne, Darcy is really at our mercy."

Ian was right—and that's what bothered Marcus the most. Darcy was highly intelligent. She must know that once she got on the plane, she was no longer in control of their destination. Hell, Ian could land in the yard of the supermax prison in Florence, Colorado.

Darcy had to have anticipated that outcome. So what the hell was she playing at? And how could Marcus ensure that he'd win—and in the end, save Chloe's life?

The door to the correctional facility opened. Marcus waited as the team from RMJ, grim-faced and silent, entered the small lobby. Julia wore her sheriff's uniform. As usual, her blond hair was pulled into a ponytail at the back of her head. She and the warden greeted each other with handshakes, and Julia took a moment to introduce the rest of the team.

"For me," said Warden Douglas, "priority number one is getting everyone out of this jail and someplace safe—for both them and the public. Can the sheriff's office help?"

Julia asked, "What do you need?"

"Manpower. More buses for transport if you have them."

"We can do both," said Julia. "I'll commandeer buses from Pleasant Pines School District."

"How many inmates do you have?" asked Luis Martinez. He stood next to Julia, close but not touching. Julia and Luis lived together now, but Marcus had no doubt that on the job, the two of them would remain professional at all times.

The warden answered, "One hundred and twenty-three inmates."

"Do you need RMJ to help get all the inmates out?" Marcus asked.

Warden Douglas shook his head. "Now that we have extra bodies from the sheriff's office, we can block the county route and park the buses well away from the facility. It's your job to neutralize Darcy Owens."

"Let's get started," said Julia. Talking quietly, the warden and sheriff retreated outside. Then Marcus was alone with his team.

"You all saw the pictures. We can't go in through the door without catastrophic consequences," said Marcus. "Does anyone have ideas?"

Liam Alexander stepped forward. His hair brushed the collar of his canvas shirt. "Ian sent the schematics of the building. I was able to print them off in the mobile HQ." Holding the paper up against the wall, he pointed as he explained. "This facility is obviously hard to get out of—and therefore, into—because of its design. The front door. A door to the exercise yard. A door to the kitchen. All are controlled by an electronic locking system. There's this one that leads to the front. The two at the building's rear lead to the exercise yards. Inside the jail, the cells are climate-controlled, so there's no venting system. Pipes for plumbing are six inches in diameter and buried in concrete."

Wyatt said, "Basically, this place is escape-proof."

"I mean, yeah. It is a prison. But there's more than just the area that houses inmates."

"Tell me that you found a way into the infirmary," said Marcus.

"I did. It won't be easy, but it's not impossible." Using his finger, he drew a circle around half a dozen rooms. "The front of the jail houses the administrative offices. Inmates are never allowed in this area, so there are some differences in the way it was built."

"Like how?" Marcus asked. Sure, he'd heard what the warden had said earlier about the renovations the state had done several years ago, but everyone on the team needed the same information.

Liam continued, "These are air ducts that run through the ceiling of the common areas. They're commercial sized, so about a foot by a foot and a half. Not a lot of room, but one of us can make it through. By accessing the conference room across the hall, we can get into the vent and drop into the infirmary through another vent. Once we have an operative inside, Darcy can be neutralized. Questions?"

"I've got a question." Marcus's primary concern was Chloe. Was that a professional way to look at the situation? Probably not. Did he care? Most definitely not. "Can we really get close to the infirmary undetected? Let's remember, there's a hostage."

Liam rubbed his jaw before speaking. "It'll be tricky, I'm not going to lie. But do we really have another choice?"

Everyone knew the answer.

"What does Darcy really want?" Wyatt asked.

"We should be asking you that question," Marcus said to Wyatt. "You're the one from the behavioral sciences unit, and you've been hunting her longer than anyone else. What game is Darcy playing?"

"Aside from avoiding justice, escaping jail, and being given seven million dollars for her trouble, you mean?" Wyatt said.

Luis asked, "You think that she just wants out of jail and to start over?"

Marcus shook his head. "Does it matter? One of our own is trapped in there with her, goddammit!"

He couldn't get the image of Chloe shackled to the bed out of his mind. He was tired of second-guessing Darcy's motives. What he wanted was action.

"It might matter," said Wyatt, answering Marcus's question. "Especially if she expects us to try to come into the infirmary. Or capture her on the way to the plane. Or not even take her where she's asked to go."

"I don't think she'll underestimate our resolve, if that's what you mean," said Luis.

"But we don't know how many other surprises she has in store." Wyatt paused and rubbed the back of his neck. "She might plan on holding Chloe hostage until she's reached her destination and then let her go. Or..."

"She might kill her once she thinks that she's safe," Marcus said, the words like broken glass in his mouth.

"It's a possibility," said Wyatt. "What we need are eyes and ears in the infirmary. At least then we can assess the situation."

"I've got that covered," said Liam, holding up a small box encased in black plastic. Marcus recognized it at once. It was a remote camera, the lens no bigger than the tip of a pen. The cable, more than one hundred yards of it, was coiled in the device. "We can attach this to a laptop and get a look into the room first."

"How big are the air ducts?" asked Wyatt. "Is it feasible for one of us to climb through?"

Liam said, "It'll be a tight fit, but I'm willing to go."

Marcus was the team leader. It meant that his job was to delegate as his operatives worked. He really should set up a mobile HQ and coordinate all parts of the plan—from the evacuation, to breaching the infirmary, to Ian Wallace's arrival.

But he'd be damned before he'd let someone else rescue Chloe. "I'll go in."

"Why you?" Luis asked. "You heard Liam. It can be anyone of us. Shouldn't you coordinate this evac op?"

Marcus should be the axle in the middle of the wheel. Sure, Chloe's life was in jeopardy, but if something went wrong, a lot of other people could die. It left him with a decision. Chloe? Or his team? "I was supposed to be with her during this interview. I promised to keep her safe. Since I messed up on that promise, I damn well intend to get her out of there alive." If anyone suspected that Marcus had feelings for Chloe, they had sense enough to keep their big mouth shut. "Wyatt, you and Luis need to set up the mobile HQ near the road. Liam, you stay with me. We'll get the camera into the infirmary."

Taking out his phone, Marcus set the timer. Eighty minutes. As the seconds began to disappear, he said, "Darcy Owens made first contact forty minutes ago. She gave us two hours to meet her demands, or Chloe will die." He held up the phone. Seventy-nine minutes, forty-seven seconds remained. "Let's go. We're running out of time."

Chapter 12

Marcus and Liam entered the conference room located directly across from the infirmary. The air was heavy with disinfectant, with an underlying stink of puke. Ignoring the odor, Marcus set his equipment on the table. In this part of the building, the ceiling was made up of drop tiles that could easily be moved.

Standing on a chair, Marcus removed the grille from the vent and exposed an duct that was small—as promised—12"x18". Little more than fifteen yards away, he spied the opposite vent.

"It's a straight shot from here to the light," Marcus said. "Hand me the camera and let's make sure this works."

The camera was a glass dome on the end of a metallic cord, and it produced a high-resolution picture.

Using a remote, Liam turned on the power. A clear image of Marcus appeared on the computer screen.

"I got you," said Liam. He held up the monitor.

Like a spool of twine for a kite, Marcus unraveled the cord into the venting system. The camera inched forward. At the infirmary vent, the lens dipped inside the grate and disappeared from view.

"I've got it," said Liam. "We can see the whole damned room."

Marcus replaced the ceiling tile and stepped off the chair. The camera picked up a bird's-eye view of the entire infirmary. There was a pool of blood on the floor, but no bodies. A curtain had been drawn around the far bed, and he guessed that Darcy had placed the corpses out of sight.

It was an odd thing that a serial killer might be squeamish.

Darcy stood at the counter. He noted that she'd donned scrubs. He made a mental note of her new attire. On the bed, handcuffed to the railing, sat Chloe. She was pale. Dark circles ringed her eyes. She looked weary. Yet she was alive—and that was all that mattered.

She glanced up, looking at the vent. For a moment, she seemed to stare straight at the camera. Had she noticed the lens?

As her blue eyes met his through the monitor, he felt that connection—the one he always felt when Chloe was around. It was the one he'd noticed from the beginning—like she was a kindred spirit, and they need not explain themselves to each other.

But there was more. She was more than a colleague,

more than a friend. More even than a one-time lover. Which meant what?

Hell, Marcus didn't have time to question his emotions—not right now.

"Looks like we should be able to get into the infirmary," said Liam. "I'll route this video to a computer and monitor your progress from the guards' break room. Sound alright?"

"Alright." Sure, Liam was making decisions that should've been up to Marcus, yet he didn't care. Watching Chloe through the monitor, he muttered under his breath. "Hold tight, Chloe. I'm on my way."

It would do Chloe no good to get smothered by her fear. She had to think of something else. To plan. To *act*. In her heart, she vowed to do everything she could to protect and save her baby. Then she reminded herself that it was Marcus's child, too.

In truth, Chloe had been attracted to Marcus from the beginning. His confidence and determination reminded Chloe of, well, herself.

For a moment, she wondered about the baby. Would it have green eyes like him? Or Chloe's dark hair? Would the child grow up to be single-minded and determined like its parents? Or was this baby destined to be a dreamer? Chloe couldn't wait to find out about her child—that is, if she survived the next few hours.

A shower of fine white dust coated Chloe's arm and lap. What the hell? Swiping her hand across her arm, she examined the powder before rubbing it together with finger and thumb.

More powder rained down from above, and Chloe

looked up. There, in the grilled of the vent, was a small, rounded piece of glass. She immediately recognized it as a camera—the kind used by law enforcement to collect evidence that she'd then used to prosecute several cases.

It had to be Marcus. He must have called in the team from RMJ. With one eye on Darcy, she wiped away the dust before the woman could see that anything was amiss.

She had to wonder—what else could Marcus see? What did he know? And how could she get Darcy to reveal her true intent?

Darcy stood at the nurse's locker, rummaging through the contents. So far, she'd found car keys, a bottle of water, a protein bar—and had set them all on the counter.

"What do you need those for?"

Darcy glanced over her shoulder. The look sent a chill down Chloe's spine. "The water for if I'm thirsty, and the protein bar in case I get hungry."

"Not any of that. The car keys. Why do you need those if an airplane is coming to take you out of the country?"

Darcy sauntered to the counter and swiped the keys into the pocket of her nurse's smock. "I don't think you should worry about that."

"Obviously I'm interested." Chloe jerked her arm hard. The handcuffs and the bed railing rattled. "What's your plan?"

Darcy looked away.

The other woman's refusal to answer only made

Chloe more determined. "Come on, Darcy. I know there's more to your plan than just getting out of jail."

"If you're so smart," said Darcy, "then you should be able to figure it out." The killer opened the water bottle and took a long swallow. Screwing the lid back on tight, she looked at Chloe. "Then again, you might not be as smart as I thought. After all, you are pregnant and not married to the father."

Chloe went cold with fear. What would Darcy to do the unborn baby? Still, she refused to back down. "You've committed murder, and you want to give *me* a lecture on morality?"

Darcy narrowed her eyes, and Chloe realized that she was at the mercy of a merciless woman. She wanted to recoil but refused to look away.

"Those men," said Darcy. "They deserved to die."

"Why?" asked Chloe. "Did they hurt you?"

"They were filthy." Darcy clenched her teeth. "They wanted to make me filth." She paused, opened the water bottle and took another drink. "I was tempted, but if your hand forces you to steal, you cut off your hand."

Chloe thought she'd caught a glimpse into the killer's mind. It was more than what'd been reported in the psych evals. More even than what Chloe knew first-hand from all those years ago.

Had she been attracted to the men, but because of the abuse she'd suffered, Darcy didn't know what to do with feelings of sexual attraction? To her, were those emotions dangerous and painful? If Chloe hadn't witnessed Darcy murder a woman in cold blood not even an hour ago, she might've felt sorry for the other woman. "But *you* didn't cut off *your* hand," Chloe said. "*You* ended their *lives*. What about Gretchen and the nurse? They weren't—" Chloe paused and tried to recall Darcy's exact word "—filthy."

"It wasn't me who did those things."

Chloe's stomach threatened to revolt. "I watched you slit Gretchen's throat. I can still feel her blood on my hands…"

"It was the Darkness," said Darcy, her voice was so low that it was almost a whisper. "It was the Darkness who told me that they had to die." She continued, "I told you about my father back in school, but it was the Darkness who said later I should lie."

"The Darkness?" It was Chloe's turn to whisper. "What is the Darkness?"

"Not what," said Darcy, her voice still low. "But where." She touched two fingers to her breastbone and then placed them on her temple. "It's inside of me."

Chloe's mouth went dry. "It's the Darkness that tells you what to do? And who to kill?"

Darcy lifted the water bottle to her lips. Her hand trembled, and liquid sloshed from the narrow opening, dribbling down the front of her shirt. "What do you think your boyfriend is doing right now?" She took a drink.

"What about the Darkness?" Chloe coaxed. "When did you first notice it was there?"

"I'd rather talk about Marcus. It doesn't seem professional for you to sleep with a coworker."

It was almost as if a flip had been switched, changing Darcy from one person to another. Almost, hell. It really had been an immediate and complete transformation. Only seconds ago, Darcy had been timid—perhaps afraid—and seemingly younger than her years.

The Darkness was what Darcy called the desire to kill. To Chloe, it seemed a terrifying moniker, given everything she knew about Darcy.

"Marcus…" said Darcy. "What about him? Tell me."

"What do you want to know?"

"Why'd you screw a coworker? Isn't there something wrong with the power dynamics of having sex with employees or something like that?"

What Chloe wanted was to reach the real Darcy, the one who was forced to take refuge in her mind after suffering years of abuse. That person might help Chloe survive. How could she get Darcy to open up again?

Until then, she had no choice but to engage with the Darkness and the person that was showed to the world. She hated to share anything personal, but what choice did she have? Finally she said, "Marcus really isn't my coworker, and he's definitely not a subordinate. We work for different organizations—it makes us more like colleagues."

"Which is another word for coworker." Darcy took another drink of water. "I know your boyfriend-slash-coworker-slash-colleague is trying to find a way into the infirmary even as we speak. What do you think he'll do?"

With a shake of her head, Chloe leaned back into the pillows. She risked a glance up at the lens and told the truth. "I have no idea."

Marcus might be able to see into the room—but that didn't mean Chloe was any closer to being rescued. In fact, she was still very much trapped with a killer.

* * *

Tucking a SIG Sauer into the holster at his hip, Marcus lifted himself into the air duct. He had a universal key for the handcuff brand used by the jail shoved into his pants pocket. His broad shoulders touched each wall. The metal scraped his skin. The air was hot, dusty and stale.

Crawling forward on his stomach, he began to sweat. His pulse raced. If hell was personal—and filled with things that were loathed or dreaded—Marcus knew his eternal damnation would be spent in tight and dark places.

His heart hammered against his chest, and sweat dripped into his eyes. He stopped crawling and forced himself to breathe. To focus. What had Liam said? It was a straight shot from the conference room to the infirmary. Five yards. Ten yards. Fifteen. Certainly, Marcus could live with his fears for a mere forty-five feet—especially if it meant getting Chloe out alive in the end.

Since the soundproofing between the duct work above and the rooms below was nonexistent, the team knew they needed to distract Darcy. The decision had been made that Wyatt would place the call, engaging the killer for as long as possible. He was located in the mobile HQ.

The vent through which Marcus would drop into the infirmary was just ahead. He heard the ringing of a phone—his cue to get into position.

Through the slats of the cover , Marcus could see a sliver of the room. He watched as Darcy glanced at the phone before swiping the call open. "I figured that I'd be hearing from you soon, Marcus. You must be having a problem getting me what I asked for."

"It's not Marcus. This is Wyatt Thornton. I'm sure you remember me."

From his vantage point in the ceiling, Marcus watched as Darcy froze. "Wyatt?" Her voice trembled. She began to pace again. "Why are you calling?"

Her reaction was everything that Marcus needed. More than a dozen metal hinges held the grille over the vent. He began to pry them loose.

He could hear Wyatt's voice. "First, how's Chloe?"

"Fine. Dandy, really." Her words were filled with snark.

"I need to speak to her." Sure, they all knew that Chloe was actually unharmed physically. But Wyatt had to stick to the hostage negotiation script.

"Is that why you called? To check on Chloe? Why am I not hearing from Marcus?"

"Marcus is working hard on making sure we can meet all of your demands. In fact, I have an update. The plane is on the way and should be here in a little more than an hour."

"A little more than an hour?" Darcy worked her jaw back and forth. She mouthed a curse before beginning to pace again. "Marcus said that he didn't know if any of my demands would be met. Also, he said that it would take time—lots of time. Now you expect me to believe that you have the money and the jet ready to fly me to a foreign country? What about the FBI? He said that they'd never negotiate. To me, this sounds like a trap."

Damn it. The last thing Marcus wanted was for

Darcy to get suspicious, especially since he was so close.

"The warden decided not to involve the Feds," said Wyatt, employing a well-practiced lie. "He wants to take care of this situation locally. We were able to get everything you asked for."

"Who's we?"

"The plane and the money come from Rocky Mountain Justice."

She snorted. "Your company has that kind of cash on hand? And a jet?"

"I knew about the jet," said Wyatt. "I didn't have a clue there was a crap ton of money lying around."

"Sounds like you should ask for a raise."

Marcus pried another bracket loose. It snapped in half, ricocheting across the vent with a *ping*. Marcus wanted to roar with frustration, but he dared not move—or even breathe. Darcy stopped pacing. Turning slowly, she looked at the ceiling.

She had heard something—Marcus was sure of it. The question was, had she heard enough?

After a moment, Wyatt asked, "Darcy, are you still there?"

Raking her fingers through her hair, she said, "I'm here."

"I thought you'd be happy that you have a plane and money. You get your freedom and a fortune."

"Of course I'm happy." Darcy leaned on the counter and picked up a bottle of water. As she took a sip, Marcus carefully pried another bracket free. "In fact, I'm freaking ecstatic."

She was lying. But why?

He removed another bracket, sweat spreading on his back. He needed to get into that room—and quick.

"We need a plan, Darcy. You have to disable that bomb and let Chloe go before you'll be allowed to get on the plane."

Darcy gave a quiet laugh. The sound sent a chill up his spine. "You really do think I'm crazy. I'll tell you this, Wyatt—I'm not. I'm taking Chloe with me. It's just like you said. Without her, you'll never let me get away. She's my guarantee."

Wyatt said, "I can't work with you if you don't work with me."

"I am taking Chloe," Darcy said again. "And the only way she's not getting on that plane is if you take her out of this room in a body bag." She slammed the phone on the counter, ending the call.

A thousand images filled Chloe's mind, snapshots she'd seen of Darcy's victims from the files of the medical examiner. None of them were good.

Sure, Darcy's M.O. had been to poison her male victims, leaving them for dead. It was a repetition of her initial crime—the murder of her father. Yet as Darcy strode back and forth in front of the counter and mumbled to herself, Chloe had to wonder—was she moments away from becoming the next victim?

"You seem upset," said Chloe hesitantly. True, it was lame. But it was all she had.

Darcy glared. "Stop pretending that you care."

"Of course I care. I want this to end peacefully so we can all go home."

"Home." Darcy snorted. "You know my house burned down, right?"

"I do." She tried to empathize with Darcy—not the killer, but the scared teenager she'd been years ago. "How do you feel about that? That must be upsetting."

"Upsetting?" Another snort. "Not at all. That place was filled with nothing but nightmares. I'm glad it's gone."

Chloe couldn't blame her, not after everything that happened during her childhood. Still, she would be wise to remember that Darcy was a criminal now—even if she'd been a victim before.

"How'd you make all of this happen?" she asked. "I was in the conference room, remember. You actually got sick. Was Gretchen an accomplice? Did she pass you a pill or something that made you ill?"

Darcy glanced at the curtain that had been pulled across the room and hid the two bodies. "Gretchen?" She shook her head. "No."

"How then?"

"Why do you want to know?"

"Until you let me go, I've got nothing to do other than talk to you. Besides, I'm curious as to how you fooled me and Marcus, considering we're pretty good at what we do." Chloe hoped against hope that appealing to Darcy's ego would get—and keep—her talking.

"Dirt," said Darcy.

For a moment, Chloe thought that the killer had gone back to talking to herself. "I don't understand."

"For weeks, I collected a little bit of dirt each time I went outside. This morning, I mixed it into my oatmeal and ate it. It made me sick. I knew it would."

"The guards never noticed that you collected a pile of soil?" How could that be? Did Darcy actually have help on the inside?

"I put the dirt into a tissue and then stashed that in my bra—as in, I pulled the threads loose and placed the tissue inside the cup." Darcy smiled. "My clothes get checked, but it's not a close inspection. Mostly they're shaken and patted. If nothing falls out, then the guards are happy."

"It's ingenious," Chloe said, being honest. Yet it was the cunning and skill of Darcy's plan that frightened Chloe the most. Her level of observation was, as usual, her greatest weapon, and if she managed to get free, Chloe fully intended to lecture Cal Douglas over the issue of incomplete searches at his prison.

"What about the bits of fabric you tied to the oxygen tank?"

"What about them?"

"What're you doing with them?"

"Why do you care?" Darcy asked again, clearly frustrated.

It was Chloe's turn to give a derisive laugh. "I just want to know how you made this happen."

"You think this is a joke? I wonder how many pieces of you I can cut away before you stop laughing."

On the counter lay a scalpel. Darcy picked it up. The handle was still stained with Gretchen's lifeblood. Chloe went cold as she realized that she'd pushed too hard for information.

Knife in hand, Darcy slowly, slowly approached the bed. Chloe pressed her back into the pillow, trying in vain to get distance from the killer and the knife. It did no good. Darcy pressed Chloe's shackled hand onto the railing and drew the blade across her palm. The metal was cold against her skin. She tried to jerk her hand away, but it was no use.

Darcy drove the blade into Chloe's flesh.

The cut burned, and for a moment, her vision filled with red. Then a seam opened in her hand. Blood began to weep from the wound. She balled her hand into a fist as her palm throbbed, and anger flooded her veins.

Chloe might've been handcuffed to a bed, but that didn't mean that she couldn't fight back.

"Damn you straight to hell," she growled.

With her free hand, Chloe pushed Darcy's chin back. At the same moment, she lifted her feet, kicking the killer in the chest. Darcy stumbled back before tumbling to the ground. Had Chloe been free, she would have had the advantage.

But shackled to the bed? Chloe had done nothing more than enrage a dangerous person.

Standing, Darcy brushed a loose strand of hair from her face. She smiled, then scoffed before echoing Chloe's words. "Damn me to hell? Hell doesn't frighten me, Chloe. Nothing does—especially not you."

Chapter 13

Marcus wasn't going to stay in the duct and watch while Darcy tortured Chloe. Driving his heel into the grille, he broke the remaining brackets. Plastic and metal rained onto the floor—and Marcus followed.

Drawing his firearm, he placed Darcy in his sights.

"Drop the knife," he said.

Lifting her hands, she let the blade slide through her grasp. It hit the floor with a clatter. Reaching out with the toe of his boot, he pulled the blade away from the killer.

"Take two steps back. Get on your knees. Keep your hands up where I can see them," he said.

Without a word, Darcy did as she was told.

In the days and weeks to come, Marcus would re-call a spark of wonder at the ease with which Darcy surrendered. Did he really believe that the killer was shocked by his arrival? In truth, he did. Or was he so worried about Chloe that he let himself be preoccupied?

After fishing the handcuff keys from his pocket, he tossed them to Chloe. "These should fit the lock. Once you've gotten the cuffs off, hand them to me."

Chloe worked the key into the lock of the handcuff and freed herself. He kept his attention trained on Darcy, who remained on the floor, kneeling with her hands up.

"Here you go," said Chloe, holding out the cuffs to Marcus. As she passed them over, the tips of her fingers grazed his hand. His body grew warm at her touch— but this wasn't the time or place to think about why.

"Aside from your hand, what else is hurt?"

"Nothing," she said with a quick shake of her head. "I'll survive, thanks to you."

"We need to get out of the room first. Then you can thank me." He tossed the restraints to Darcy. They hit her in the chest before bouncing off and clanking to the floor. "Put those on."

After reaching for the handcuffs, she wrapped one cuff around her wrist and pressed it closed, then slipped into the second cuff. Marcus slid his firearm into the holster at his hip. He walked over and pulled on the links, making sure that Darcy was truly restrained. He patted her down and pulled a set of keys from Darcy's pocket. He didn't know what they were for, but he placed them on the counter.

Certain that the killer was free of contraband and weapons, he stepped away.

Marcus's plan had been straightforward. Step one:

get into the infirmary. Step two: place Darcy in custody. He'd checked both of those boxes. But step three was a bit more complicated. He had to disarm the bomb without triggering it.

"You stay here," he said to Chloe, pointing at the far side of the bed. "I want you as far away from the bomb as you can get in case something goes wrong. You can use the mattress as a shield if you need it."

With a swallow, Chloe picked up her purse and moved to the far side of the bed. Darcy still knelt on the ground and kept her eyes downcast.

Marcus examined the improvised explosive device. The air tank was wedged against the door and strapped to the handles. A frayed electrical cord was wrapped around the tank's release valve. The prongs had been plugged into an outlet, and the opened end spit sparks as a current ran through the cord. It was a crude mechanism. But, like he had feared from the beginning, if the door was opened, the bomb would explode—the blast killing anyone unlucky enough to be inside the room. Could he simply unplug the wire? Maybe. Then again, maybe he'd get electrocuted in the process.

If he wanted to save Chloe, he had to disarm the bomb. But how?

Darcy knelt on the floor at the foot of the bed, her hands shackled and hanging in front of her waist. Sure, she had given up—yet, she was far from giving in.

"Now," the Darkness whispered. *"It's now or never."*

"Marcus," Chloe screamed. "Look out!"

The warning came a fraction of a second too late.

Darcy launched herself at Marcus and grabbed him around the waist, her fingers grazing the grip of his gun. Marcus swung around. His fist connected with Darcy's temple.

The pain radiated out from the side of her head. The blow left her dizzy and stole her breath. Her ears began to buzz. Her vision dimmed. She hit the floor.

Then she realized she held the gun.

Wrapping her fingers around the grip, Darcy placed her finger around the trigger. Then, rising to her knees, she aimed the barrel at Marcus's chest. "Gotcha, you stupid bastard."

He slowly lifted his hands. "You won't get away with this, you know?"

"I won't?" Darcy shook her head and smiled. "It seems like I already have."

He took a step to the side. And then another. Marcus stopped, standing directly in front of the door.

"I can guess what you're thinking," she said. "You think that if you're in front of the bomb, then I won't shoot. I'll be worried that the bullet will punch a hole through you and cause an explosion."

"Darcy," he said, drawing out her name. "You have no idea what I plan to do next."

Reaching behind his back, Marcus opened the air tank. "Chloe, get down," he yelled. The electrical cord was pulled tight, like a live thing, trying to escape.

Marcus vaulted over the bed.

There was a noise like thunder, but hundreds of times louder. And then there was light. And fire. And pain.

Then nothing.

* * *

"Chloe? Can you hear me?"

"Marcus?" She choked and began to cough. Her skull throbbed, the pain radiating outward until her teeth ached.

"You fell and hit the back of your head on the floor. You might have a concussion. Can you stand? We need to get out of here."

She opened her eyes and remembered everything. "Where's Darcy? She had your gun!"

With his hand under her elbow, Marcus helped Chloe to her feet. "She was over there."

The metal cabinets, which had lined the wall, were now a pile of rubble that blocked the door. Was Darcy beneath all that debris? Marcus lifted one of the cabinets. There were fingers. A hand. Another hand along with a set of handcuffs. The flesh on the wrists was pale.

He felt for a pulse on one wrist and shook his head. Then, he reached for the other. "Nothing."

"She's…dead?" Chloe wasn't sure what she should think or feel. She tried to say something, but her throat was too raw to speak.

That's when she noticed the thin tendrils of smoke floating in the room. The air turned hazy. Chloe's eyes began to water.

"Is there a fire in the hallway?" she asked, her pulse racing. Even if they could get around the twisted metal cabinets, they could hardly go out of the door. "We're trapped."

Marcus looked up, and Chloe's gaze followed. "The vent," he said. "It's how I got in. Crossing back to the conference room won't help us if there's a fire in the corridor, but the vent will lead somewhere else, too. We have to get out of here."

"We can't leave Darcy here," said Chloe. "She's our responsibility."

"She's dead, Chloe. Are you willing to die with her? Because we're stuck in a room that's filling up with smoke and that's what's going to happen."

Well, Chloe hadn't thought about it that way. Maybe she was suffering from a concussion. Besides, it was more than Chloe's life at risk, but the baby's, too.

"Marcus, I…" How was she supposed to tell him about the pregnancy? "I don't like leaving Darcy behind."

"This isn't optimal," he said, his voice hoarse. He coughed. "But what other choice do we have? Honestly, tell me what else to do and I'll do it. As soon as we get out of here we'll make sure a medical team recovers her body, first thing."

Chloe drew in a breath. Her lungs burned. She didn't have any other options—and that was the problem. Her gaze traveled to the ceiling. "How do we get into the vent?"

He pushed the bed frame directly beneath the hole in the ceiling and said, "I'll lift you up."

Chloe climbed onto the mattress and reached for the sides of the opening. A hissing sound filled the room. Sparks erupted from the wall. She took one last look over her shoulder at Darcy before Marcus helped her into crawlspace. The overhead lights flickered.

Then everything went dark.

* * *

Luke Winston stretched out on the top bunk in his cell. His cellmate, Rex Vanguard, lay on the bottom bunk. At this hour, Luke and Rex typically worked in the kitchens and assisted with lunch prep.

But not today.

All inmates had been sent back to their cells and told nothing more.

"You know what I hate more than jail?" Luke asked.

"What?" Rex replied, even though Luke's answer was always the same.

"That bitch prosecutor."

"Chloe Ryder?"

"You know another?" Luke paused a beat. "You know what I wish I would've done?"

"No. What?"

"Broken her freaking neck that day in the courtroom."

"Then you'd be in jail for murder," said Rex, like always.

"I'm in jail now, ain't I?" Luke paused. "Or if I'd just had one more second, I could have choked her out. Guaranteed."

"Except that big guy from Rocky Mountain Justice flattened you like roadkill."

"Shut up, douche."

"I'm just saying."

"Well, don't," said Luke. "Besides, you know what I'd do if I ever got my hands on that guy again?"

"Beat his ass?" guessed Rex.

"Damn straight." Luke rolled to his side.

The overhead lights flickered before going out. Sunlight streamed in through a barred window set high into the wall. There was a click as the electronic lock disengaged, and the door opened a fraction of an inch.

"What in the hell?" Luke dropped to the floor and pushed the door open. All the cells in the block surrounded a single common room where meals were served. Several other inmates were opening the doors to their cells. Each of the men stared at each other.

"What's going on?" Rex asked, sitting up.

"Well," said Luke, pushing the door open all the way. "Isn't this interesting."

Standing outside of the Northern Wyoming Correctional Facility, Julia McCloud pushed her sunglasses higher onto the bridge of her nose. She hadn't intended on staying in Pleasant Pines, much less keeping the job as sheriff. She'd originally accepted the position to remain involved in the hunt for Darcy Owens. Yet as she recovered from injuries both physical and emotional, she'd come to realize that Pleasant Pines needed a leader—and she needed a home.

It was mid-morning, barely beyond ten o'clock, yet it seemed like weeks had passed since she'd gotten the text from Marcus. Darcy had once again taken a hostage. Julia truly knew what Chloe was enduring.

The facility's evacuation had been going without incident—so far, at least. The corrections staff, fourteen in all, worked in teams of two. Each pair took an inmate from the jail. Wrists bound with flex-cuffs, the convicts were delivered to a school bus being used for prisoner transport. So far, over one hundred inmates had been safely removed from the jail. A few more than twenty remained—and those individuals were the most violent, and therefore the most difficult to control. They were coming out last.

Wyatt Thornton was monitoring the situation in the infirmary via remote video in RMJ's mobile HQ. Julia had commandeered Luis and Liam to help with the jail evacuation, and they were now inside the correctional facility.

In the days and weeks to come, Julia could not recall what she saw, smelled or heard first. Was it the sound of a distant explosion? The stench of smoke? Or was it the red light above the front door that began to flash?

In her mind, time splintered, leaving Julia to examine each fragment. An alarm began to sound. The wailing stretched out across the plains until it disappeared beyond the horizon.

"What the hell?"

The scent of smoke was strong. The door to the jail burst open. A duo of guards ran out, hustling a group of inmates between them.

Julia stepped forward. "What happened?" She had to yell to be heard over the alarm.

"That bomb exploded," said one of the guards. His face was ashen with fear. "There's a fire."

And then the alarm stopped. The light ceased to flash.

Julia went cold. Had the worst case scenario just happened? The bomb had exploded. A fire was raging inside the building and people were still trapped inside. But she had a job to do. There were still prisoners to evacuate, and she couldn't get distracted until they were out safely.

Except…it seemed no one else was exiting the building. At all. Marching to the front door, she pulled on the handle. Locked.

Wyatt stepped out of the mobile HQ—a white van that was parked at the end of the long drive. He sprinted from the van to where she stood.

"What's happening?" he asked.

"I have no idea. There's the alarm, and now this." She gestured to the door. "It won't open."

Wyatt pulled on the door. It didn't budge.

Julia's phone began to ring. Her caller ID said Cal Douglas, the warden. "What's going on?" she asked after swiping the call open. "We're locked out of the jail."

"There was a surge in the electrical system. It seems like the backup generator worked for a minute, but then it crapped the bed. Here's the real problem. The jail is on automatic lockdown." He paused and drew in a shaking breath. "What's worse, all the cell doors have been disarmed."

Shock rippled through Julia's body. She stared at the door, realizing that one of those locked inside was the love of her life, Luis Martinez. She rubbed the stubs of her two missing fingers. A sensation ran up her arm that registered as an ache in her elbow. "Are you telling me that you and some of the other guards are locked inside, and the inmates are free?"

"That's exactly what I'm telling you."

There was yelling in the background.

The phone beeped. The line went dead.

Julia redialed the number. The call went to voice mail. She cursed and didn't bother leaving a message.

Wyatt had overheard the conversation, so she didn't need to relay the details. "We have problems bigger than one killer and a single hostage." With an inhale, she looked at Wyatt. "That door needs to be opened. Now."

"Of course. But how?"

It was a good question—and Julia didn't have an answer for him.

On her belly, Chloe slid through the vent. The metal under her flesh was hot to the touch, and she knew it meant one thing. Fire. Thankfully, Marcus was on her heels.

"According to Liam, the overhead venting system is only in parts of the jail where inmates don't have free access—like the infirmary, conference room, offices…"

"Hopefully the front door."

"You read my mind," he said. "Just keep moving forward. I think the door is where the duct work will end. Besides, the further we move away from the infirmary, the more distance we put between us and the fire."

Elbow. Elbow. Knee. Knee. Progress was slow and painful. Sweat collected at Chloe's hairline before dripping down her face and dampening her shirt. Through everything, she'd stupidly kept her purse. Now she wore the straps over each arm like a backpack.

And yet, this wasn't the worst decision she'd made all day.

She knew this was definitely not the time to tell Marcus about the baby—in fact, she could hardly imagine a place and time less ideal. Yet she'd hesitated before—and almost lost her chance. Well, she was going to make damn sure she didn't miss her chance a second time. The instant they were free of this building, she was going to tell him she was pregnant. And she hoped with all her being that he would feel the same growing excitement that she did.

Light shone upward from an exhaust vent that led to a room below. Chloe slowed before asking, "How do I get around that?"

"Check it out first," said Marcus. "This may be our way out of the jail."

A few more crawls and Chloe stopped several feet from the grille. There were voices. Several men were in the room. Someone was yelling. She couldn't tell what he said, but gooseflesh rose on her arms. A scream echoed through the vent.

Looking over her shoulder, she whispered, "What was that?"

Marcus placed his fingers to his lips for quiet. From behind, he moved to be next to her. They were pressed into each other, squeezed into the tight space. The metal underneath creaked and bent, but thankfully didn't give way. The hole was in front of them. She moved forward and looked into the room below.

It was Cal Douglas's office—the same place they'd met with the warden this morning.

The small room was filled with more than a dozen men. All of them wore the baggy orange NWCF jumpsuit. Chloe's blood ran cold as she recognized several. In fact, she'd been the one who personally prosecuted the cases that sent them to jail.

The warden was in a seat behind his desk. Yet the meeting was far from friendly. Two men held his shoulders to the chair's back, while another two held out his arm. His fingers were placed on the desktop. Despite being outnumbered, the warden struggled against his captors.

"You ready for this?" an inmate asked.

A round of mean-spirited laughter followed.

Fear, which registered as a wave of nausea, washed over her. She whispered, "Is that Luke Winston?"

"Looks like it," Marcus whispered back. "What I want to know is how in the hell all of these inmates are out of their cells."

Before Chloe could answer, yet another man slammed a letter opener into the warden's hand. Blood spurted from the wound.

As the warden screamed, the men all laughed.

Luke said, "That's just the first cut as we take you apart, piece by piece."

Bile rose in the back of her throat. "We can't just let them torment Douglas," she whispered. "We have to do something."

"We will," said Marcus. Removing his gun from the holster, he aimed through the slats of the vent.

"Wait. You aren't going down there."

"I can't stay up here and watch a man get tortured."

Marcus was brave—it was one of the things she admired most. But was this really the smartest thing to do when it would be one against so many? "What's your plan?"

"Liam and Luis are somewhere in the building. I need backup." He removed his phone and glanced at the screen. "Damn, there's no bars." He paused. "It means that I have to go it alone."

Chloe bit the inside of her lip hard. "Alone?"

"You stay here. And stay quiet. I don't want you involved."

Chloe had no intention of facing a room full of enraged—and suddenly empowered—men she'd put in the jail. It meant that the stakes had changed since this morning. About everything.

"Wait," she whispered. "I need to tell you something important."

Douglas was hauled to his feet. One of the men slammed his head into the warden's face. From her vantage point, Chloe could hear the snapping of cartilage as his nose broke. Blood streamed down Douglas's chin as the warden's agonized cry reverberated in her chest.

"Important?" Marcus echoed. "What is it?"

Despite what she had to say, Chloe couldn't let Douglas be hurt anymore. She couldn't let Marcus be distracted, either. "Nothing," she said. "Just be careful."

Driving his heels through the grille, Marcus knocked the covering to the ground. Gun in hand, he slipped through the opening and disappeared.

Chapter 14

In all honesty, Luke didn't think that he'd ever get out of jail. In fact, he knew that torturing the warden was eventually going to make things worse for him—much worse.

The thing was, he didn't give a crap.

In fact, it put a smile on his face to see someone else suffer. And nothing could make him stop.

There was a soft thump behind Luke, and he turned. In the moment, he didn't have a clue what might have made the noise. In all fairness, he never would have guessed that Marcus Jones would drop from the ceiling like a comic book hero. And he definitely didn't think that the dude would have a gun.

"Whoa," he said lifting his hands. Luke had been arrested more than once, and he knew what to do. "Where the hell did you come from?"

"Hell. And I'm taking you back with me," Jones said. "Move to the corner. Keep your hands up where I can see them."

Everyone else had been arrested more than once, too. In unison, all the other inmates—his fellow chapter members from the Transgressors—lifted their hands. In a tight knot, they shuffled to the corner.

"We have to get out of here," Jones said to the warden.

"That's just the thing," said Douglas. "We can't get out. The jail is on automatic lockdown. The front doors can't be opened until the electrical system is reset—and that's in the basement."

"Can you call someone and get them to fix it?"

The warden shook his head. "The first thing they did was break my cell phone and disable the landline. What about your phone?"

Marcus gave his head a quick shake. "I don't have it."

Luke kept his hands up and his ears open. If they were really all trapped inside, with no hope of help coming anytime soon…well, then the dynamics of the situation just changed.

Luke might never have graduated from high school. He still knew a thing or two—like the fact that Jones couldn't shoot twelve men at one time. He nudged Rex. Leaning in close, Luke whispered, "We all rush them at once. Go for the bald guy with the gun. If we take control now, we can use these two as bargaining chips. We all want out of jail. We deserve our freedom, right?" He paused to make sure that the others had heard. They all exchanged glances. "One," Luke whispered. "Two. Now."

The members of the Transgressors rushed forward, screaming like demons.

Marcus turned and fired twice. He hit the guy to Luke's right. The back of the man's head blew off. Blood splatter covered the wall behind him. He dropped to his knees, the scream dying on his lips as he fell facedown.

The small room contained the blast of gunfire and left Luke's ears ringing. The smell of gunpowder filled the office.

Firing again, Marcus hit another guy in the shoulder. The bullet shredded his flesh and broke bones, while the force of the blast spun him around and knocked him down.

Even for a guy with a gun—who was also a hell of a shot—ten to one were lousy odds.

Luke and his fellow prisoners fell on Marcus like a pack of wolves. Knocking him to the floor. Kicking. Biting. Punching. The gun was fired twice more. The bullets struck the wall.

Cal Douglas joined the fight. But he, too, was overpowered.

Luke stepped on Jones's arm, pinning the firearm to the floor. Rex kicked the gun away, leaving the operative from RMJ unarmed. Two guys lifted Marcus to his feet.

"Guess who we have here, fellas?" Luke asked. "The bastard who shot up the compound and then took away all the ladies."

"Bastard," Rex echoed while driving his fist into Jones's stomach.

The punch bent Jones over double and left him

wheezing. Lifting his head, Marcus stared at the open hole that he'd jumped through. Luke wasn't sure, but it seemed like Jones shook his head—just a little. Glancing over his shoulder, Luke stared at the broken grille. There was nothing to be seen.

"Guess you regret trying to be the hero now," he said to Jones. "'Cause life ain't like a fairy tale, and not everyone gets a happy ending." He paused. "You sure won't."

The clock was ticking. Each second that passed put lives in jeopardy. The FBI agents were on the way but had yet to arrive.

It meant that those on site had to take control. Liam and Luis were in the guards' break room when the explosion happened. There wasn't an exterior window, and the room was black as pitch. Luis placed a call.

Julia answered on the first ring. "Where in the hell are you?"

The air was thick with smoke. The hallway was filled with the screams of those who'd gotten out of their cells—and those that they'd found. "Hell sums it up nicely," he said, keeping his voice low. How long did they have until someone found them in the break room?

"What happened?" Luis moved closer to Liam so both men could hear the call.

"I only spoke to the warden for a few minutes before we lost contact, but he said the bomb exploded. The electric circuit's been overridden. The doors coming into the building are locked. The doors inside the building are open."

Luis didn't have a lot of time to waste, but he needed

to know what assets were in place. "What about Marcus? Wyatt? Chloe?"

"Wyatt is with me. Chloe and Marcus are in the jail and incommunicado."

"Damn," Luis muttered. "What's our plan?"

"I don't have one." He could hear the strain in Julia's words.

Liam held up the building's schematics and used the light from the phone as he spoke. "This is the main electrical grid. It's located in the basement. If we reboot the system, we might be able to restore power to the building—or at least enough to open the doors."

"How are we supposed to get into the basement?" he asked.

"That's where we've actually gotten a lucky break," said Liam. He shone his light in a back corner. "That's the door, tucked into the secured area so inmates won't have access."

"It's a shaky plan." Julia exhaled. "But it's all we've got."

"Then let's get after it," said Luis. "And Julia?"

He waited for her reply. It never came. He looked at the phone. There were no bars. The connection was lost—which meant that he and Liam were on their own. "You know how to get an electrical system started?"

Liam's face was illuminated by his phone. "In theory, yeah."

"In theory?" he repeated. That wasn't exactly the answer he was hoping to hear. "In reality—what kind of equipment do you need?"

"Goggles. A multimeter to test amperes. A generator—if we can get one." Liam shone the light from his phone around the guards' break room. In a back corner was a door. Utility closet.

"That's the best place to look," said Luis, already moving across the room. He opened the door. "Hot damn." Sure, there were the expected items—mops, buckets, cleaning supplies and such—but there was also a shelf filled with power equipment. "Any of that work for you?" he asked Liam.

"Oh, yeah." Liam grabbed a canvas sack that was shoved into a corner of the closet. "Let's see what we can find."

It took only a few minutes to gather what they could. At the back of the guards' break room, a set of metal stairs led to the underbelly of the jail. The first two steps were visible before the rest were lost in the gloom.

"You ready?" Liam asked.

"You're my brother in arms, man. I'll follow you to hell and back."

"Good," said Liam. They'd collected wire strippers, gloves and a set of goggles from the utility closet. It'd all been stowed in a pack, and Liam slipped one of the straps over his arm. "Because I'm in the mood to kick the devil in the balls."

Darcy's head pounded. Her mouth was dry, and her face was wet and sticky. Lifting a hand to her head, she found a gash in her forehead. The pain intensified as she touched the wound. She sucked in a breath and immediately began to cough.

Was that smoke?

She opened her eyes. A piece of bent and twisted metal shielded her and she lay on a cold tile floor. A cinder block wall was at her back. Tendrils of smoke snuck under the door before dispersing throughout the room.

Darcy tried to recall where she was and what had happened. Thinking hurt, and the effort left her slightly nauseated.

She began to cough again, her body wracking. The pain in her head increased, leaving her nauseous. Darcy slumped against the wall, wanting nothing more than to sleep.

"Move," a voice whispered in her ear.

She forced her eyes to open, yet she was alone.

"Move," the voice said again.

Then Darcy remembered. She'd had Marcus's gun. Before she had a chance to shoot, he had done the unexpected—and detonated the bomb.

The voice spoke again. *"Get up or you'll die here. Then they will have won, and soon, all of those bastards will stand over your body and gloat."*

All of those bastards. Chloe Ryder. Marcus Jones and the rest of the team from RMJ. She couldn't let them have a victory at her expense. She could well imagine the pious shaking of their heads at her demise. The feigned horror of disbelief and the manufactured sadness.

Darcy would never give them the satisfaction by perishing alone, snared inside a trap that she'd set. She'd live, escape and finally defy them all.

Bracing her feet on the wall, she pushed herself forward. One inch and then another. Crawling on her belly, she freed herself from the rubble that covered her. Darcy lay on the middle of the infirmary floor and looked around. She was alone.

Where were Marcus and Chloe?

Her hands were still shackled together—and that was the most immediate problem. Slowly, she rose to her feet. The smoke was thicker and burned her eyes. Still, she could see the two dead bodies at the far side of the room. The question was—did Gretchen still have a spare key to the handcuffs?

Stumbling around the debris, Darcy collapsed next to the guard's corpse. She patted down her pants and shirt pockets, but they were empty. Then, from the belt that hung around her waist, she discovered a large set of keys. Her fingers were stiff as she fumbled with the carabiner that held the key ring in place. From there, she found the handcuff key and unlocked her restraints.

At least her hands were unshackled, but she was still trapped in the infirmary, with a fire just outside the door. Now what?

"Deal with the smoke," the Darkness told her.

"How?" Darcy's lungs burned. Her vision was blurry. Just walking across the infirmary had stolen all her energy. What she wanted now was to sleep.

"No!" the Darkness screamed. *"Never."*

Then it told her what to do.

The remnants of a tattered sheet lay on the floor. Darcy shoved the fabric into a stream of water that spilled from where the sink used to be. Soon the fabric was doused, and she spread the cover along the seam between the floor and the door. The air began to clear as smoke rose upward and disappeared. Next she stripped a pillowcase from a pillow and likewise soaked it through. After wrapping the sodden pillowcase over her face and mouth, Darcy's breathing came easier.

Yet where were the firefighters? Why was there no alarm?

She clambered over the metal cabinets and placed her palm on the door. The metal was warm, but not hot. Pushing, she opened the door a fraction of an inch and peered through the crack. There were scorch marks along the walls. Part of the ceiling had collapsed and was now smoldering and scattered across the floor. The conference room door—made of wood—was charred, but whatever had been on fire was now nothing but ashes.

She stepped into the corridor. Just beyond was the door leading to the small entryway and beyond that, the door to outside.

It meant only one thing—freedom.

Darcy crept into the hallway, looking both left and right. She saw no one. She heard nothing. She took one step and then another. The glass-enclosed guard office was empty. The monitors were all black.

Where in the hell had everyone gone?

For a moment, Darcy wondered if the hit to her head caused her to leave her senses.

The door was so close. She leaned forward. Her fingertips brushed the handle. She pushed down, and the door slowly opened.

The lobby was filled with smoke, but through the haze, Darcy could clearly see the front door. It was the only way in—or out.

She rushed across the tiled floor. Her heartbeat raced and repeated a single word. *Escape.*

She gripped the handle and pushed.

Nothing.

Darcy jerked on the handle again and again. It wouldn't budge.

She rammed the door with her shoulder. She kicked it. She pulled on the handle and screamed.

Nothing.

It was then that Darcy realized she might be out of her cell. But she was still just as trapped as she had been before.

Chapter 15

Chloe stared into the room below. Her heart thumped wildly in her chest. Her pulse resonated in her ears. She wanted to retch, but she dared not breathe.

Despite the fact that Marcus had killed one of the inmates and injured another, he'd been disarmed. Now his arms were bound with duct tape that had been found in the warden's desk. Likewise, his shins were taped to the chair's legs. One convict after another took turns punching him in the face.

Another fist slammed into him. His head snapped back, and blood spattered from his mouth.

Her heart ached for him. Marcus had to have known that it would be impossible to control a dozen desperate men. Yet he had sacrificed himself to help the warden—and to keep her safely hidden.

Chloe looked away.

Where was everyone? Obviously the inmates had gotten out of their cells. But why hadn't the rest of the guards come in? Or deputies from the sheriff's office? Or even the operatives from RMJ?

Carefully, Chloe slipped her bag from her back. Was there any way she could make a call without the men in the room overhearing her conversation? No. Still, she could send a message. After muting her phone, she pulled up her contact list and found the number for Julia McCloud.

She typed out a message. Where are you? Need help in the jail.

She hit the send icon.

A wheel began to spin, and a message appeared on the screen. Sending… Sending… Sending…

Chloe held her breath.

The wheel disappeared. It was replaced with a red exclamation point. Message failed to send.

By hiding in the vent, was she without coverage? Were Chloe and Marcus really all alone, with no hope of getting any help?

She tried again.

Inmates out of their cells.

Send.

Transgressors have taken Marcus and Cal Douglas hostage in the warden's office. Both men are injured.

Send.

If you get this, help. Please.

Sending... Sending... Sending...

Message failed to send.

Biting her lip hard, she tried to stanch the tears of frustration that stung her eyes.

Chloe was stuck inside the vent with no way to connect with the outside world. Without help, could she hope to get to Marcus and survive?

The front door of the jail was reinforced steel, with four titanium bolts that had been engaged. In short, it was impossible to break out of—and therefore, hard as hell to break into. It didn't mean that Julia wasn't going to try.

Since her short conversation with Luis, Julia hadn't been able to get in contact with anyone inside the jail. She hoped like hell that he and Liam were in the basement and working on the electrical system. While waiting for news, she and Wyatt had brainstormed several ways to get the door opened. Now Wyatt held a rotor saw. His eyes were covered by safety glasses. The saw's engine whined. Smoke rose from the gears, and sparks flew from the blade.

As he let off the power, the saw slowed and stopped. He leaned in close to examine his handiwork. "Nada on the progress, unless you count making the blade dull."

Julia wanted to curse. "What other options do we have? Can we drill a hole in the wall?"

"Big enough for a person to climb through?"

"Okay, that was a stupid idea." Julia looked at the door. "There has to be something we can do."

"There is no way to break those bolts, short of blowing the door clean off its hinges. The only thing that will work for that is C-4, which is something that I don't have and cannot get."

"Wait," said Julia. "I think you've figured it out. If you can pry the hinges loose, we can open the door that way, at least a little."

Wyatt ran his hand over the faceplate that was bolted into the concrete wall. "Actually," he said, drawing out his word, "in theory, yeah. But it'd take some time to break through the cinder blocks."

"How long?"

"Hours," he said.

"We don't have hours," said Julia.

"No," he said with the shake of his head. "We don't."

"Do you have a shotgun?"

"Back in the van, sure."

Julia turned on her heel. "Let's go."

The van was completely unremarkable from the outside and gave RMJ perfect cover for surveillance. Yet as the old saying went, appearances were often deceiving, and it was true in the case of the mobile HQ.

Several cameras were located on the exterior and gave a three-hundred-sixty-degree view for up to one thousand yards. The van was also equipped with sensitive audio equipment. They could listen to, and record, a single conversation up to seventy-five yards away.

Inside, a small arsenal of weapons—handguns, rifles and a shotgun with a four-round chamber—hung on one wall. A bench ran along the middle of the van. Half a dozen monitors filled a connected table. The van had Wi-Fi and could connect with the main RMJ server in

Denver. From there, everyone on the team could access the internal sites for the FBI, CIA, NSA, and MI6, just to name a few. In short, there wasn't a shred of information that RMJ couldn't access.

For now, all the fancy equipment meant nothing.

Wyatt pulled the shotgun from the wall and racked a round into the chamber.

The sound sent a chill up Julia's spine.

"I don't know if this is going to work," he said. "The base for each hinge is buried pretty deep."

"There's only one way to find out," she said.

At a jog, they returned to the front of the jail.

"Ready?" Wyatt pulled the trigger. A cloud of dust filled the air as the blast rolled across the plains.

As powdered concrete settled to the ground, Wyatt and Julia stepped forward. There was a hole where wall used to be, but the hinge was still securely inside the brick.

"Damn it," said Julia. "It didn't work."

Stepping back, Wyatt racked the shotgun once more. Aiming at the second hinge, he pulled the trigger. Same for the third and the final hinge. Without another word, Wyatt strode toward the road.

Jogging, Julia caught up with Wyatt. Grabbing his shoulder, she spun him toward her. "Where are you going?"

"To get my truck. We might be able to pull the door loose now."

Julia was willing to try anything. "Go," she said. "What are you waiting for?"

Wyatt was back in minutes, the bumper of his truck

pulled close to the door. He wrapped one end of a chain around the handle and the other around a hitch.

"Ready?" Wyatt asked while slipping behind the wheel of his pickup.

Julia stepped back. "As ready as I'm going to be."

Wyatt put the truck into Drive. The engine whined as the tires spun and the scent of burnt rubber filled the air. The door didn't budge. The handle bent, the metal groaning. Damn it. The last thing she wanted was to pull the handle clean off the door.

Waving both arms, Julia stepped forward. "Whoa. Whoa. Whoa. It's not going to work."

Wyatt turned off the ignition and leaned out the window. "We just have to keep thinking," he said. "There has to be some way to get into the jail."

The phone in Julia's pocket vibrated with incoming texts. Must be that she'd connected Wi-Fi from the RMJ van. After pulling out the phone, she glanced at the screen. All of the messages were from Chloe. She opened the app and her mouth went dry.

"What is it?" Wyatt asked.

Julia held up the screen for him to see.

He worked his jaw back and forth as he read. "We have to get into that jail."

Of course they did. But how?

Julia hated the idea of leaving people in the facility for a single minute. Yet what bothered her more than the delay—and the possible danger to the inmates—was that their friends and the rest of the prison staff were stuck inside the jail with the likes of Darcy Owens and the Transgressors. Then there was the worst problem of all—for the moment, she could do nothing to help.

Still, she had to give Chloe some kind of hope. She typed and sent a message.

Stay strong. There was an override on the electrical system. Should be fixed in a minute. Then we're on our way.

She hit Send and watched as the text was delivered. Her stomach clenched, not only because of what her friends were enduring, but because Julia knew that she'd lied.

There was no help to be had now and possibly not enough time to make a difference for those inside.

Chloe's phone lit up with an incoming message. She read Julia's words and breathed a sigh of relief. This nightmare would soon end. But how much more could Marcus endure?

His face was bloodied. His nose was flattened and definitely broken. One of his eyes was swollen shut, and his bottom lip was split open. Yet there was nothing he could do to defend himself against his tormentors while he was bound to the chair.

She had to let Marcus know that help was on the way—and if he could hold on for just a minute more, he'd survive.

Scooting on her stomach, Chloe peered into the room.

Was it rotten luck, or fate wanting to make matters worse? Chloe would never know. At the same instant she looked down, Luke looked up. Their eyes met, and for a moment, neither of them reacted.

"What the hell?" Luke rushed forward.

Chloe tried to move back, further into the ventilation system, but wasn't fast enough. Luke reached into the vent and grabbed Chloe by the hair. Her scalp filled with pain. She struggled to break free. He was stronger, and he pulled her closer to him. She skidded along the vent.

Grabbing his wrists with both of her hands, she dug in her fingernails and squeezed.

Luke screamed a curse and shoved her wrists back. She saw a flash of white. Before she knew what happened, Luke had pulled her to him enough that he had a hold on her arms.

Fighting Luke was like holding back the tide. Inch by inch, she lost the battle and ended up on the floor, flat on her back. The air left Chloe's lungs in a painful gust and she couldn't draw a breath. One of the men raised a foot as if to kick her in the abdomen. "Don't, please. I'm pregnant."

She knew that she never should've admitted to her condition, but now she couldn't take the words back. Yet she looked up and her eyes locked with Marcus's. Without having to say a word, he knew that the child she carried was his.

That is, if they all made it out of the jail alive.

Marcus couldn't believe it.

He and Chloe had created a child. He didn't have time to wonder how he felt or marvel at the new life. But he now had one more reason to make sure that both he and Chloe survived.

Luke jerked Chloe up by the shoulders.

She screamed. "Let me go!"

"Let you go?" Luke taunted. "The way you act is like you ain't to happy to see me, Madam District Attorney."

She struggled in his grip. "You'll regret this for sure, you bastard."

Luke slapped her face. "Shut up, bitch."

She spun backwards with the impact and slammed into the desk, scattering pens, tape and the letter opener used to stab Douglas. A trickle of blood leaked from the corner of Chloe's mouth. She wiped it away with her shoulder and said nothing.

Marcus wanted to roar and tear Luke apart bit by filthy bit. But he was bound tightly. He needed to get free.

Warden Douglas, slumped on the floor, leaned into Marcus's chair. The older man's face was bloody, and his fingers were broken. Stab wounds littered his body. His brown suit had turned black with blood. The older man was unconscious and would be no help.

As all the Transgressors gathered around the desk, the warden moved his hand—it was just a fraction of an inch. Reaching out, he slipped his palm over the letter opener. Then, without moving anything beyond his arm, he silently and deftly placed the blade in Marcus's palm.

Flipping the blade around, Marcus had but a few seconds. The tip pierced the tape, and once he'd ripped open a seam, Marcus worked his hands free.

"Ready?" the warden whispered.

Ready for what? Then again, the exact plan didn't

matter. Marcus was ready for anything. "Yessir," he whispered back.

With a roar, the old marine launched himself from the floor. He grabbed Luke around the middle and shoved him back. They toppled to the ground, struggling.

"Go, Chloe," Marcus yelled over the melee.

Chloe ran for the door, but Rex stepped in her way. She dodged to the left, trying to get around him. Rex grabbed her by the waist. "No, you don't go anywhere, sugarlips."

Luke punched the warden in the face, knocking his head into the hard tile floor. "Sonofabitch," the inmate growled. "You're too much trouble, you know?"

Marcus's gun sat on a shelf. Luke retrieved it.

Warden Douglas sat up. Holding his hands in front of him, he said a single word. "No!"

Pointing the barrel at the warden, Luke pulled the trigger. Once. Twice. Three times. The older man slumped to the ground, the echoes of his final word mixing with the gun's report.

Marcus swallowed down his revulsion and fury. In the last seconds of his life, Warden Douglas had been a hero in more ways than one. He'd sacrificed everything to give Marcus a chance to save Chloe. It was a chance he wasn't going to waste.

Marcus had gotten his hand free. Despite his legs being taped to the chair, he could now enter the fight. Reaching out, he stabbed the closest inmate in the thigh. The man yelled in pain and surprise. Gripping his leg, the guy dropped to the ground.

Marcus began to saw at the tape between one of his ankles, using the moment of confusion as cover. Rex sprinted toward Marcus. He lifted his fist, ready to strike. The last bit of tape ripped just as Rex came into range. Marcus lifted his heel, catching the guy's crotch.

Rex hit the ground like a sack of potatoes.

Standing on one leg. Marcus spun around and rammed the chair into another inmate. The chair splintered with the impact. Marcus picked up the chair's back and unleashed his fury, striking the man in the head and the back. He, too, fell to the ground, unconscious.

A blast of gunfire filled the small room as heat sliced the top of his ear. He turned. Luke held the gun, and smoke rose from the barrel. Luke pulled the trigger again and again. Marcus flattened himself on the floor as the bullets whizzed by and punched holes in the wall. He counted as his heart thundered. Marcus had pulled the trigger four times—killing one and injuring one more, with two misses.

Luke shot the warden three times, then wasted four bullets trying to kill Marcus.

The gun held one more bullet.

Marcus kicked Luke in the knee. The other man cursed. Grabbing Luke around the middle, Marcus knocked the other man into the desk. His torso hit the edge with a satisfying crack. Luke cried out in pain but lifted the SIG Sauer. He aimed at Marcus's head.

Reaching for the other man's wrist, he squeezed.

Rough hands grabbed him from behind and pulled him back. Luke brought the gun down and aimed at Marcus's chest.

He froze.

At this range, there was no way that Luke would miss. And then what? Chloe would be without protection. Her life, and the life their child, would be in the hands of a group of dangerous and deadly men. He flicked his gaze in her direction. One of the inmates held her by the shoulder and pressed her back into his chest. Her gaze didn't hold sorrow or fear, but defiance.

Even in the face of a certain and horrible death, she would fight. He loved that about her. In truth, he loved everything about her. Now it was too late.

Then he realized what had given her such courage. Wrapped into her palm was the letter opener. Without looking away, she brought up her blade and stabbed her captor in the hand.

The man howled in agony and disbelief. Chloe rushed at Luke with the letter opener held high. Marcus reached for the gun and wrested it from the inmate's grasp. A single shot rang out as the bullet tore through the ceiling.

Chloe fell on top of Luke. The letter opener protruded from the inmate's eye.

Marcus grabbed Chloe by the waist and pulled her from the room. The warden's office led to the hallway. Marcus slammed the door shut. He toppled a filing cabinet in front of the door, wedging it between the handle and the wall, blocking the Transgressors inside. Despite the closed door, Luke's screams could still be heard. One leg of the chair was still taped to his ankle. He ripped it away and tossed it aside.

Chloe threw herself into his arms. He wrapped her into a tight embrace.

She said, "Thank goodness we made it out of that room alive."

Marcus pulled her in close. God, it felt good just to hold her. "When were you going to tell me about the baby? Is that what the call was about this morning?"

"It was, but are you sure this is the best time for this conversation?"

"It's not," he said, "but let's have it anyway."

Chloe licked her lips before pressing them together. "Honestly, I was going to tell you as soon as I found out, but you didn't answer. And then, I think I was just so...stunned. I didn't know how I felt at first. We got here, and everything happened, and..."

"We're in this together." He placed his hand on her shoulder. Should he do more? Say more? After all, it had taken the two of them, together, to create this new life. "All three of us."

"You aren't upset?" she asked. Her voice was small, the words all but disappearing as soon as she spoke.

"Surprised? Sure. Upset? Hell, no. What about you?"

"Me? Well, I'm..."

The door to the warden's office shook. The filing cabinet rocked. Marcus walked another cabinet over, wedged one end under the handle, and pressed the other end against the opposite wall. "Let's get out of here in case that lock and barricade don't hold," he said.

"I got a text from Julia. They can't get any of the exterior doors opened." Chloe shook her head. "It's some kind of electrical override."

The door rattled again. "We still need to get out of here."

"And go where?" asked Chloe.

He didn't know. Until power was restored to the building, they were stuck inside—with the inmates free.

Chapter 16

Darcy sat on the floor, slumped next to the front door. Three rounds of gunshots sounded from outside. From a different direction came screams of agony and the sound of footsteps approaching fast. She had no idea what was happening throughout the jail, but she did know that none of it was good. Drawing a deep breath, she waited for the voice of the Darkness.

Nothing came to her.

She waited a minute and then a minute more.

"Hello," she called into the recesses of her mind. "Where are you?"

Silence.

It was there, in the shadows, where the Darkness dwelled.

"Hello?" Her voice was small, as it had been when

she was young and had no protection. When there was nobody to care or to guide the way—except for the Darkness, that is.

Still, the Darkness did not answer.

Darcy squeezed her eyes shut and pressed her knuckles into her temples. "Where are you? You cannot go. You cannot leave me. Not now. Not when I need you most."

Then she recalled that she had told Chloe Ryder about the Darkness. Because of that indiscretion, was she now forsaken? The possibility left her sick and gasping for air.

If she was right, it brought up an even more terrifying question. Who would Darcy be if not for the Darkness?

Then again, she knew. Darcy would cease to be herself.

Rocking back and forth, she begged the Darkness to return. It didn't. And from somewhere came a notion. She could not remain in the lobby while masquerading as a nurse. She had to act. But what could she do?

A plan came to her—it was imperfect, but it might work.

Rising to her feet, Darcy retraced her steps and returned to the infirmary. The room stank, smelling of smoke and blood and rot. She gagged but refused to retch. Two corpses lay on the floor. Their throats were open. Their eyes were wide. The pupils had already gone milky.

"Gretchen," she said, her voice clear and strong. "I need your uniform." Pulling on the large nurse's uniform, she said, "This is too big. It'll be more noticeable than if I borrow what you're wearing."

Holding up her hands, Darcy continued, "I know, you might get in trouble. I doubt they'll fire you because, well, you know—you are already dead."

Darcy chuckled. The small joke gave her some measure of courage, and she knelt in front of the guard's body. Gretchen's jaw and neck were tight, but rigor mortis had yet to spread to other parts of her body. It took several minutes to strip the guard out of her uniform.

Darcy then undressed, discarding the baggy uniform. She put on the pants first. They were a bit long but fit around the waist. She took a moment to roll the cuffs and knew that at a quick glance, the pants would look as if they were made to fit.

The shoes were two sizes too big, but again—who would notice?

Blood splatter dotted the legs and had dried, making the fabric stiff. The shirt, however, was a different matter. The gray fabric was tacky, cold and blackened with blood. Darcy shoved the top into the sink and turned on the tap full blast.

The water changed to red and then pink as the fabric was rinsed clean.

She donned the cold, wet shirt and pulled her hair back into a ponytail with an elastic band that she'd found on the floor. There was no mirror in the infirmary, but Darcy assumed that she looked official. The nurse's keys lay on the floor. Darcy scooped them up and dropped them into her own pocket.

Finally, she cut the ID band from her own arm. Using

surgical tape on the back of the band, she taped it around Gretchen's wrist. Darcy's prison jumpsuit, covered in blood and barf, was balled up in a corner. She struggled to dress the guard in the garment—taking extra time to zip up the neck to the chin and hide the wound at Gretchen's throat.

If she got lucky, the NWCF jumpsuit and wristband would be enough—at least during an initial once-over. Hopefully, whoever found the body would believe that the serial killer had perished. Sure, in time they'd figure out what really happened, but by then, Darcy planned to be long gone.

Liam and Luis stood in front of the master panel for the electrical system that controlled the entire jail. It was a tangle of wires and switches. Dozens of lights, all dark, stood in two rows.

"Where do we start?" Luis asked.

"We need to check the amperes. Even if we have a little bit of juice, we can rig this system with enough power to get us back online—temporarily, at least." He touched the metal sensor to one of the switches. Despite the gloom, they could see the reading.

"Zero," said Luis. "Now what?"

"Thank goodness I brought this with me." Liam slipped off his pack and removed a small plastic box.

"A generator," said Luis. "There can't be enough energy inside that thing to power the entire jail."

"Thankfully we only need enough power to release the lock on the front door. That takes, what? A second? Two? Once the door is open, help can get inside."

"Does somebody have to be next to the door to pull it open?"

"They do." Liam paused. "But we only have one shot at this."

Luis pulled a phone from a side pocket in his pants. "There's barely any coverage."

"Then keep the conversation short," said Liam. "Just make the call."

Liam waited while the other man opened his contacts and placed the call. After several seconds, the phone began to ring. He activated the speaker function.

"Hello?" Julia's single word was broken up with static.

"I need you to be ready to open the door." Luis spoke louder. "Did you hear me? Open the door."

"Open the door?" Julia repeated. "I can't get it open."

Liam attached the generator to the electrical grid. The small box hummed with contained power. "All set? Tell me when."

Luis screamed into the phone, "You need to open the door in three. Two…"

Liam turned on the generator. Every light on the panel was illuminated.

"Now," said Luis. "Pull the door open now."

The lights went dark, and the generator went silent.

"Did it work?" Liam asked. "Was Julia able to open the door?"

"Julia?" Luis asked. "How'd that work?"

Nothing.

Luis glanced at his phone. "Damn it. There are no bars. The call dropped."

Liam muttered a curse. Had Julia even heard the orders? Or had all of this been for nothing? Were Liam and Luis truly trapped inside the jail, with no hope of escaping?

Julia caught enough of Luis's static-filled message to know they had one chance to open the door. What's more, she had to pull the handle at just the right time.

But nothing happened when she did.

The notion of failure—of her team, her friends—was unacceptable. Army rangers never failed, and despite having retired years ago, she was still a ranger, through and through. She pulled again. Nothing.

Kicking the door, she cursed.

Softer than a whisper, she heard a click.

Julia reached for the handle and pulled. The door opened. Smoke billowed into the sky as Chloe rushed from the lobby with Marcus at her heels.

Both were beaten and bloodied. Marcus was definitely in worse shape—one eye swollen shut, nose crooked, lip busted and fat. Yet Julia had never been happier to see anyone than she was to see those two.

"You guys look awful," said Julia, pulling them into a hug.

"Then I look a lot better than I feel," said Marcus, his words slightly slurred.

"You being able to make a joke, even a bad one, counts for something." Julia hugged them again. "What in the hell happened?"

"I guess you got it right," said Marcus. "Hell broke out inside the jail. It's going to take everything we've got to bring back sanity to all of that madness. But even worse, Darcy's on the loose—in there—somewhere. She's the one who caused all this chaos, and it's time to make her pay."

There were several things that concerned Marcus. The death of the warden. The inmates, who now controlled the jail and roamed freely throughout. But mostly Marcus worried about Darcy Owens. Was she really dead?

Then again, he hadn't had much of a choice. Still...

"What happened in there?" Julia asked. "Where's Darcy?"

Marcus ignored the first question, yet Chloe answered the second. "She's gone. Marcus checked her pulse." She shook her head.

"What happened to you guys, then?" Julia asked.

Picking up the story, Marcus continued, "With the fire in the hallway, Chloe and I escaped through the vents." He paused. "There's some things you need to know, Julia."

"Like what?"

"Warden Douglas is dead."

"Damn." Julia sighed. "That's a shame. He was good people."

"He died a hero." Marcus knew that the loss of Cal Douglas would be felt by many, but now was not the time to be distracted by grief—not with so much at stake.

"Well, wait a minute," Julia said. "If Cal is gone, then who is in charge? Most of the staff were outside helping with the evacuation. Didn't he have a second-in-command?"

Marcus didn't know the answer to that question. "Until we figure that out, we need someone to be in charge. You're the sheriff, so logically the responsibility is yours."

Julia nodded. "If I'm in command, what will you do, Marcus?"

"I'm going back in the jail to find Darcy's body."

"Are you crazy?" Chloe asked. She reached for his hand, linking her fingers through his. Did she know how nice it felt just to touch her? Or how hard it would be to leave her again? "It's total chaos in there. You don't even know how many inmates are in that building."

Julia had that information. She said, "According to the records, there were one hundred and twenty-three inmates before the bomb exploded. All but twenty have been safely removed."

That meant the math was easy. "If eleven Transgressors are locked in the warden's office, there's only a dozen more inmates that need to be accounted for—Darcy included."

"I'm going to organize a team of guards to restore order, but you—you've taken quite a beating."

"And then some." Marcus wiped his nose with the cuff of his shirt. Blood stained the fabric, and his eyes watered. Definitely, his nose was broken. But what were a few bumps and bruises when compared to recovering the body of Darcy Owens.

"Which means you need medical treatment," Julia said.

Marcus ignored her comment. "Where's Wyatt? Get him to see if he can get power to the CCTV. If we have cameras working inside, we can get an accurate assessment of the situation."

"And while he does that," said Chloe, "you see a doctor."

Great. Now it's two against one. Marcus wasn't about to be deterred. "I'm going back to the infirmary. Once I've recovered Darcy's body I'll see the doctor."

A handful of inmates, along with a group of guards, must've realized that the front door was now open. To the man, they were bruised and bloody. They limped into the parking lot. Marcus could feel the tension in Julia—a cord pulling her toward her duty. "Go," he said. "You're in charge. I can take care of myself and Darcy."

Julia lifted a brow. "I'm in charge, eh? Then I order you to stand down. Get seen by the NWFC doc. You won't do anyone any good if you play cowboy and pass out."

Ordered to stand down? Did Marcus hear her right? "Aww, hell no."

The sound of a dozen sirens wailing at once could be heard in the distance. The horizon was filled with strobing lights of blue and red. It was the help that his little brother had promised to deliver.

"Looks like the cavalry finally showed up." Chloe gave Marcus's hand a squeeze before letting her fingers slip through his. "Instead of disagreeing all day, why don't we compromise? Obviously the jail needs to be searched. Let Julia assign someone. They can report back to you."

Julia added, "You can get a report in an ambulance

same as you can standing—and that's a pretty generous term—in the parking lot."

Marcus wanted to argue—but he knew when he was beat. "Agreed."

"I hate to leave you both, but I need to deal with all of the new arrivals." Julia looked over her shoulder at the incoming emergency vehicles.

Then it was just Marcus and Chloe. There was so much to discuss—what should he say? What should he do?

His fingers itched with the need to touch her stomach—to connect with his child, even if just a little. He placed his palm on her middle—and sure, it felt like a stomach. But really, it was so much more. There was a new life, one that he and Chloe had created during a night of passion. "How are both of you?" he whispered, unable to keep the wonderment from his voice. Before he had a chance to say anything else, a man in a Wyoming Highway Patrol uniform approached.

"You Jones?"

"I am." He read the man's name tag. "Nice to meet you, Captain Franz. This is Chloe Ryder, DA from Pleasant Pines."

"I got briefed on everything that happened. Sounds like you two have had a heck of a day so far," said Captain Franz. He was a large man with wide shoulders. "I've been tasked with searching the correctional facility and have been asked to coordinate with you."

"Eleven inmates took over the warden's office. One's dead and three are severely injured. Just now, four other inmates exited the front door and are in the custody of the guards. That leaves five on the inside who's status is unknown."

"Five doesn't sound so bad," said the captain. "What can you tell me about them?"

"One of them is Darcy Owens."

The big guy blanched. "Darcy Owens? That serial killer?"

"She was injured in the explosion at the infirmary. I checked for a pulse." He shook his head. "She was gone."

Captain Franz wrote in a spiral notebook. "Sounds like the first place we need to search is the infirmary so we can recover her body."

"Agreed," said Marcus. "I'm coming with you."

"No can do, Jones. That's a direct order from Sheriff McCloud." He paused. "And if you don't mind me saying, you look like crap on a cracker."

Marcus chuckled at the description. A knife of pain stabbed his face, and he winced. "I've never heard that one before."

"You don't get a doctor to look at all those injuries and clean you up, you're going to hear it a whole lot more." Pen and pad in hand, Captain Franz asked, "Where's the best place to reach you?"

Marcus pointed to the ground. "Right here." Sure, he knew that he was being stubborn. And what's more, a halo of light surrounded the trooper. It meant that he was probably concussed, and everyone was right—he did need to see a doctor. But he damn well wasn't going anywhere until Darcy Owens was brought out in a body bag and this entire episode ended.

* * *

Captain Franz led a team of seven troopers into the correctional facility. He'd served a tour overseas with the Wyoming National Guard in a combat zone. Yet he never imagined seeing the same kind of damage back in the US.

The walls were covered in scorch marks, and the ceiling had collapsed. "Thank goodness this place is made of cinder blocks or the whole thing would have gone up in flames," he said to a junior patrol officer.

"Roger that, sir."

To get to the infirmary, Franz led his team down a corridor. He paused at the door. "Everyone get ready," he said, removing his firearm from a holster at his hip. "This is the last known location of Darcy Owens. I want everyone prepared for any eventuality."

"Yessir," came the reply.

He waited as all the troopers drew their weapons as well.

Franz pushed the door open slowly and peeked through the seam between jamb and wall. Cabinets had been blown off the walls. Blood covered the floor. A set of handcuffs lay in the corner. And at the back of the room—there were two corpses. One wore a nurse's scrubs. The other had on an inmate's orange jumpsuit. From the pallor of their skin, the unseeing eyes and the blood that covered them both, Franz was fairly certain the women were deceased.

The question was—was one of them Darcy Owens?

With his gun still drawn, he stepped into the room and approached the corpses. His team followed. Franz knelt next to the body of the inmate. He checked the wristband. Name: Owens, Darcy.

He stood. "Looks like we have her, fellas. This'll be one of those days you can tell your grandkids about— when you found the body of Wyoming's most notorious killer. Adam, call someone to collect these bodies so they can be processed with DNA and such. Tommy, go tell Marcus Jones that Darcy Owens is deceased."

"Marcus Jones? Who's he?"

"Just go outside and find the guy who looks like he took the worst beating in the world. That's him." He paused. "I want the rest of you to go in teams of two to search this entire facility. You've all been emailed a document with name of each guard, along with identifying information. We want to find everyone—good guys and bad. Now, go."

"Yessir."

Standing in the middle of the infirmary, Franz made a notation in his notebook with the time.

Body of Darcy Owens discovered in infirmary.
ID made by wristband.

He'd wait until the bodies were collected, and then he'd speak to Jones personally and answer any questions—that is, if the guy hadn't been taken to the hospital already.

Chapter 17

Darcy took refuge in the conference room across the hall from the infirmary. The room stank of vomit and smoke. It was enough to make her sick all over again. Yet the sounds of people moving up and down the corridor were unmistakable. What was she supposed to do now? She pressed her back against the wall and waited for the voice of the Darkness to return.

It didn't. For the first time in years, Darcy was truly alone.

She sank to the floor. Time held no meaning, and she sat for what seemed like days, but really, only minutes passed.

The door opened, brushing up against Darcy's shoulder.

She quickly rose to her feet.

A round-faced state trooper peered into the room. "What are you doing in here?" he asked.

Damn. All her plans for freedom and vengeance were gone. She was going to rot in a cell—that is, until she was executed. "I..." she began.

"Jeez, just look at you. What the hell happened?" He held the door open. "I guess it doesn't matter right now. This place is crawling with cops. You're safe. Just come with me."

It was the uniform. Her ruse had worked. Darcy's legs were stiff from sitting, yet she stepped into the hallway. "Thanks," she said.

"What'd you say your name was?"

"Um, well, I..."

"Gretchen," whispered the Darkness. *"Your name is Gretchen."*

Her eyes stung and her throat was sore. "Gretchen," she said, her voice still small. "Gretchen Harper."

The man consulted his phone, running his finger down the screen. "Gretchen," he said. "Here you are. Who's your next of kin?"

Darcy felt like she'd been sucker punched. "What?"

"Next of kin. We need to verify everyone's identity. I get that it's a stupid rule, but my captain will rip me a new one if I don't."

How in the hell was Darcy supposed to know who Gretchen's next to kin?

"But you do," the Darkness coaxed. *"Remember?"*

Darcy had a flash of memory from first thing in the morning, though it felt like the moment happened years ago.

"Why are you so nice to me?" she had asked the guard. *"You actually treat me like a person."*

Gretchen had said, *"I was brought up to believe that everyone has value."*

"Everyone?"

"It was what my grandma Ruth always said while raising me."

Darcy stood taller and cleared her throat. "Ruth," she said. "My Grandma Ruth is my next of kin."

"Thank you much, ma'am." He tucked his phone into the pocket of his uniform pants. "I'm glad we found you. Really, I don't know how to tell you this, but Warden Douglas was murdered." The trooper placed his hand on her arm. He led Darcy to the front door. She stepped outside and inhaled her first breath of freedom in months. The car keys she had thought to take with her were heavy in her pocket. She exhaled and thanked the Darkness for always having a plan.

"We need to get you checked out." The trooper led her toward a waiting ambulance.

To her left, a gravel parking lot was filled with cars. A sign, attached to the fence, read Employees Only.

"I'm okay," Darcy said. Then she quickly added, "I can get myself to the EMTs. You go and help other folks."

"Are you sure? I don't mind staying with you."

"I'll mind if you treat me like an invalid and don't help the people who need you."

"Okay then," said the trooper.

Darcy walked toward the ambulance. Her gait was slow. Glancing over her shoulder, she waited as the trooper returned to the jail's front door. He didn't pause or look back before disappearing inside. She turned, going left, heading to the employee lot—the most likely place for the nurse to park her car. All she needed to do was find the right one, and then she'd truly be free.

Chloe persuaded Marcus to wait for news about Darcy near RMJ's mobile headquarters. It'd taken some convincing to get him away from the front doors.

Now, if she could only get him to see a doctor...

All the operatives from RMJ were gathered. Liam and Luis had given a report on how they'd rebooted the electrical system. Until the power was fully restored, the CCTV wouldn't be online—although Wyatt had tried. Chloe and Marcus filled everyone in the Transgressors, who had turned the warden's office into a sanctuary.

It was the removal of those inmates they now discussed. Yet Chloe could feel the anxiety of each person—along with the unasked question. Where was Darcy Owens?

Liam had a set of schematics on a tablet computer. Pointing to a row of windows, he said, "Those lead to the office. They're thick, but not reinforced with wire. With the right kind of firepower, we can break through."

Luis continued with the rest of the plan. "Then we throw in a flash-bang grenade. While everyone's disoriented, a team can kick in the door."

"Simple but effective," said Marcus. "I like it. Liam and Wyatt, you get the munitions through the window. Luis—connect with Julia and get a team to come in through the building."

"And what will you be doing?" Wyatt asked.

Chloe knew that he should be going to see the doc, but she doubted that would happen until everyone who'd gotten loose was apprehended and accounted for.

A trooper from the highway patrol approached the group. "One of you Marcus Jones?"

Chloe's heart ceased to beat. Was it news about Darcy? It had to be.

"I'm Jones."

"I thought you were supposed to be by the main entrance." He sighed. "Captain Franz sent me to tell you that we found Darcy Owens's body."

"Where is she now?" Marcus stepped forward. "I want to see her."

Was it over? Was the Darcy Owens case truly closed? Chloe stood at his side. "We need to see her."

"Captain Franz was having EMTs collect the body. She's probably been loaded into one of the ambulances by now." The trooper tipped his hat to Chloe. "Ma'am." And then he left.

Chloe reached for Marcus's hand. He squeezed her palm into his and looked her in the eye.

"I…" She could feel the need for confirmation. "I need to see her body."

Marcus turned to scan the rows of ambulances. She could guess what he was thinking—which one of those held Darcy Owens?

"Go," said Wyatt. "Both of you. The three of us can take care of the Transgressors."

Marcus opened his mouth, ready to argue. He wouldn't want to leave his team without their leader.

Before he could speak, Liam said, "You know we

are all professionals. We can take care of this. Go." He paused. "And since you're going to be with all of those EMTs, get yourself checked out."

Marcus ignored the last comment. "I'll be in touch."

Chloe and Marcus hustled across the parking lot. A young man wearing a blue jumpsuit from Pleasant Pines emergency services stood near the rear doors of an ambulance. "Hey," Marcus called out. "I need some information. Which one of these has the body of Darcy Owens?"

The EMT swallowed. "I'm not authorized to tell you that."

Chloe's tone was like flint. "Do you know who I am?"

The young man nodded. "The DA."

"I'm authorizing you—where's Darcy?"

The kid pointed. "Third one from the front." And then, "Hey, man. You want me to check you out?"

"Not now," said Marcus. He was already jogging to the waiting ambulance.

Chloe had to run to catch up. The back doors were closed, and a trooper stood guard. "DA Chloe Ryder," she said as she approached. "I need to see the body of Darcy Owens." Sure, she'd lost her ID—probably it was with her bag somewhere in the vents—but thankfully the trooper didn't ask for proof.

She opened the rear gate and stepped aside. "Owens is on the left."

Two stretchers stood side by side in the back of the ambulance. A black body bag was strapped to each stretcher. Marcus climbed into the ambulance and held out his hand to Chloe.

"You ready?" he asked.

Chloe nodded.

Marcus reached for the zipper and pulled. Chloe drew in a deep breath before she looked.

"What the f—" Marcus breathed.

What the f— was right. Chloe was sucked back to this morning when she held the guard as she died. It was the same woman who lay in the body bag. "It's not Darcy," said Chloe, stating the obvious. She unzipped the other body bag and exposed the head and torso of the second corpse. For the span of a heartbeat, Chloe went numb.

"That's the nurse." Even she heard the tremor in her voice.

Yet, what she didn't know was much more important. Where was Darcy right now? And if she'd gotten out of the jail, how far might she have gotten before they'd realized she had escaped?

"I checked! She had no pulse, goddamn it!" said Marcus for what felt like the hundredth time. He recalled the chaotic moment as the infirmary filled with smoke. Darcy's flesh was already cooling.

Wyatt gave a sympathetic grunt. "I know you did, man. But—the likely scenario was that her pulse was just too faint for you to feel. Besides, who'd have thought she'd survive an explosion? Or the fire? Especially if she was standing so close to the bomb."

It was the same answer that Marcus had been given each time. And sure, it might be true. Yet, it made him feel no better.

His insides burned with self-loathing. "I screwed up."

"We'll get the chance to make this right." At least Wyatt didn't give him a pandering answer about it not being Marcus's fault.

Then, Marcus asked the only question that really mattered. "How?"

For that, Wyatt didn't have an answer.

The alarm had been raised. None of the bodies belonged to Darcy Owens. The infirmary had been searched. Her body wasn't there.

People were now searching for the missing serial killer. It meant that everyone had a job—and it left Chloe wondering how she could help. Eventually she'd be needed, but not until someone who'd been accused had their day in court.

Walking alone from the line of ambulances to the RMJ mobile HQ, she had a moment to wonder—where had she gone so wrong? Sure, Chloe was confident. But had Chloe been so certain in her own abilities that she'd failed to correctly assess the threat that was Darcy Owens?

What had she missed? Anxious to come up with some kind of useful clue, she examined each moment with Darcy.

She started with her arrival, to Darcy's illness, to the guard's murder. To Darcy forcing Chloe to change her clothes. She took another step forward and stumbled. She recalled a moment when Darcy had laid out several items on the counter. The phone. The scalpel. A water bottle and protein bar.

A set of car keys.

Her eyes were drawn to the employee lot. There,

at the end of a row of cars, was a woman wearing a guard's uniform.

Darcy. It had to be.

Chloe reached for her phone. *Damn.* She didn't have her bag.

She searched the crowd for Liam. Or Luis. Or Wyatt. Or Julia. None of them were to be seen.

Chloe didn't have time to consider the consequences. She knew there were only two outcomes—act now or lose her chance. When she thought about it that way, she didn't really have a choice at all. She sprinted toward the parking lot, where the killer stood at the side of a car.

"Darcy." The single word rang out like a shot. "Don't move."

For a moment, the two women stared at each other. Then the killer pulled open the door of an older sedan and slid into driver's seat.

Forcing her legs to move faster, Chloe grabbed the door as Darcy tried to pull it shut. "You aren't going anywhere." Sure, her words were tough. But she wasn't Julia McCloud. She'd never been trained in any form of combat. Reaching for Darcy, she grabbed the other woman's hair and tried to jerk her out of the car.

The killer kicked Chloe's knee. The impact of the blow dropped her to the ground. She landed hard on her rear and gravel dug into her palms. The driver's door slammed shut, and Darcy started the engine.

Chloe refused to let the killer get away. Rising to her feet, she reached for the rear door and pulled it open.

Darcy backed out of the parking spot, the tires kicking up a cloud of dust. The door slipped from Chloe's grasp but remained a gaping hole. She had but one second to act. Then, without thought, she jumped into the back seat as Darcy sped away.

"What a freaking goat rope," Marcus said, as he rubbed the back of his neck—the cords of tension were unmistakable. Marcus and Wyatt stood next to his SUV. "I'm not sure which problem is the most urgent. The Transgressors have taken over the warden's office. A perimeter needs to be created around the jail. Or that each and every cell has to be searched—again."

Wyatt said, "You need to see a doctor."

"Not you," he groaned. His whole face hurt. "I got my butt whipped. Big deal. I'll survive."

"It has been a hell of a day—worst one I can remember."

Sure, things were bad here. But he had gotten some good news. "Chloe's pregnant." Marcus hadn't meant to blurt out that bit of information, yet sharing the fact made the whole situation—oh, hell, he didn't know. More real?

"Chloe? Pregnant?" Wyatt spluttered. "And the father?"

"Is me. Chloe and I are having a baby."

"How? When?" Wyatt held up his palms. "Never mind with the how."

"Remember the night I took her out to dinner at Quinton's?"

"Yep."

"Yep," Marcus echoed.

"Well, congrats. What happens now?"

"Jesus, I don't know. We get the perimeter set up—maybe a roadblock half a mile in every direction."

"Not that! I meant you guys! You know what—leave it for a better time and place." Wyatt shook his head. "I can't even believe we're back in the middle of this again. You think Darcy's going to drive away? If she made it out, wouldn't she try to disappear into the woods?"

"Since it went so well for her the last time, you mean?" Marcus asked as he scanned the parking lot. More emergency services had arrived. Cars and SUVs, with their lights flashing, were parked at different angles around the parking lot. Then there were the unmarked sedans in black and gray that circled the lot. Everyone wanted to help, sure. But was anyone even in charge anymore? "Jesus, it *is* a freaking goat rope."

His gaze was drawn to a single car that sped from the compound. "Holy crap." He grabbed Wyatt's shoulder and pointed. "Are you seeing what I'm seeing?"

"Is Darcy driving that car?"

"Yes," he said, his voice full of disbelief.

The two-toned hair was hard to miss, even at a distance. But the back door was flung open—and a person struggled to stay in the back seat. The figure was indistinct—little more than a shadowy female. Yet Marcus's pulse spiked, and he knew. "And she's got Chloe with her."

"Come on," said Wyatt, opening the passenger door of the SUV. "Let's get her."

Marcus slid behind the steering wheel and started the big engine. He drove across the plain that separated the jail from the road. Then, using his in-car system, he placed a call.

It was answered before the first ring ceased.

"What's your ETA?" Marcus asked before Ian got a chance to speak.

"We've caught some tailwinds, and I'm in your area," said Ian. "I have the money in three suitcases. All I need is clearance to land on the road."

"Don't worry about landing. Darcy Owens escaped from the jail complex. She's in a car." Marcus gave Ian the make, model and color—enough information for the Brit to locate the sedan at five thousand feet in the air with nothing more than binoculars.

"How the blazes did she escape?"

"It's a long story, but she's not alone." Marcus paused. He tried to swallow down the self-loathing for not taking better care of Chloe. "She has a hostage— the same one from earlier. The local DA, Chloe Ryder. I need to know where they're headed."

A few moments went by, and then Ian chimed in. "I have eyes on the vehicle. They're heading north on County Route 17."

"What's the plan?" Wyatt asked.

Ian said, "We can force the car off the road."

"I don't give a damn what happens to Darcy Owens," said Marcus, "but there are two more lives at stake."

"Two more?" Ian paused. "Are you saying that the hostage is pregnant?"

Marcus was silent.

"You have to level with me," said Ian. "Is that child yours?"

Marcus drew in a deep breath. "It is."

"You won't do any good if you're emotionally compromised. Can you lead the rescue?"

Not lead the rescue? Emotionally compromised? What BS. Marcus gritted his teeth and glanced at Wyatt. The other operative lifted his brow. Marcus didn't know how to read the look. Did Wyatt agree or disagree with Ian?

"I've got this," Marcus said. His jaw was sore.

Or did Ian have a point?

Marcus hated to admit it, but the Brit might be right. As much as he tried to steer clear of the sexy district attorney, Marcus had found it nearly impossible. Oftentimes, he'd wait until after-hours and stop by the county office building, simply to see if Chloe's car was in the back lot.

Almost without fail, she worked late. It gave him the opportunity to give her the latest news with the Darcy Owens case. Even he knew the updates were just an excuse to see her. What was worse—he was certain that Chloe knew it was an excuse, too.

Over the past several months, not an hour passed during the day when she didn't come to mind. She was the last thing he thought about at night, and her face was the first image that came to mind in the morning.

Was Marcus emotionally compromised? Yeah, he guessed that he was. Yet his feelings weren't his weakness, but rather—his strength.

"I have to save Chloe and the baby," he said after a pause that had gone on for far too long. "The question is, Ian, are you willing to break the rules—again—to help me do the right thing?"

"You know I will," said the Brit. "Stay on the phone with me and I'll get you to that car."

Chapter 18

Chloe couldn't believe she'd willingly jumped into a car with a serial killer. But it was too late to second-guess her thinking now. Then again, the real question was—what should she do next?

The car increased its speed. The road passed in a blur. Darcy swerved left. Chloe slid across the back seat and toward the open door. She grabbed the seat belt and wrapped her arm in the webbing. The belt held fast. Chloe pulled herself back inside the car. She slammed the door shut just as Darcy reached over the seat and struck her with a fist.

The blow was awkward, glancing off the side of Chloe's ear. Before Darcy could retreat, Chloe grabbed her wrist and pulled her arm over the seat back.

"Pull over!"

"Never," Darcy screamed. The car swerved wildly. Left. Right. Left. Chloe could hold on no longer, and she slid to the floor. "You'll never force me to go back to jail."

It was then that Chloe realized the chilling truth. Darcy would rather perish than surrender. And that meant only one thing—Chloe was going to die, too.

Marcus was behind the wheel of his big SUV. For miles, the road ran without a bend or an incline. Then, abruptly the foothills rose from the terrain. The pavement dipped and swerved while following the slopes and leading ever upward. Marcus stayed in contact with Ian Wallace as he drove—routing the call through the in-car phone system. With a bird's-eye view, the Brit saw everything.

"Your girl seems more like a nuisance than a hostage," said Ian. Before Marcus could ask why, the other man continued, "The car's swerving like crazy. My best guess, there's a fight going on in that auto, and whoever is driving is losing."

Marcus shuddered at the possibilities and pressed his foot harder onto the gas. The SUV's large engine roared as the speedometer climbed. Seventy-five miles per hour. Eighty. Eighty-five. Ninety. Ninety-five miles per hour.

"I can see you now, too," said Ian.

"How far back am I?" Marcus asked. He needed to focus on the task at hand and not worry about the danger facing his unborn baby and the woman he loved.

Woman I love? The realization knocked the air from

his lungs. Marcus was in love with Chloe. When had that happened?

Then again, he knew. The minute he saw her sitting in the diner, something elemental, deep down inside, had told him she was the one for him. He just hadn't been ready to acknowledge it yet.

Chloe was not just a woman who completed him. She also challenged Marcus and made him the best version of himself.

God, he hoped he got the chance to tell her as much.

"You've got two miles to go," said Ian, in answer to Marcus's earlier question.

The Brit had been right. In less than a minute, the older model sedan came into view. The car fishtailed as it shot down the road.

"I think you're right," said Marcus. "I think there's a fight going on in the car."

It was more than the erratic driving. Marcus was close enough to see the shadowy figures engaged in battle.

He floored it and prayed he'd get to them in time.

Chloe's chest tightened as she thought of all the things she'd never do. Yet her biggest regret was Marcus. Why had she not let him into her life? Why had she not opened herself up to him from the beginning, given him a chance? What good was a promising career without someone to share her success?

Well, if she was going to die, she sure as hell was taking Darcy Owens with her.

Chloe scrambled onto her knees and reached over the seat. Darcy had thought to put on her seat belt—a small blessing. Grabbing two sides of the belt, Chloe pulled it across the killer's neck.

Darcy fought with one hand. Scratching. Punching. Chloe ignored the assault and pulled tighter.

Single-handed, Darcy tried to steer the car.

The road, once stick-straight, now wound through the foothills. The car slid off the road and onto the shoulder. The tires kicked up dirt until they were surrounded by a dun-colored cloud. Chloe bounced and jostled as the undercarriage slammed into the dirt. The seat belt slipped through her fingers, opening the cut across her palm.

The pain did nothing to deter her from her mission. Scrambling back to the seat, she grabbed Darcy by the hair. It was then that she saw a shadowy reflection in the sideview mirror.

Letting go, she turned in the seat and looked out the back window. It was Marcus in his black SUV, coming up from the rear—and fast.

Darcy saw him, too. "How in the hell did he find us?"

"You won't get away," said Chloe. How could she have been ready to die just moments before? Especially since what she wanted most was to live her life with Marcus. "Give up now, before you get hurt."

"I'm not going back to jail."

Ahead, there was another curve that hugged the side of a steep hill. Darcy dropped her foot on the accelerator and gripped the steering wheel. A moment before they were airborne, Chloe knew what was happening. She didn't have time to react—only say a prayer that perhaps somehow—everything would turn out alright in the end.

* * *

Darcy pressed her foot on the accelerator as the car shot over the side of the hill.

The seat belt contracted, pinning her in place. It was like an iron band, constricting her lungs—her heart—and trapping her in the car. The roof collapsed a bit more each time the car tumbled over. The steering wheel pinned her to the seat and held her upright. A shard of glass gouged her arm.

Then the car came to a stop, resting on its hood. Darcy hung upside down, and blood dripped from her arm onto the cracked windshield. She tried to let go and slip her earthly bonds. Yet every part of her body ached and throbbed. She remained tethered to her physical self. She pushed on the seat belt's latch. The button depressed, but she remained strapped in. She tried again. And again. It was no use.

Darcy had stumbled into a trap that she'd set—and now, she'd never escape.

Marcus dropped his foot on the brakes, skidding to a stop at the same place Darcy had catapulted her vehicle off the road.

"Ian, you see that?" Marcus asked, his chest tight. "Call for help?"

"I'm on it," said the Brit.

Slamming the gearshift into Park, he leaped to the ground and scrambled to the edge of the hill. Wyatt was at his side.

Heartbeat hammering, Marcus stared down into the valley below. The car lay at the bottom of the ravine and on its hood. The tires, though shredded, still spun. The axles still rotated as the engine revved. The stench of gasoline filled the air. Could anyone survive that crash?

"Holy crap," Wyatt said, his words nothing more than a whisper.

Marcus's throat was too tight to speak. His eyes burned. He ran. Loose gravel underfoot gave way, and he skated the last few yards. Dropping to his knees, he looked in the back seat. The window was shattered, and pebbles of glass littered the ground.

Chloe lay on the interior roof of the car. Blood streamed from a gash in her forehead.

Darcy was in the driver's seat. A seat belt held her in place. Her hair hung in front of her face. She moaned. Not unconscious—or dead. Yet he wasn't worried about Darcy—not as much as he cared about Chloe.

Reaching through the smashed rear window, he brushed his fingertips on Chloe's outstretched hand— the only thing he could touch. Her skin was warm. Her chest rose and fell. "Chloe." He patted the back of her hand. "Chloe, can you hear me?"

Her lids fluttered. "Marcus," she croaked.

"We have to get you out of here. Can you move?"

"I think…" She inched forward. It wasn't enough.

"Wyatt, help me out."

"Sure, man." Wyatt knelt next to Marcus. Like a mantra, he repeated, "Slow and steady. Slow and steady."

Together, they grabbed Chloe's wrists and pulled her forward. Sure, he'd taken first aid classes, and he knew enough to be worried about a head or spinal injury. It's just that the stench of gas stung his eyes, and he was more worried about a fire.

Inch by inch, they pulled Chloe forward, until she was free of the car.

Lying on her back, Chloe panted. "Darcy. Where is she?"

Wyatt looked through the driver's side window. "She's still here—alive." He reached inside the car and tried to unbuckle the seat belt. "It's stuck," he said. Reaching into his pocket, he removed a multi-tool that included a sharp blade. Flipping it open, he began to saw through the webbing.

Chloe rolled to her side. Her arms were scraped. Dirt stuck to the blood and patches of raw flesh. One eye was blackened. There was a bruise on her chin. Her shirt was ripped, and she'd lost one of her shoes.

"You want to take it easy?" Marcus said. "You've just been in a car accident. You don't know if anything's broken. Besides, in your condition."

"Nothing's broken," said Chloe.

"Just do me a favor and stay put." He knelt at her side.

"We have to get Darcy out of that car." She pushed to sitting. Marcus knew that no matter how much he tried—he'd never keep Chloe down.

There was a whoosh as the undercarriage of the car caught on fire. That was immediately followed by the screams of the killer, who was stuck inside the inferno.

From a young age, Darcy had been told that the wicked suffered for eternity while being consumed by flames and existed in constant torment. Was she now in hell? Would Darcy forever roast alive, broken and bruised, inside the hull of a burning car?

No. It was impossible.

She'd been righteous in her quest to rid the world of those would-be defilers. Sure, others had gotten hurt. But a little pain was to be expected during an unholy war.

The flesh on her ankles blistered, sizzling with the heat. The agony was so great, she could do nothing but scream and release her suffering. Yet the pain remained.

Only moments ago, Darcy had been ready to die. That was when she imagined death to be sailing through the sky and painlessly crossing over to the other side. Now that she was trapped in an inferno, she wanted nothing more than to live and for the agony to end.

Through the flames and waves of heat, three figures rushed toward the car. Were they here to deliver her? As they drew closer, she recognized Chloe Ryder, Marcus Jones and Wyatt Thornton.

Had they all come to gloat? To laugh, as Darcy breathed her last breath?

"I'll get you out of here," said Wyatt as he cut through the seatbelt. "It'll just be another second." The last of the fibers ripped.

Gravity took hold, and Darcy flopped onto the roof of the car. Marcus reached into the burning car and pulled her through the broken window. There wasn't an inch on her body that didn't hurt, yet she was alive. He carried her away from the inferno and set her on the ground. As she lay on the dirt, panting, she couldn't help but wonder what had motivated Wyatt and Marcus to save her life.

Was it grace? Forgiveness?

Actually, Darcy knew. The two men—along with

Chloe—wanted to avoid guilt. She took in her surroundings.

Ten paces away, Chloe was tucked into Marcus's embrace. He spoke to her, his words so soft that Darcy couldn't hear what he said. Yet the cozy tableau left her ill. She refused to let them win. Pushing upright, Darcy marshaled every bit of strength she could find and rushed forward. As she ran, she picked up two shards of glass.

Grabbing Chloe by the shoulder, she spun her around. In the same movement, she drove the shank into her chest. Chloe's face went white, her eyes wide, her mouth open.

She stared, disbelieving, at the piece of mirror protruding from her breast. Like a blooming rose, blood spread across her shirt. She gasped. "Why do this to me now?"

Darcy swayed where she stood, drunk on the final victory and her never-ending pain. "You never could save me, Chloe. That was the whole point." She lifted the other piece of glass and aimed for Chloe's throat.

Marcus shoved Chloe to the side and reached out for the killer's arm as Darcy's hand sliced through the air once more, the glass in her hand shimmering in the sunlight.

There was an explosion that echoed off the hills. It felt like a bolt of lightning had struck her in the chest, leaving her vision fuzzy. She could just make out Wyatt Thornton, arm extended, pointed a gun at her. Smoke rose from the barrel.

"Wyatt? You did this?" she asked. "Why? Without me, who are you?"

"I told you a long time ago," he said. "I don't need you. Not now. Not ever."

She tried to speak, but blood leaked from her lips. As she lay in the grass, the last of her strength leaving her, The Darkness came and whispered in her ear. *"Follow me."*

And then she was no more.

"You take Chloe and go," Wyatt shouted. "I'll stay with the body until the cops show up."

Marcus didn't need to be told twice. He walled off all his emotions and just reacted. Following years of training and his instincts, he scooped Chloe into his arms. Holding her to his chest, he sprinted up the side of the hill. As if thunder erupted from the bottom of the ravine, an explosion shook the ground. A column of smoke rose skyward, and a wave of heat pushed him from behind.

The car had finally blown up.

His heart raced. Had Wyatt been hurt in the explosion? Marcus pivoted on the hillside. In the valley below, Wyatt was still on his feet.

Even from the distance, he must've been able to see the alarm that Marcus felt.

"Go," Wyatt called out. "I'm fine."

"I can help," he called back.

"No. You just go."

In his arms, Chloe groaned. Thank God she was still alive. Blood soaked her clothing from her chin to her knees. A piece of mirrored glass stuck out of her chest.

"Stay with me," he said.

Her head rested against his shoulder.

"Chloe," he said, louder this time.

Her eyelids fluttered.

"Stay with me."

"Tired," she whispered. "I'm so tired."

He couldn't let her fall asleep—especially since she might never wake.

The sound of sirens, faint but distinct, filled the quiet mountainside. He wasn't the praying type, but he thanked all that was good in the universe that the EMTs Ian called were on the way.

"I can hear the ambulance now. You're going to be okay. The baby's going to be okay, too." He paused, not sure if he was ready for what he wanted to say next. Yet there was nothing else that needed to be said more. "Chloe, I love you."

She placed her hand on his cheek. "I wish I would've let you kiss me sooner."

Her eyes closed and her hand slipped from his face. His chest contracted, and Marcus sprinted the last few yards. He stepped onto the blacktop just as the ambulance came into view.

A pair of EMTs rushed toward Marcus. One carried a foldable stretcher, and the other held a medical kit. Behind the ambulance was a sheriff's cruiser. One of the EMTs took Chloe from Marcus's arms.

"She's pregnant," Marcus said at first. But there was more, "She's been stabbed. Beaten. In a car crash." His voice was rough with emotion. Could anyone survive everything that Chloe had been through?

"We've got her, sir," said the EMT.

Sheriff's Deputy Travis Cooper parked his car next to Marcus's SUV. "What happened?"

Marcus kept an eye on Chloe as he spoke. "It was Darcy Owens," he said. "She got away from the jail by posing as a guard. Chloe forced her way into the car. There was a crash. Long story made very short—Darcy stabbed Chloe. Then Wyatt shot Darcy."

"Where is she now?"

"Dead, at the bottom of the ravine. Wyatt's with the body."

"Are you sure?"

Marcus had watched as the light left Darcy's eyes and the serial killer breathed her last. "Positive," he said. "She's dead."

"Well, I guess I need to identify the body. You can walk me through the scene." Travis stepped over the edge of the hill and paused. "Are you coming with me?"

Chloe was placed in the waiting ambulance. Never had Marcus felt such a tug to be with another person. As if they were bound, one to the other, and wherever she went, he was compelled to follow. It was more than the fact that she was pregnant with his baby. He needed to be with Chloe.

She was his other half.

"Are you coming with me?" Deputy Cooper asked again.

Marcus shook his head. "Wyatt's down there, and he can tell you everything you need to know. You can get him back to Pleasant Pines," he said, not quite an order, not quite a request. "I've got someplace else to be."

"What's more important than the investigation into the death of a serial murderer?" Travis called as Marcus jogged to his SUV.

"Lots," said Marcus. He jumped into the back of the ambulance and slammed the doors shut. Settling into one of the jump seats, he reached for Chloe's hand as the vehicle sped away.

Chapter 19

By the time Marcus arrived at the hospital, a team of surgeons was standing by to take Chloe straight into emergency surgery. He was told by a nurse's assistant, Zhang Wei, that abdominal wounds were difficult to treat because so many organs were located in the stomach area.

"She's in good hands," the guy explained while leading Marcus to a waiting room. "I'll let you know as soon as she's out of surgery."

A registered nurse was kind enough to visit Marcus in the waiting room, bandage his cuts and clean his scrapes. He also gave Marcus an over-the-counter painkiller, which turned the throbbing in Marcus's face to a dull ache. The nurse suggested he see a specialist about the broken nose. Marcus made a vague promise to follow up.

That was two hours ago.

Since then, Marcus had heard nothing. He'd received several calls asking about Chloe's status. He gave the same non-update to everyone.

Wyatt called. "It's official. Darcy Owens has been declared dead by Doc Lambert."

Sure, he already knew she was dead. Still, he had several things on his mind, and he said them rapid-fire. "I gotta thank you for what you did out there. If you hadn't taken that shot…" Marcus pinched the bridge of his nose and pushed aside the worst-case scenario. He started again. "What happens next? Will Julia hold an inquest or anything?"

"I spoke to her briefly, and she wants to meet and go over the situation in detail. It sucks that I had to shoot, but I know she needs to investigate. The facts will speak for themselves, and she'll do her job. I wouldn't expect any less of her."

"I've always got your back."

"I know. Thanks, man. How about you? How're you holding up?"

Before Marcus could answer, the nurse's assistant, Wei, stood at the threshold of the waiting room door. "I have to go," said Marcus, abruptly ending the call and getting to his feet. His mouth had gone dry. "How is she?"

"She's out of surgery, awake and wants to speak to you."

"Of course." Marcus rose from his seat and hustled to the door. In the corridor, he paused. "What about the baby?"

"You'll have to talk to her," said Wei. "I'm sorry, I can't tell you anything more."

From his years with the Bureau, he knew all about confidentiality. He also knew that arguing would do no good. "Where is she?"

"Second floor. Room 257."

Marcus took the stairs two at a time and found Chloe's room in minutes. She lay on the bed, an IV attached to her arm. Looking up as he entered, she gave a weary smile. "Hey."

"Hey yourself. How are you?" Moving to her side, he took Chloe's hand in his.

"I'll survive," she said, "truly, thanks to you."

His eyes burned. It was a sensation Marcus had come to recognize as gratitude intermingled with dread for what might've been. Marcus smoothed the hair from Chloe's forehead. "You're too strong for someone like Darcy to get the better of you," he said, joking but also telling the truth.

"I hate what happened to her. Not just years ago, but today."

"When she was a kid, she was a victim. But now?" He paused a beat. "All those choices were ones that she made. Nobody else."

"I guess you're right. I feel like this case is going to stay with me for a while, like the rest of my days."

"I expect it might." Marcus took a knee at her bedside. He wanted to be supportive, but what he really needed to know was about the baby. "How is everything else?"

"They did an ultrasound, Marcus. He…"

"Or she," he said.

"Or she," Chloe repeated, "is fine. The pregnancy is progressing as it should. I'll need to take it easy for several days and then go to Laramie to see a specialist. But for now, there's no need to worry."

"Oh, thank God." He pressed her hands to his lips.

"We'll be okay," she said. Her eyes drifted closed, the tiredness a side effect of the anesthesia administered during surgery, no doubt.

He stood and placed his lips on her forehead. "You rest. I'll be here when you wake up. I promise you, Chloe. I'm not going anywhere."

Two weeks later.

Marcus sat beside Chloe in the doctor's office. A hard knot of dread had settled into his stomach. Sure, there was no reason to think there was anything wrong with Chloe or the baby. But until he spoke to the doctor, Marcus couldn't relax.

It was in total juxtaposition to how he felt for the past two weeks. Since she'd been discharged from the hospital, he'd been staying at her house and helping her through the recovery from her injuries—and the psychological recovery. He fell asleep with Chloe in his arms every night and woke up with her at his side every morning. Sometimes, Chloe had nightmares about Darcy or the Transgressors. And that's when he held her tighter and let her cry.

He hadn't been to work in two weeks—just kept in contact with Ian and Wyatt sporadically. And honestly, he'd never been happier.

He nodded toward a side. "That's a lot of diplomas,"

he said, mentioning the framed documents that lined the wall.

"Doctor Hatathli comes highly recommended."

"That's good," he said, his nerves jangling. Marcus reached for her hand and gave it a squeeze. Chloe wore a pair of leggings, winter boots, and long tunic in a deep blue that matched her eyes. "Nothing but the best for you. And for the—for our—baby." He really had to get used to saying that. And he would. In time.

"Thanks for coming with me," said Chloe.

"Where else would I be?"

Before she could answer, the office door opened. The doctor slipped into the room. Long, dark hair hung loose around her shoulders. She held a laptop, the screen up and illuminated. Looking up, she set the computer on her desk and held out a hand to Chloe. "I'm Doctor Hatathli. It's a pleasure to meet you both. Of course, I've seen all the media coverage of what happened at the correctional facility. If it was half as bad as the news reports, then I'm thrilled to see you at all."

Chloe shook hands with the doctor. "It was wild, that's for sure."

The doctor then offered her hand for Marcus to shake. She had a firm grip. He was already impressed. "Thanks for seeing us, doc. I was told that it's hard to get an appointment with you."

"Well, who am I to turn away two of Wyoming's favorite heroes?"

She sat behind her desk and pulled the computer to her. "It looks like they ran blood work in Pleasant Pines and had the lab send us the results. Based on those, and the ultrasound we did here when you arrived, I am happy to report that everything looks normal. The baby is healthy, and so are you. I'll want to see you once a month. As we get closer to the due date, we'll discuss birthing plans. For now, what questions can I answer?"

Chloe and Marcus regarded one another but said nothing.

"Come on," said the doctor. "You must have at least one question for me."

"Is it still too early to know the gender?" Marcus asked. "I don't care, honestly. I just—"

"I get it," said Dr. Hatathli, smiling. "But yes, it is early. At about twenty weeks, we'll do another ultrasound and if the baby cooperates, we can tell you if it's a boy or girl."

The doctor then went on to discuss nutrition, exercise—which should be coordinated with Chloe's physical therapist, along with how to handle stress and the need to rest. Marcus held on to each word the physician said. Yet, there was only thing that really mattered. Everything was okay.

His phone pinged with an incoming text. Not many people had the number to his new phone. He stole a glance at the screen. The message was from his brother, Jason.

How's the appointment going?

Marcus was happy to see that his little brother was excited to be an uncle. He'd fill him in later but for now, he sent a thumbs-up emoji.

The appointment continued for another twenty minutes. Armed with several pamphlets about pregnancy, prenatal care and childbirth, Chloe and Marcus shook hands with the doctor. She directed them to the scheduling desk. An appointment card in hand, they left the medical building, located in downtown Laramie.

"That was all good news." They walked down the street and Marcus pulled a knit cap down on his bald head.

"It was," Chloe agreed, shoving her hands deeper into her coat pockets.

"You want to grab a cup of tea before we get back on the road?" He pointed to a small shop with a striped awning that sat across the road. "There's a little bakery over there."

"Sounds good."

Marcus reached for her hand. They waited for a break in traffic before crossing the street. He pushed the door open and stepped inside. The interior of the bakery was warm and smelled of sugar and cinnamon. It was mid-morning. Chloe and Marcus were the only patrons. A young woman in a blue apron stood behind a glass and chrome case that was filled with scones, cookies, and cupcakes. Half a dozen round tables were scattered around the room.

"Earl Grey tea?" Marcus offered.

"And a cranberry-orange scone." Chloe placed her hand on her belly and gave him a wink. "After all, I am eating for two."

She moved to a table and sat as he ordered.

In the small space, it was impossible to miss the sound of Chloe's phone as it began to ring. She swiped the call open.

"Hello?" And then, "Yes, I'll hold for the attorney general."

"Hello, ma'am. Thank you for calling." Pause. "Yes,

it was a harrowing experience." She glanced up at Marcus and mouthed the words, *It's the AG calling.*

He smiled and turned back to the counter to pay and collect a tray with the drinks and food. After walking the short distance, he set the tray on the table as Chloe said, "Of course I remember working for your office. I loved that experience." She glanced at Marcus as he handed her a cup of tea. "It's a tempting offer, but I have to decline. My personal life has taken some unexpected turns and I need to stay in Pleasant Pines..."

Was Chloe turning down her dream job for him? There was no way that he could let her pass up on the opportunity of a lifetime. He grabbed a paper napkin that had been placed under one of the scones. He found a pen in his coat pocket and quickly scribbled a note. *Take the job.*

He held the napkin up for Chloe to see.

She waved him away.

He wrote another note under the first one. *Tell her you'll think about it, at least. We can talk.*

Chloe sighed. "Can I think about your offer? I'll call you back by the end of the week." She paused. "Thank you. You have a nice day as well." She ended the call and set her phone aside. "Well, you know what that was all about."

"I do and I think you should take the job."

"In case you forgot, I'm having a baby. I don't think I want to take on the responsibility of being a new parent and a new job at the same time." She took a sip of her tea. "It's too much for one person."

"Yeah, but you won't be alone. Chloe, I'll be at your side every step of the way." It was then that he realized what he'd been feeling for days—but had been too afraid to say aloud. "Marry me."

She looked stunned. "You don't need to propose because I'm pregnant, Marcus."

"I love you, Chloe. I love you because you're smart and strong, because you're professional and compassionate at the same time. I love you because I want to be a better agent—a better person—because of you. I think I fell in love the first moment we met. I'm so lucky that you're going to be the mother of our child."

Chloe pushed her tea away. "Marcus. It wasn't so long ago that you told me that you were an agency man. That you didn't think you were the marrying type. You've sacrificed a marriage to the job. What makes you think it'll be different this time? Is it just—" She swallowed. "Is it because of the baby?"

Marcus took her hands in his. "Chloe—you're right. About everything. But—there's so much more. Before—I think I didn't understand what it meant to really share a part of myself with my partner. With my partner in heart. In life. With you… it's different. I get it. And I'm in it—for good. And yeah, I want to be a dad to our child. But I want to be a husband to *you*, because I love you. And I'll do anything to prove it to you, every day that we're together." He held her gaze. "So—will you marry me?"

She squeezed his hands, then smiled as a tear slipped down her cheek. "Hell yes, I will. I love you too, Marcus. So much."

He came over to her and wrapped her in a tight embrace, holding her as though he'd never let her go. When he finally did, he gestured to her phone. "Call the AG back. Take the job."

Chloe stared at him. "What about you? What about RMJ?"

"Me? I need a cell phone and a car. I can do my job anywhere."

She wiped a tear away, then sat down again. "I'll call her back on one condition."

"What's that?" he asked.

"Tell me again how much you love me."

"Let me show you instead," he said before placing his lips on hers. They might have closed the case of the infamous serial killer of Pleasant Pines, but Marcus knew that this was just the beginning of their happily-ever-after.

Epilogue

The suite of offices had one time been a prison for Luke and the other guys. For hours now, it had been their sanctuary. A loudspeaker had been pushed up against the door. A voice ordered everyone inside to surrender peacefully or be forcibly removed. Sitting on the floor, Luke held his head in his hand.

"What do we do?" Rex asked.

Luke's eye hurt so bad he couldn't think. "Stop bothering me. How the hell am I supposed to know what we do next?"

"Without Booth around, you're in charge."

The other gang members stood around Luke, staring down with blank expressions. They were all like sheep, unable to make a move without a leader.

"You're in charge," Rex said again. "You gotta make up your mind, man. Do we give up? Or fight?"

Well, when he put it that way... "We don't ever give up."

Rex rubbed his chin. "Then what do we use for the fight?"

Before Luke could answer, there was a crash as a window set high in the wall shattered. It was followed by a metal tube that landed on the floor. The canister rolled to a stop by Luke's foot.

"Flash-bang grenade," Rex yelled. "Take cover."

Luke had time to do nothing but gape. The room filled with light so bright, it left him blind. The explosion rendered him deaf to every sound but a ringing in his ears.

Hands gripped him under the arms and hefted him to his feet. He was handcuffed and dragged out of the room. By the time his vision returned, he was in the back of a police van with Rex at his side.

A guard looped a chain through a steel ring on the floor, securing Luke's handcuffs to the vehicle. Leaning in close, the guard whispered, "I heard from Booth. He said to be ready." The guard glanced at Rex. "Both of you."

Instead of fastening the chain with a lock, he slipped the final link under Luke's foot, giving the appearance of security.

The van could seat more than a dozen men, yet Luke and Rex were the only passengers. The back door was slammed shut, plunging Luke into darkness once more. The van's engine rumbled a moment before the vehicle started moving. It was only a matter of time—and he'd be free. In fact, freedom was so close, he could taste it.

Booth. Was he really coming? How long were they supposed to wait? They'd been in the back of the van for a long while. Certainly they were close by now. If a rescue operation was on the way, it had better hurry the hell up.

Luke asked, "Who in the hell was the guard anyway?"

"Didn't you see his hand? He had the Transgressors tat on his wrist. He's from a different chapter of the club."

"See? What's the matter with you? Are you the one who got stabbed in the eye? Because you sure seem like you're freaking blind." Luke spat on the metal floor.

The van lurched to the side, and Luke flew across the aisle before slamming into the opposite bench. "What the hell?"

"Must be Booth," said Rex, pulling Luke to his feet. "Get ready to run."

From outside the van, there were shouts, curses, and the report of handgun fire being exchanged. Then there was a long *rat-a-tat-tat* of an automatic rifle's magazine being emptied. He heard one long scream and the silence that followed.

Luke's pulse echoed in his ears. Someone had won the battle. But who? The cops? Or the Transgressors?

The doors to the van were pulled open. Sunlight filled the dark and cramped cell. The light burned Luke's eyes. He held up his arm and scooted back to a corner.

"What in the hell happened to you?" It was Booth.

He was thinner than when Luke saw him last, and his blonde hair hung past his shoulders. Still, it was good to see his friend. "What do you mean? I just broke outta jail."

"No, your eye. You look like a pirate. It don't matter. We gotta go. One of the officers got off a radio call. Every cop in the county is on the way."

Luke jumped to the ground. "Good to see you, brother," he said, embracing Booth.

Booth slapped him on the back. "Good to see you, too. But I ain't joking, the heat will be here in minutes." Booth turned to Rex as he, too, jumped to the ground. "Thanks for taking care of him while he was away."

"It's nothing, man," said Rex.

A red muscle car was parked across the road, blocking the van. The driver was still behind the wheel, and the engine still ran. Two guards, both dead, were sprawled across the pavement. The sounds from several approaching sirens were faint, but the wailing grew louder with each second.

"That didn't take long," said Booth, pulling open the passenger door. "Get in."

Luke slipped into the cramped back seat, scooting to the spot directly behind the driver. Rex followed. Booth sat in the passenger seat and slammed the door shut.

The car raced down the road. "Now what?" Luke asked.

"I've already got plans." Booth turned in his seat and smiled. "Big plans. For the right price, we might be able to even some scores."

Luke wasn't sure what was about to happen next, but being free—even if wanted by the law—held a definite appeal. At the same time, he had the chance to get revenge. Really? Now, that was his real reward.

* * * * *

Look for the first book in Jennifer D. Bokal's new miniseries Texas Law,
Coming in 2022 to Harlequin Romantic Suspense.
Catch up with the previous books in the
Wyoming Nights miniseries

Under the Agent's Protection
Agent's Mountain Rescue
Agent's Wyoming Mission

Available now, wherever Harlequin books
and ebooks are sold.

WE HOPE YOU ENJOYED
THIS BOOK FROM

✦ HARLEQUIN
ROMANTIC
SUSPENSE

Danger. Passion. Drama.

These heart-racing page-turners will keep you guessing
to the very end. Experience the thrill of unexpected
plot twists and irresistible chemistry.

4 NEW BOOKS AVAILABLE EVERY MONTH!

#2191 COLTON'S SECRET SABOTAGE
The Coltons of Colorado
by Deborah Fletcher Mello

Detective Philip Rees is determined to catch the person leaking secrets to the Russian mob. When television producer Naomi Colton wrangles him for her reality TV series, saying no isn't an option. He can't risk blowing his cover, so sliding into the saddle and her heart are his only options.

#2192 OPERATION PAYBACK
Cutter's Code • by Justine Davis

The Foxworth Foundation has stepped in to help Trip Callen before, so when a brutal crime boss targets him, they're willing to step in again. He doesn't know they're helping him because of a past connection to Kayley McSwain, the woman he's beginning to care more for than he ever expected. Will Cutter and the Foxworths be able to keep them both safe?

#2193 AMBUSH AT HEARTBREAK RIDGE
Lost Legacy • by Colleen Thompson

When a family vanishes in the dangerous wilderness, Sheriff Hayden Hale-Walker will stop at nothing to find them before it's too late, even if that means calling Kate McClafferty, the former lover with the search-and-rescue skills he needs—regardless of the long-buried secrets that put their hearts at risk.

#2194 HER DANGEROUS TRUTH
Heroes of the Pacific Northwest • by Beverly Long

Lab scientist Layla Morant is on the run—until a car accident threatens not only her identity but also her life. She can't allow herself to be found, but her injuries need immediate attention. And Dr. Jaime Weathers is determined to help her, not knowing the danger he's putting himself in...

HRSCNM0622

"If it's necessary," he said, undoing Banner's lead rope, "I'll take care of business."

"Maybe I should take that for you, Hayden. Since you're—"

Tossing aside his ruined hat, he gave her a look of disbelief. "Have you lost your ever-loving mind? I'm not handing you my gun. It might be your job to find these people, but I'm sworn to protect them. And you, for that matter."

"I get that, but I don't believe you're currently fit to make a life-and-death call or even to be riding."

Turning away from her, he grabbed a handful of Banner's mane along with the saddle horn and shoved his boot into the stirrup before swinging aboard the gray.

HRSEXP0622

If it were anyone else, she might have missed the way he slightly overbalanced and then hesitated, recovering for a beat or two, giving her time to mount her mule to face him.

"You're clearly dizzy. I can see it," she challenged. "So please, Hayden, you need to—"

The engines' noise abruptly dropped off, but they could still barely make out the low rumble of the motors idling. With the ravine's rocky face amplifying the sound, she knew it was tricky to judge distance. Though the vehicles couldn't be far, they might be just literally around the next bend in the creek or more than half a mile downstream.

Before Kate could regain her train of thought, shouts, followed by an anguished human cry—definitely a woman's—carried from the same direction. The terror in it had Kate's breath catching, her nerve endings standing at attention.

"Call for assistance. *Now!*" Hayden ordered before kicking Banner's side and leaning forward.

Don't miss
Ambush at Heartbreak Ridge *by Colleen Thompson,
available August 2022 wherever
Harlequin Romantic Suspense books and
ebooks are sold.*

Harlequin.com

HRSEXP0622

Love Harlequin romance?

DISCOVER.

Be the first to find out about promotions,
news and exclusive content!

Facebook.com/HarlequinBooks

Twitter.com/HarlequinBooks

Instagram.com/HarlequinBooks

Pinterest.com/HarlequinBooks

YouTube.com/HarlequinBooks

ReaderService.com

EXPLORE.

Sign up for the Harlequin e-newsletter and
download a free book from any series at
TryHarlequin.com

CONNECT.

Join our Harlequin community to
share your thoughts and connect
with other romance readers!
Facebook.com/groups/HarlequinConnection

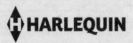

HARLEQUIN

Heartfelt or thrilling, passionate or uplifting—Harlequin is more than just happily-ever-after.

With twelve different series to choose from and new books available every month, you are sure to find stories that will move you, uplift you, inspire and delight you.

SIGN UP FOR THE HARLEQUIN NEWSLETTER

Be the first to hear about great new reads and exciting offers!

Harlequin.com/newsletters